FAE:LOST

EVA BLACKWING

CHAPTER 1

*C*hapter One

Mor stared blankly down at the magazine on the counter, idly turning pages as she leaned her head in her hand. She wasn't really paying any attention to what was on the page. Just another day not in paradise. Waiting for something - anything - to change what was happening. Small towns sucked. Technically, she did live close to a city, but no one really stopped in her town of Castroville, Texas. The occasional person would visit, but most people didn't venture further inside the town to find the local coffee shop. And she didn't really have time or the money to go into town.

She was zoned out. The locals had cleared out after their morning 'rush' and now Mor was just doing nothing until she could close the shop at two. When she would go home and watch spotty Netflix on shitty WiFi and dream of ways to get out. Mor had done the whole college thing. She had gotten a degree in teaching from Texas Tech but then couldn't find a job. Finally sucking up her pride, she had come home to Castroville and gotten a job from her obnoxious brother in his side business coffee shop. That he only kept around for taxes since it was always in the red. But at least she was given the apartment above the shop for free because she was family.

With a groan, she laid her head on the counter and gently thumped her head a couple of times against the counter. "My life sucks."

"Does it now?" A deep voice rumbled above Mor.

"Holy fuck!" She jumped up, stumbled backwards and tripped over her stool barely managing to catch herself before she fell over. "Shit, I'm sorry. Sh-I mean. Damn." Pinching the bridge of her nose she said, "I am so sorry, please don't tell my brother I cussed at work. He'll flip out and then I may lose this job and my apartment and I really don't have anywhere else to go." Mor glanced up and her jaw dropped. In front of her was the hottest man she had ever seen. At least six and a half feet tall, black t-shirt straining across his chest and biceps, forearms braced against the counter with a smirk gracing his lips. His infinitely kissable lips. Ice blue eyes, lightly brown skin, and black hair flowing to his shoulders. Holy. Shit.

He leaned toward her and whispered, "I don't give a fuck how much you cuss. It's cute." He grinned at her and tapped her under the chin.

Mor snapped her jaw shut"Th-thank you?" The words were forced out and her cheeks burned. What was wrong with her? She never had this response to guys. Not even the super hot ones. Of course, she had never met a man this hot. And now Mor was rambling in her head and just staring at him. "Fuck. I mean. What can I get you?" Her voice had gone a little squeaky.

"What's your name?" He reached out and tucked a piece of blonde hair behind her ear where it had fallen out of her messy bun.

"Mor Williamson. Well, its Moreen, but who names their kid that? It's awful. So. Mor is all I respond to...." Mor trailed off. Word vomit much? *Real smooth Mor. Real smooth.*

"Mor. I like that. Why does your life suck?" He sat down on one of the stools.

"That's a boring story. I'm sure you don't want to hear that." She looked around for a menu and pushed one to him.

He ignored the menu. "No, I definitely want to hear it. Can I get a black coffee?"

"Any sugar or cream?" She poured him a cup and set it in front of him.

"I'm good." He took a sip, closing his eyes and purring? No. Definitely not. Men didn't purr. Cats purred and never around her because cats hate her. "I'm ready for story time."

Mor kept her jaw firmly closed when he flashed his smile at her again. "Not much to tell. Grew up here, went away to college with dreams of becoming a teacher, couldn't find a job and ended up back here. Working for my asshole brother in his failing coffee shop that he keeps purely for taxes. And I live in the semi-crappy apartment above it with shitty WiFi where I'm not allowed to even have a goldfish much less the puppy I want. I have no friends and no boyfriend even though Robby McFarlan keeps asking me out but I won't go out with him because he smells like fish has a beer gut at twenty-four and its been a really long fucking time sin - " Abruptly she shut her mouth.

"Since what?" The man had a gleam in his eye, almost predatory as he looked Mor over.

"Nothing. Nothing. So, um, that's my boring story. Small town girl who tried to get out and inevitably got sucked back in. Sorry. Apparently I have a case of word vomit today."

"I like it. Even if you do seem to hold back the good stuff." He grinned. "So what's keeping you here?"

"I barely make enough to get by, much less save enough to get out of here." With a sigh she sat on her stool, putting her head back down on the counter.

"Moreen! What are you doing?"

She flinched, stood up and would have fallen if hotty hadn't grabbed her arms and kept her upright. "Heeeeey. Tom. What are you doing here?"

Tom rolled his eyes. "It's my shop. I can do whatever I want. I think the better question, little sister, is why you had your head on the counter with a paying customer in front of you." His voice dripped disdain and anger.

She was so fucked. "I'm sor - "

"Shut up. Sir, I apologize for the unprofessional behavior of my sister. Please, whatever you want is on the house and I assure you she will be thoroughly reprimanded." Hotty's face was shocked as Tom's eyes cut to her. "As for you, I will be docking your pay since you obviously aren't doing much work. Do you understand?"

"Yes, sir." Her voice was barely above a whisper, mortification making her face burn as she held in tears.

"What did you say?" Tom's voice cracked across the room.

A rumble sounded from hotty as he stood casually turned toward Tom, towering over him. "Are your ears broken?"

"What?" Tom redirected his attention to the man, his smarmy business face immediately taking over.

"I said. Are. Your. Ears. Broken?" He enunciated each word. "After you so rudely talked to your sister and are docking her pay for having a momentary break, I want to know if you couldn't hear her? She spoke plain as day. And was way more polite than you deserve." He stood to his full height, towering over Tom. "I suggest you apologize to the lady before I decide to intervene."

Definitely growling. Wait, growling? How is that happening? And why did that make a shiver run down her spine? Not a fear shiver. Nope. Not if the pulse between her legs was any indication. Shit.

"Moreen. I apologize for yelling. I think it would be best if you found another job. And somewhere else to live. You have one week." Tom gave the man a nasty glare before turning and marching out.

"Oh fuck." Hotty turned to Mor. "I am so sorry. I didn't think he would do that."

"I'm not sure if I'm happy or about to spiral into a bout of hysteria. Maybe both?" She paused and took a deep breath, suppressing the sob that threatened to bubble out. "Definitely both. Oh fuck. Fuck. Fuck. Fuck. What am I going to do? That asshole is kicking me out! His sister!" A sob broke through. "What am I going to do?" Tears were definitely flowing now.

"Shit." She heard a thump and then was wrapped up in a pair of strong arms. "Shhh. We'll figure this out. It's ok. Shhh."

Mor's sobs slowed as a hand slowly stroked her hair. "What am I going to do?" She went from hysteria to hopelessness. "I really have no where to go. My parents are assholes just like Tom, and I'm sure he's already on the phone with them telling them what a fuck up I still am." Tears started falling faster again and she started to sob. "I c-can't s-s-stop c-crying."

"Where are your keys?" When she pointed, he reached under the counter and snagged them. "Do you have to go outside to get to your apartment?" When Mor shook her head no, he swept her up in his arms and walked over to the front door. He flipped the sign to closed and then locked the door before marching into the back room and heading up the stairs.

He pushed Mor's door open and then sat down on the couch with her in his lap. Mor cried a little harder. She had never had anyone take care of her like this. Or at all. Her family wasn't exactly the nurturing type. Or the nice type. Slowly, her sobs slowed and her eyes closed as she nestled into the arms holding onto her.

"It's ok, Mor. Sleep. I've got you."

***

Mor slowly woke up, feeling worn out. Why did sh- oh. Tom. One week. And hotty? Bolting up right, Mor looked around her small living room. She was laying on the couch, a blanket covering her legs. A movie was playing on silent with captions but no one was in the room with her.

"You're awake." She jumped as hotty came out of her bathroom. "How are you feeling?"

"Um. Better? I guess?" She fidgeted with the fringe on the blanket. "Not that I'm not grateful to you for getting me up here, but what's your name?"

Hotty burst out with a laugh and her heart thumped a little harder. "Damn, I didn't realize I hadn't told you! My name is Atreyu."

"Seriously? Like the Neverending Story?" She gaped.

Atreyu rolled his eyes as he came to sit next to her on the couch. "Like the book. My mom loved that book and hated the movie."

"I love that movie." Her voice was breathy and she fought the urge to lean into him.

"Me too." He grinned. "So. Do you have any idea what you want to do?"

Mor took a deep breath. "Nope. My parents are assholes like my brother. I didn't go to a fancy private university so I could meet someone with a suitable stock portfolio and I refused to marry the son of one of my father's investors because he is a misogynistic womanizer who wanted me to stay home and pop out at least two children for him." She lifted a shoulder. "So basically I'm disowned. If I go back, they'll want me to marry John and then my soul will slowly die."

"Well, we can't have that. I think I like your soul." Atreyu brushed her cheek with a finger. "How is it you and your brother look nothing alike?"

Now she did smile. "I'm adopted. They wanted a daughter to show off and my mother refused to have another baby because it would 'destroy her figure.'"

"Seriously? That's fucked up."

"Yeah. But I take comfort in it since I'm not genetically related to that asshole. But..." She slumped back into the couch. "It is also why it's likely they *will* totally disown me now." They were silent for a few minutes. "Well, I don't have a lot in my fridge but I can go down to the shop and get us something. Because fuck - " She cut off when her phone buzzed.

"Speak of the devil." Mor pulled her phone out. "Hey Mo - "

"Don't you 'hey mom' me, young lady. You are a disgrace. Who was that trash who was so rude to your brother? You better not be sleeping with him. We expect you to be a - "

"A virgin. I know." She put her head in her hands, leaning forward. Mortification made her cheeks flush, knowing Atreyu was hearing half of this conversation.

"Good. Now that this ridiculous farce of you working at that awful shop is over, you can move back home. I will inform John you are ready to accept his proposal and then we can get started on planning your wedding."

"What? No! I'm not marrying that jackass." Atreyu wrapped his arm around her and pulled her head into his side.

"You will marry him or you will be disowned! It's time you do your duty to your family. Enough of this playing around."

"Mom - " She tried to cut in.

"No! And when you get here, I will have Dr. Robertson check to see if you are intact."

Mor sat up. "Excuse me?" Her voice was quiet.

"You heard me, young lady. Dr. Robertson will ensure you are still a virgin. John wants a wife that is not a whore."

"A whore? That piece of shit fucks anything that walks!"

"Do not speak of your future husband that way! It is his right as the man to do as he pleases. You are there to provide heirs that will join our families."

"Do you even hear yourself? It's the year twenty-nineteen! I am not a piece of property to be sold to the highest bidder for a life of popping out babies and staying home while my husband fucks everything that walks!"

"Language!"

"I'll talk however I want, mother." She spat the words out. "You only care for what I can bring you. Well FUCK YOU! I will not be moving home. I will not be marrying that piece of shit John. And guess what, mom? I'm not a virgin!" Mor was shouting by the end. She went to throw her phone across the room, but was stopped by a hand closing gently around hers and then plucking the phone from her hand.

She could hear her mother shouting on the other end. Mor went to take it from Atreyu but he just grinned and lifted it this ear. "Ma'am? This is the trash that spoke back to your worthless son." Mor gaped at him. "Just wanted to let you know, in case you care, that Mor will be taken care of. In every way possible." His voice deepened into a sexy rumble, wicked grin on his face as he winked at her. "It's a shame she was stuck with you for her family, because Mor is one amazing woman who deserves better than you. Enjoy your miserable life." He hit the end button and handed the phone back to her.

7

"What just happened?" Eyes wide, Mor stared at him.

"You just told your mother off for being a selfish prick. And I couldn't help but tweak her a little further. I won't say sorry because I'm not." He grinned. "You did good!"

A grin stretched her face. "Thank you!" Then it fell again. "Oh shit. She is really going to cut me off. Where am I going to go? Oh shit." Panic started creeping back into her.

"Hey. It's ok." Atreyu rubbed her back in slow circles and that deep purr came from him again. "I know we just met, but you could come with me until you figure things out. I live with my brothers - well, they aren't blood brothers, but close enough. I got you into this mess, the least I can do is help you out of it."

"I don't know. I just met you. And everyone would say this is a bad idea. Going with a strange man to his house? Horror movie in the making."

"What does your gut say?" His hand stilled but the purr continued.

"That I can trust you." She looked up at him. "Are you purring?"

The sound cut off, "What? Of course not." He flushed.

"Uh-huh." She smirked at him. "Well, I literally have no other options and frankly, even being ax murdered at this point would be better than crawling back to my parents and marrying John." Mor shuddered.

"Why don't we order some takeout and then I can help you pack in the morning?"

"Um, I can't afford to do that." Mor felt a flush creeping up her face and was so glad he couldn't see her.

"My treat. Since I got you disowned by your family."

She laughed. "Okay, if you put it that way. There are two places that deliver. Pizza and Mexican. Which would you prefer?"

"Uhhh whatever you want is fine."

"Pizza it is! I'm feeling the need for some comfort food. Put on a movie while I order." Mor pulled up the number for the pizza place and called it in. Atreyu requested three pizzas so he would have at least two to himself.

She went into the kitchen and pulled out her emergency bottle of whiskey and two tumblers. Grabbing two whiskey stones from the freezer and plunking one into each glass she poured two glasses and started to bring them out to the couch before thinking better of it and taking the bottle too.

"I may get drunk. Fair warning." Mor set the bottle on the coffee table, handed him his drink and clinked his glass before tossing back half of her drink. "Something else mother and father dearest never approved of, but I'm pretty sure I'm part Irish because I do love whiskey."

"I promise to hold your hair back when you puke." Atreyu grinned and took a sip. "Damn, girl! This is some good shit."

"My one splurge. I was saving it for when I made it. But, since I seem to have hit rock bottom..." She shrugged and downed the rest, reaching for the bottle and pouring herself another drink. "Did you pick a movie?"

"I wasn't totally sure what you would like, so I picked one of my favorites." He pushed play and sat back, arm across the back of the sofa.

Mor grinned when Thor: Ragnorak started playing. "Yes! I love Marvel!" She leaned her head back on the couch, turning her head to look at Atreyu. She started to say something but was distracted by the tendrils of ink peeking out from his shirt. Without thinking she reached up and traced one with her finger. "Oh my gosh. I'm sorry. I didn't think."

Grinning, Atreyu nudged her. "Don't worry about it. Maybe one day I will show you the rest of it." His eyes darkened and he leaned down towards her.

Mor held her breath, hoping he would kiss her. Aaaand then the doorbell rang. Atreyu shook his head ruefully and pulled away, walking to get the door.

"Hey Mor, ready to let- who are you?" Robby McFarlan stood with his mouth hanging open like the fish he smelled like holding their pizza.

"Fuck. I forgot he delivered on Wednesday." With a groan, she made her way over to the door. She nudged Atreyu who refused to move out the way. He did sling an arm around her neck and pull her to him before kissing the top of her head.

"Babe. Do you know this guy?" His eyes laughed down at her.

"Atreyu, this is Robby. We went to high school together."

"What are you doing with my girlfriend?" Robby started to bluster, his face turning splotchy.

Atreyu growled. Straight up growled. Without thinking, Mor wrapped her arms around him and squeezed. His body relaxed and the growling stopped. "Robby, we've been over this. I have never been your girlfriend and will never be your girlfriend."

Atreyu took the pizza out of Robby's hand and handed it to Mor before shoving cash in Robby's surprised hands. "Keep the change." He shut the door and turned around. Atreyu took the pizza out of her hands, placing it on the table. Stalking slowly toward her and he trapped her against the fridge. "No wonder its been a long time since you've had sex."

"What? I never, I mean, I - " Mor stopped talking and just looked up at him. Damn, he was sexy with those ice blue eyes and all that black hair. She started to say something else but stopped when Atreyu slowly lowered his head toward hers. He paused, giving Mor another second to say no before gently pressing his lips against hers. It started slow but didn't stay that way. Atreyu slipped an arm around her waist and pulled her to him, his other hand slipping into her hair and holding her in place as his tongue stroked her lips. She opened on a gasp and his tongue invaded her mouth. Time stood still. Mor had never been kissed like this. Like she was being savored. Like they had all the time in the world. He pulled back and placed another gentle peck on her lips.

"Come on. Let's get some food in you so you don't get too sick from all that whiskey." He wrapped her hand in his, grabbed the pizzas and led her to the couch. Once she was settled against him with pizza and whiskey, he started the movie over and dropped a kiss on her head.

CHAPTER 2

*M*or woke slowly, with her head pounding. Groaning, she rolled over and smacked into Atreyu's hard body. "Good morning, beautiful." Atreyu grinned at her. She froze, her arm draped over his naked, muscley, beautiful chest. Her hand stroked his side. She couldn't stop. "How are you feeling this morning?" He smirked like he knew she couldn't stop.

"Um, my head hurts."

"I'll get you something." He stood up and her mouth dropped. He was only in his boxers. Her eyes travelled the length of his body and she prayed she wasn't drooling as she took in the swirls of tattoos around his shoulders, down to perfect abs and then the perfect V leading down to - oh shit. Well, it was probably just because it was morning. Surely not because of her. But Mor would dream of what was hidden under those boxers because damn. He leaned in to her, took one finger and tapped under her chin. "Close your mouth, beautiful. I'm getting ideas and you don't feel good."

She snapped her mouth closed and yanked the sheet up to cover her face. He laughed and she heard him walk away. After a moment, the bed dipped as he sat down on it. With an exasperated laugh,

Atreyu tugged the sheet away from her face. "Take some Advil, beautiful. We have to get you packed up today." He grinned.

Mor sat up and took the Advil and water from him. "Um, did we, um..."

He smirked down at her. "No. Not that I don't want to, but I wasn't about to take advantage of drunk you. Especially since you had such an awful day. And I would prefer you responsive."

"Oh. Um." She took a breath and winced.

Taking the cup from her hand, he pushed her gently back down onto the bed before pressing a kiss on Mor's forehead. "Sleep a little more, my brother's will be here soon to help load up your stuff."

"Wait, wh-?"

"Sleep."

Before she could say anything else, she plunged into a dreamless sleep.

* * *

MOR WOKE up to voices coming from the living room. Deep voices. Sexy voices. Wait, what? Fuck. Why was every other thought about sexy things? She had never thought like this before. Mor sat up, feeling much better after Advil and a nap. But how did he get her to sleep so fast? She stood up and started to walk out of her room but realized she was in her bra and panties. Granny panties. Ugh. That means Atreyu saw them. *Nooooo!* Okay, she had to get ready fast.

Dashing into her bathroom she made sure it was locked on both sides since it led into the living room too. She took a fast shower (but did take time to shave), brushed her teeth and walked naked into her room towel drying her hair.

"Oh shit!"

Snapping her eyes up, Mor saw a man standing in her room, carrying some empty boxes. His eyes were a deep green and he had red hair falling across his forehead. Freckles were scattered across his chiseled features, breaking up his pale skin. She stood frozen as they gaped at each other.

Finally waking up from frozen status, she yanked the towel in front of her body as the man mumbled something, dropped the boxes and hurried out of the room. She stood there a moment longer before hurrying to her dresser and pulling out a matching set of blue lace bra and thong. Because with men like that in her house she damn sure was going to be wearing something pretty. Even if only she knew about it. Shrugging, she pulled on a pair of shorts and a tank top, ready to get to work.

"Come on, Mor. Atreyu saw your granny panties and that red headed hotty saw you naked and hunched over. But it's okay. You are smart and sexy and you are going to put on your big girl panties and go out there. It's moving day." She took a breath and walked out.

"Hey, beautiful! How're you feeling?" Atreyu set down the cup he was busy packing up and walked straight over to her, wrapping her up in a hug.

Snuggling into him, she sighed. "I feel much better. I have no idea how you got me to go back to sleep like that." She had a passing moment where she thought about how she should feel weird about being so affectionate. Mor had only known him for less than a day. Snuggling with strangers had never been her thing. But Atreyu didn't feel like a stranger. It didn't scare her like it logically should have.

He chuckled but didn't answer, merely dropping a kiss on the top of her head and then turned her to face the others in the room. "These are my brothers. You already sort of met Max." He pointed over to the redhead who sheepishly ducked his head.

"Sorry about that."

"It's okay, honest mistake."

"I must say, I am rather jealous of that mistake." Another man with an English accent walked forward. His deep blonde hair perfectly styled and eyes so brown they looked black. His skin was flawless and he was wearing slacks with a button down dress shirt rolled up to show inked forearms. He stalked over to Mor, lifted her hand, flipped it over and kissed her palm. "But I am grateful for the view of those legs."

She barely suppressed a moan as a pulse went from her palm to her clit. Maybe moving in with Atreyu was a bad idea. *Or the best idea I've ever had!*

"This jackass is Sebastian." Atreyu chuckled and lightly shoved his shoulder.

"Uh huh." She looked around. "Aren't you a little overdressed to be packing and moving?"

"Darling," He looked her over slowly, "One can never be under-dressed in the presence of such beauty." He winked at her before moving back to the box he was packing up.

Atreyu chuckled and pulled her into the living room, nudging her to sit on the couch. A moment later, a steaming cup of coffee was put in front of her by Max, who gave her a shy smile. "I found some creamer in your fridge, so I put some in. Is that okay?"

Lifting the cup with a smile, Mor looked up at him. "Thank you, Max. It's perfect."

He ducked his head with a smile and disappeared back into the kitchen. A second later, Atreyu handed her a plate of bacon, eggs and biscuits. "Eat up! It's a big day. Your first full day of freedom!"

"Where did you get all this? I know I didn't have this in my kitchen." She dove in for the bacon and moaned as she took a bite. "I fucking love bacon." She looked up to find Atreyu's eyes on her mouth.

"That would be me, darling, although our dear Max did the cook-ing. He is a wiz in the kitchen."

Max grunted behind Mor and she turned to look at him. "This bacon is perfect." A smile briefly appeared on his face before he ducked his head and went back to work.

"Eat up, beautiful. Let's get this big day going!" Atreyu jumped up and rushed off to the kitchen.

She stared at the plate for a minute, dumbfounded. "I'm confused."

"What are you confused about, darling?" Sebastian came and sat next to her.

"Why are you all here?"

"Our dear brother Atreyu called, explained your situation and your awful family, and we could do nothing but come and help you spread your wings and fly." He smirked.

"So y'all didn't have anything going on? Work, lives, whatever?"

"We own a mechanic shop." He stared at her. "Why aren't you eating, darling? You need your strength." His voice roughened. He picked up a forkful of eggs and held it to her mouth. "Open up."

Mor's mouth opened before she could think and she took the bite from him. Oh shit, those were good too. She couldn't help the moan that slipped out. "Oh fuck, Max you are a genius!" She grabbed the fork from Sebastian and started stuffing her face, totally focused on the craziness in front of her. Shit, literally the best food she had ever eaten. Holy fuck.

When she had finally scraped the plate clean, Mor sat back with a groan to find all three men standing in front of her. Sebastian licked his lips, Max was smiling softly at her and Atreyu had a wicked grin on his face like he wanted to eat her. "Um. I think that's the best food I've ever eaten."

"I thought your family came from money, darling." Sebastian raised an eyebrow at her.

"Well, true. But I was the daughter adopted to eventually marry well." She shrugged. "I was on a very strict regime of healthy, terrible food, and proscribed exercise including running, yoga, and martial arts. Which I only got to do if I did everything else they said and smiled pretty for pictures. Not that I actually got to spar. Can't risk the face." The change that came over the guys when she said that was intense. They were - angry? "Are y'all okay?"

Atreyu started to say something when someone pounded on the door. Without waiting for her, Sebastian strode over to the door and opened it. "You aren't the movers I hired." His voice was sharp, his accent making the words sound harsher than what was said.

"Who are you?"

"Oh shit. Tom." She plastered a smile on her face and hurried over. "Tom, what an unpleasant surprise. And Dad. You're here too."

"What is the meaning of this? Who are these men? Your mother made it very clear what was expected of you."

"And I made it very clear to her that I wouldn't be coming home." Her voice took a sharp turn.

"We are here to move you home. Where you will do your duty to your family and marry John Davis!" Her father's face was splotchy and he was sputtering.

"I do believe you are mistaken." Sebastian's voice was deadly but his smile was wicked as he wrapped an arm around her. Mor tried not to jump as Max slid up on her other side and slipped his arm around the other side. When a warm body pressed up behind her, she leaned her head back onto Atreyu's chest. "As you can see, we are taking very good care of Mor."

She shivered as Max leaned over and nuzzled her neck. "Very good care." Mor couldn't help but to tilt her head to give him better access.

"So as you can see, you are not needed." Atreyu's hands squeezed her shoulders.

"You - you - get your hands off my daughter!" Her dad reached out and grabbed her arm. "She is coming with me!"

Before she could try to pull away, Mor was standing behind a wall of men. What a view of seriously perfect asses. "Um, guys?" They were growling. All of them.

"You will not touch her ever again." Atreyu snarled. They took a step forward. "You will never bother her again." Another step. "Or you will deal with us." One last step, and now Tom and Dad were halfway down the stairs. "She's ours now."

They turned and ran. Literally ran. Mor started laughing, a little hysterically. "You guys. That was amazing!" She started jumping up and down. Literally jumping. "I'm free. I'm free! I'm totally broke, have no where to go, but I don't have to go back to that awful house where they wanted to check my virginity and marry that awful man!" She collapsed on the couch, giggling like a madwoman. She closed her eyes, holding on to this delicious feeling of freedom.

When she opened them, the guys had gathered around her and were looking at her like she had lost her mind. "Thank you. Seriously, thank you!" She grinned.

"You may be broke now, but you do have somewhere to go." Max's voice was soft. "We got you."

"You don't even know me." She sat up on her elbows. "Why are you all doing this?"

"Aside from it being the right thing to do since it really was Atreyu's fault, it feels right." Sebastian smiled. "Now, come on darling. Let's get everything packed so you can start on your new life." He reached his hand down to her.

She grinned and let herself be pulled up. "Let's do this!"

* * *

THE MOVERS HAD SHOWN up just as they taped up the last boxes and now she was following behind Atreyu's sleek black car with Max riding shotgun. Sebastian's fancy red car was behind them. It was as if they felt the need for her to be surrounded at all times. It should have made her feel uncomfortable, but all she felt was safe. Protected. Loved. She shook her head. No way in hell would she ever say that to the guys.

"Are you okay?" Max's soft voice barely carried over the sound of the radio. His fingers gently brushed her leg before going back into his side. All day long the men had been finding reasons and ways to touch her. Not in creepy ways or anything inappropriate. Just reassuring touches as if they knew she craved it. Touch had never been on the radar of her parents with hugs and gentleness totally off limits.

"I'm good. Just - excited? Terrified? Definitely sad, too. They're my parents. They should have loved me, but...but I was just a tool to them." A sob built up in her but she held it back. One tear escaped, but she pushed down the rest. Driving and crying was always a bad idea.

"I know how that feels." Max was staring out the window.

"You do?" Mor wasn't sure what to do with that, so she waited, hoping he would tell her more.

"My parents were much like yours. I was expected to fulfill certain duties and to provide my House with heirs, but I couldn't do it. Especially not with the awful woman they wanted for me."

So much to unpack in that. "That's awful. Although, kind of nice to know I'm not alone." She reached over and squeezed his hand. "We aren't alone." Releasing his hand, she moved her hand back to her lap. "So, um, how long do we have until we get to your home?"

"Our home." He reached over and laced his fingers through hers. "We have about an hour drive until we get to our home."

She smiled and kept driving. Almost exactly an hour later they pulled off the highway and started traveling further out. "Where are we exactly?"

"We don't live in town. We live a little farther out of town. It feels too hectic. We need...space."

"Space sounds amazing right now." She grinned. A few minutes later they turned right again and kept traveling. A few miles down the road, Atreyu slowed down and turned into a drive, pausing to punch in some numbers on a key pad before pulling through the seriously fancy - and thorough - gate.

"Code is seven-two-one-three." Max said.

"You're giving me the code to your home?"

"Our home." He squeezed her hand again. "Get used to saying it." He smiled softly at her.

She gulped, taking a shuddering breath. "Our home." Mor hadn't even seen it yet, but it already felt more like home than anywhere she had lived before. Parking next to Atreyu, she stared out at the beautiful stone home in front of her car. "I still don't understand why y'all are doing this." She had barely spoken, but he heard her anyway.

"Because you're worth it."

Mor swallowed hard. "You don't know me."

"I know enough. I know you didn't break when those people that pretended to be your parents raised you. I know you did everything you could to stand on your own. I know you didn't try to hurt or use anyone to get your own way. And I know that you stood up to your adopted family when they pushed you too far." He leaned toward her and reached a hand up to cup her cheek. "You are a strong, kind, fierce, and beautiful woman. That's what I know." He leaned in and kissed her. It was so different than Atreyu, but damn if she didn't love it. His lips moved softly against her mouth as she opened for him. His tongue smoothed across hers, dancing with it gently. He pulled back with a gentle smack. "So fierce." He pecked her lips. "So kind." Another peck. "So beautiful." One more and she was melting. "Let's get you settled in your new home."

She sat frozen in place until he walked around, opened her door, and held his hand out for her. Snapping herself out of it, she put her hand in his and let him pull her out of the car. He pulled her into his arms and kissed her softly one more time. "We had our housekeeper clean up a room for you. I hope that's okay?"

Before she could say anything, Atreyu walked up next to them and tugged her from Max's hold and into his arms. "If he gets a kiss, I get one too." He grinned, leaning toward her and pausing for a second before kissing her, giving her a chance to pull away. She couldn't move even if she had wanted to. He closed the distance and kissed her softly, licking the seam of her lips and then pulling away before deepening it further "Hey, beautiful. Welcome home."

"Well, this just isn't fair." Sebastian had just gotten out of his car and was staring at them, hand on his hip. He marched over, took her hand and hooked it through his arm. "Come, darling. I will show you your new home and let these boys organize the unloading of your things." Sebastian pulled her hand to his lips, kissed it, and then placed it back in the crook of his arm to lead her into the house.

"I think I'm having a mental breakdown."

"Why is that, darling?" His velvet voice washed over her.

"Your brothers both just kissed me." They walked in the door and she stood gaping at the beauty of the home. A double staircase arched up in the entry way. There were doors on either side of the entryway and she could see couches in one, and what looked like a bar in the other.

"They did. I'm feeling a little jealous." He patted her hand. "That's okay. I'll have my time."

"I don't understand." Her head felt like it would explode. "Your brothers. Both. Kissed. Me."

"Yes, darling, I know. I was there."

"Both of them."

"Darling, at the risk of raising your ire, you are sounding a bit simple right now." Sebastian quirked his eyebrow at her. "Are you quite alright?"

"I don't understand. How are they not mad right now? Why aren't you mad right now?"

"Ah. I see what you are confused about now. Darling, my brothers and I have always understood that if we did manage to find someone to complete our set, then we would be sharing."

"Wait. What?" She couldn't have heard that right.

"Sharing." He stopped in front of a door and pulled her into him. "My brothers and I have a special bond. It is not one that would easily accept the addition of mates. But one special, wonderful person?" He tucked a strand of her hair behind her ear. "One person could complete us. Now, let us see what Trisha set up for you, shall we?" He opened the door and gestured for her to go in.

She started to ask who Trisha was but then she walked in and her jaw dropped. "What's this?"

"Your room, of course, darling."

"But there's all this furniture." She gestured to the beautiful four poster bed that looked as soft as a cloud with the matching night-stands and dressers.

"When Atreyu told us what happened, we thought you might like this space. It was never a room any of us used and it felt right for you to have it. If you'd prefer your own furniture in here, I can have the movers comeback tomorrow and set it up for you." His voice was anxious and his face looked tight as he watched her take in the room.

"It's perfect." Mor walked over to the bed and softly touched the duvet covering the bed. "This is my favorite shade of blue."

The smile that came over Sebastian's face was breathtaking. "I'm so happy you love it. I'll go get your suitcase so you have something for tonight anyway. We'll let you get settled, and then we can all have dinner together. And maybe a movie? Wonderful." Mor nodded and Sebastian went out the door with a smile, leaving her to herself in this beautiful room.

The guys were so sweet - weird, but sweet. Who took in total strangers? She shook her head and noticed a door on the left side of the room. Mor opened it and walked into heaven. It must be heaven because where else would have a tub that could double as a small pool? And a shower of stone that was so big, it didn't need a door and had a seat running around it? Not bothering to close her mouth, she wandered further in and found a closet that was almost as big as her old apartment. Holy. Shit. She didn't have enough clothes to fill that closet, but she didn't care. It was the most amazing bathroom she had ever seen.

"Heaven. I'm in heaven."

A chuckle sounded behind Mor and she whipped around. "We have your bags." Atreyu smiled. "We'll leave them on the bed and let you get settled in. Dinner is in two hours." He winked and walked out of the door.

"Right. First, trying out that shower. Then dealing with everything else." She nodded to herself. She could do this.

CHAPTER 3

*T*wo hours later she was feeling refreshed and maybe ready to handle things. She had taken an excessively long shower and was now dressed in clean pajamas. She had braided her long blonde hair and peeked her head out of the room. Hearing the voices of the guys, Mor headed down the hall. She followed their voices to a room and hesitated outside of it, hand raised to knock. Should she bother them?

"Beautiful, why don't you come in?" Mor froze. Surely he couldn't know she was outside of the door? "Yes, I know you are outside of the door." The door opened. "Come in." How did he know she was there? These guys were so strange. She was currently ignoring that she should feel weird about how comfortable she was with them.

Mor was tall at five foot nine, but she felt dwarfed by these guys. And she loved it. "I heard you and I wasn't sure where to go, but I don't want to intrude."

"You can come in my room anytime you want, beautiful." He gave her his wicked grin and pulled her inside, lacing his fingers through hers. His room was all dark browns and golds with a leather couch and chairs on one side facing a TV. Max and Sebastian were on the couch playing a game and yelling at each other.

"Is that Smash Brothers?" She couldn't help the excited jump in her voice.

"Hell yeah, want to play?" Atreyu grinned and pulled her over to the couch. He grabbed a controller and tossed it to her. "Next round you are going down!"

"You need to work on your smack talk, Atreyu." Mor smirked at him. "You have no idea what you are getting into." They watched as Sebastian and Max did their best to destroy each other.

When Max finally won, Sebastian yelled "That's bullocks you dirty rotten cheater!" He jumped up and put Max in a headlock, both of them laughing. She stood there behind the couch with Atreyu laughing until her sides hurt. Finally, they stopped and looked up at her.

"Way to settle that like grown men." Mor smirked at them.

"Hmmm, I'd like to see you be calm in the face of such blatant cheating." Sebastian pointed dramatically at Max.

"Come join us, Mor." Max smiled softly at her and scooted over on the couch, leaving room for her to sit down between him and Sebastian. She sat down between the guys and Atreyu settled in at her feet, leaning back against the couch.

"If I sit here will you two behave?"

"Of course, darling, wouldn't dream of misbehaving with you." His voice was a low purr making her think of all the ways she would love for him to misbehave with her. Which was probably his point.

She grinned as the guys picked their characters. So typical. Atreyu picked Donkey Kong, Sebastian picked Star Fox and Max picked Marty. Pretending to take her time, she went through each one before picking Peach. They had no idea what was about to happen to them. She was going to take them out. Mor kept a confused look on her face, wanting to draw it out for as long as possible. They set it for no time limit, so she could play it off for as long as she wanted.

Max looked at her so sweetly as she died the second time and said, "Don't worry, sweetie. We'll teach you how to play." She almost felt bad for what she was about to do. Almost.

"Sure. Sounds great!" Mor said as Peach regenerated. Immediately she went on the offense and managed to take out all three of them within thirty seconds. Within one minute she had killed them all and was the winner. "I am the champion!" She stood up, hands straight up in the air and started singing, "I am the champion, my friends. And I'll keep on fighting til the e - " She cut off when Atreyu snapped an arm around her waist and pulled her back onto the couch.

"You are a dirty rotten cheater!" He worked hard to keep a scowl on his face but the corners of his mouth kept twitching up.

Sebastian smirked at her. "That will never work again. I demand a rematch!" His British accent was crisp and formal, almost like he was challenging her to a duel.

"Mor." Max just shook his head at her.

She couldn't help the grin that exploded across her face. "Y'all I haven't had fun like that in years!" She giggled. Straight up giggled! Mor hadn't giggled in years, either. Not since graduating and having to move back home. Really, she hadn't had reason to smile since moving back home. It was all 'you're too fat' and 'marry this guy' and so on.

"What's going on in that head of yours?" Atreyu cocked his head making his hair fall to one side.

"It's just nice to have fun. For once. I haven't smiled like this, much less laughed, since I moved back home." He didn't move, so she kept talking because apparently she had still had word vomit around him. "I should be terrified. I've lost my family. I have no idea who you are. There is no reason I should be this comfortable with you all. You're strangers. But I'm more comfortable with you than I have ever been with my family."

Now a smile cracked across Atreyu's face as he pulled her upright. "It doesn't sound like they were ever your family."

Slinging an arm around her Sebastian said, "We can be your family, darling."

"Sometimes the family we choose is better than the family chosen for us. I think there are people out there that match our souls and we just know it. We don't always acknowledge it because of fear." He nudged her arm. "When I met Atreyu and Sebastian, it felt like coming home. You feel the same." Red crept up his neck and he abruptly hurried out of the room.

"He's shy." Atreyu grinned and plopped down next to her on the couch. "He has a hard time opening up to us and never does to new people. He must like you. Let's play while he gets it together."

"We shouldn't go after him?" Mor started to stand up only to be pulled back down between Atreyu and Sebastian.

"No, he likes to have space." Sebastian shrugged as they started selecting their players.

She played another couple of rounds but Max still hadn't come back. Mor excused herself to 'use the restroom' and went to find him. The thought of him feeling uncomfortable in his home because of her made her stomach twist. She wandered around and finally found him in the kitchen. He was on the phone ordering Chinese food. When he put down the phone he leaned on the counter. "Gotta love Uber Eats. We wouldn't get anything delivered otherwise." He didn't look up.

"I love Chinese food." Walking over Mor leaned her hip against the counter. "I know you don't want to talk about what you said, earlier." She hesitated until he looked at her from the side. "Thank you. I'm sorry to come crashing into your lives like this."

Max turned, leaning into her. "I'm happy you came. We needed shaking up."

"How long have you lived together?"

"We moved in together after - well, about five years ago."

Ignoring his pause, she said, "But you've been friends for longer, right?"

He turned fully toward her, now, a real smile lighting up his face. He had a dimple - shit. She loved dimples. And with that smile across his face, damn. So sexy. She felt a flush, creeping up her neck and face. She really hoped he couldn't tell. Why was she so attracted to all of them? Ridiculous. It must be because she hadn't been around hot guys in so long. Or gotten any in longer than that. Talk about a dry spell of several years.

"We've been friends since we were kids. Sebastian and Ben grew up together, and Atreyu met them when they were ten and he was nine. Then I met them a year later when I was nine."

"Wait, who is Ben?"

"Ben lives with us too. He was called away by his family to deal with…some…things."

"Huh." She wanted to ask him about what it was, but it didn't feel right digging into the private life of someone she didn't know. "How have you liked living here? I used to hate having roommates, but that was probably because they were girls selected by my parents."

"I love living with the guys. They're like my brothers. I always have someone I can depend on."

"I can already tell you they're better than my brother."

"I know what shitty family is like." He hung his head for a moment. Before she could ask anything he said, "What were your roommates like?"

"Ugh. That is the nicest word I can think of for them." Max laughed at that and she smiled at him. "Seriously, they were only there to get a token degree so they could run whatever charity their future husband would approve of. And to find said husband if their parents had not picked him as long as he met the correct tax bracket and name qualifications."

"That doesn't sound too different than most of our families."

"What do you mean?"

Max opened and closed his mouth, clearly debating whether he was ready to tell her whatever had taught him about shitty families. Just then, the doorbell rang, effectively ending their conversation. "Go on up, I'll bring dinner up."

She went back to up to Atreyu's room and settled in one of the reclining chairs. "Rather long bathroom break, beautiful. How's Max?"

"Um - I - "

"Please don't insult our intelligence." Sebastian's voice was prim. "We are not censoring you for going to find him." He sent her a heated glance. "I rather love that you did."

Before she could form a reply to that, Max came in the room and set several bags and paper plates on the coffee table. "Yes! Good call, Max!" Atreyu dove in and started digging through the bags. Before he could get very far, Max pushed him away.

"Let Mor pick something before you two try and see who can stuff their faces the fastest."

Atreyu and Sebastian just stared at him, their mouths hanging open slightly. "Um right. Darling, do you have a preference?" Sebastian looked at her expectantly.

"No. Well, I love egg rolls. And fried rice. And orange chicken. And - "She cut herself off. Lamely, Mor added, "I'm not picky."

They grinned and started dishing up a plate for her. Once they were happy with the plate they passed it to her. "Any movie choices?"

"Our girl here is a Marvel fan." Atreyu winked at her.

"True story. I really hate rom coms. They just keep doing stupid shit that could easily be fixed by a simple fucking conversation. Usually with just a stupid question. I just want to punch them all. I'd much rather watch things with a lot of action and swords and stuff." She moaned as she took a bite of fried rice. "This is so good."

Mor looked up to see the guys staring at her. Atreyu had paused with chopsticks half way to his mouth, Sebastian had an egg roll hanging out of his mouth and Max was pushing down on a button on the remote control and the screen was flickering through movies without stopping. "Max? Are you going to pick a movie?" Three jaws snapped closed.

"Right. Movie." Max turned back to the TV and picked one. "Everyone okay with Fantastic Beasts?" When there were no objections he started the movie and plopped himself on the ottoman her feet were on. He leaned back against the arm rest and looked back at her. "Is this okay?" His arm rested across her legs.

"Definitely." Mor's voice was soft and he turned back to the movie. She wasn't sure how much of the movie she was going to pay attention to with his hand resting on her leg and his thumb rubbing soft circles on her calf. She glanced at Sebastian and Atreyu to see them watching them with little smiles. Without a word, they turned back to the movie.

They had all stopped eating, well Mor had stopped eating the guys were still working their way through the mountains of food, when Sebastian's head came up. "Here comes trouble." He grinned.

"Trouble?"

"Did anyone tell him?" Max looked over at Atreyu.

"Erm. No. I may have forgotten. It was all rather last minute?" He looked like a shamefaced puppy.

"This is going to be interesting." Max sighed and put his hand on her leg, gently squeezing it.

"I feel like I'm missing something." Nervously, she looked around at the guys.

"It's fine." Atreyu grinned. "Maybe I should just go and - Oh, heeeey Ben!" His voice got overly cheerful and he bounded up from his seat. "How's the family?"

Ben stood in the doorway, eyes locked on Mor. She gave a small wave from where she was sitting and struggled out of the chair, only not falling because Max caught her by her waist and held her up. Ben was tall and intimidating with more muscles than any of the other guys. He stood well over six and a half feet tall, making her feel oh so tiny. His dark hair was cropped short and his arms were crossed making his biceps bulge. She wanted to lick them. Wait. Shit.

"Who's this." Ben's voice was like velvety gravel. She wanted to drool.

"This is Mor! She's staying here." Atreyu grinned at him.

"So now you're bringing your bitches home?"

There went any sexy thoughts. "Excuse me. I am no ones bitch." Her voice snapped out.

"No no no no. She's not my bitch. I may have screwed up her life so she's staying here so we can help her." Atreyu smiled triumphantly at Ben.

"She needs to go." Ben's glare hadn't left her face.

Mor felt herself pale. Again, she wasn't wanted. That was okay, she'd figure it out. The guys were yelling at each other. Max had pulled her behind him and his growl was back. They were yelling at Ben that he was being a dick, unreasonable. But really, she was in his space. This was his home. She was coming between the brothers. Mor couldn't do that. "Guys." They didn't stop their yelling. "Guys. GUYS!" Finally, they stopped and looked at her. "It's fine. I'll go. Just let me stay tonight? Then I can go in the morning."

"What? No!" Sebastian's face softened as he looked at her. "Darling, you are *not* going anywhere. We promised to help you."

Ben had a haughty look on his face as he stared at her. "I refuse to get between you and your brothers. I'll leave tomorrow." Ben's face changed to almost look…regretful? But then the guys started arguing again. Atreyu, Max and Sebastian were yelling at Ben and he was yelling right back. "Guys! My choice. I won't cause a family to break apart. Mine is already broken. I won't make that happen to another one."

Before they could say anything else, Mor ducked around Max and Ben and ran out of the room. She ran into her room and shut the door. Leaning against the door she closed her eyes, trying to force her tears back. Mor couldn't help them leaking out when there was a soft knock on the door.

"Beautiful? I know you're there." She turned around and leaned her forehead against the door. Tears were falling freely now. She had hoped for just a moment that maybe she would be okay. That she had found someplace to be accepted. But she should know better. Good things didn't happen to her. "Please open the door. Ben won't be a problem, I promise." She still didn't answer. "Please, let us in."

"Mor, it'll be okay. We'll make him understand." Max's sweet voice came through the door.

"We won't lose him. Ben is our family just like you are." Sebastian's clipped voice came through.

"Please." Atreyu almost broke her he sounded so sad.

But she pushed away from the door and went to the closet, quickly packing the clothes she had brought in. After she was finished, Mor crawled into bed and cried herself to sleep. Tomorrow would be here sooner than she was ready for. She didn't know what she would do or where she would go. She would get through this. She just prayed that she wouldn't have to go back home to do it.

The next morning, Mor woke with bleary eyes and with a pounding headache. Sighing, she stood up and trudged into the bathroom. Time to face this super shitty day. Maybe she could find a job. She'd have to sleep in her car, but that would be fine. It would still be better than going home and having to marry John. Pretty much anything was better than that. And she could mostly stretch out in her back seat. So it wouldn't be too bad.

With that super comforting thought, Mor grabbed her bag and opened the door. She walked out without looking at the guys sitting across the hall from her. As soon as she walked out they jumped up, stumbling over themselves to get to her. Mor didn't look at them as she walked downstairs to the front door. Their voices sounded desperate as they talked over each other trying to get her to stop. She stepped out to find Ben waiting by her car with a look of confusion on his face.

"Mor." He looked over at her. "I - um." He shook his head. "I'm sorry. Please don't go." He grimaced when he said the words.

Mor shook her head and put her bag in the backseat of her car. "You made your feelings perfectly well known last night, Ben. No need to fake it now."

"I'm not faking it. I came home in a bad mood because of my family and I took it out on you."

"Thank you for that, Ben. But I believe that you spoke your truth. You don't want anyone else added to what you have here. And I understand. You have a wonderful thing here. Brothers that love you and a place of your own. A safe place." Mor looked at the ground. "I don't know what it's like to have that. But I do know what its like to not have a safe place, to be unwelcome and uncomfortable." Now she looked him directly in the eye. "I won't take that from you."

Without waiting for a response she got in her car and drove away. Tears started falling as she drove away. She refused to look in her rear view mirror at the line of men standing by the door. She turned out of the driveway and drove down the road. After several minutes Mor couldn't see through her tears so she pulled over and let her tears fall. She didn't know how long she sat there but she didn't hear the car pulling up behind her. And she didn't see the man walking up to her door. And when the door opened, Mor was too slow to notice the hand coming in front of her face until it was covered by a cloth. And then…she didn't notice anything.

CHAPTER 4

or the third time she woke up with bleary eyes and a pounding headache. Mor sat up slowly and looked around. She was - home? What was she doing home? She looked down and was wearing - a nightgown? What in the actual fuck? She crawled out of bed and looked around for her suitcase. She didn't find it, but she did see a fifties style dress laying on a chair. Fuck. How did she end up here?

After several minutes of arguing with herself about whether or not to put the dress on her door opened and her mother walked through. "Good. You're awake. Why aren't you getting dressed? We don't have a lot of time."

"Back up. What am I doing here?"

"You don't remember? Your brother brought you home." She clicked her tongue. "Honestly, you should know better than to drink and drive."

"I didn't. I was crying in my car and...I was drugged!" She turned to stare at her. "You had me drugged! How did you even know where I was?" Mor was yelling now.

Her mother didn't bother to deny it. "Honestly, Moreen. You are being ridiculous. Obviously we had a tracker placed on your car when you moved out of our house. We wanted to make sure you stayed pure." She shot her a nasty look. "Which Dr. Robertson confirmed you did not do! How dare you? You had very specific instructions to stay pure!"

"You sound insane. I'm leaving." She marched toward the door, not caring that she was in a nightgown. It covered everything, anyway. Long sleeved, high necked monstrosity that it was.

"Moreen. You will put on that dress and you will go down to dinner. I've managed to convince John that your lack of virginity is a plus since you will not be totally clueless in the bedroom. And we had Dr. Robertson ensure you are not pregnant."

"I'm not marrying that piece of shit!" Now she was yelling. There was no way she would marry him.

"You will marry him! We have clothed you and fed you for your entire life. Now you will pay us back for that or I will see you destroyed." She stalked across the room to her. "Put on the dress. Come downstairs. Be agreeable. Or so help me I will make you regret it for the rest of your life."

She left the room, slamming the door. Mor ran to it but heard a click just as she got to the door. She locked her in! *What the hell?* She stared at the dress for a little longer, slowly growing resigned to her lot. Well, at least she would play the part until she could figure out what she was doing. At least it would buy her time.

Taking a breath, she went into her bathroom and got changed into the hated dress. Mor hated wearing these. Mechanically she went through the motions of doing her hair and makeup. Once she was done, she went and sat down in the chair and waited. Eventually her mother came to get her. She looked her over, nodded once and gestured for Mor to come.

Suppressing a sigh, she followed her downstairs. Mor could hear her father, brother, and John chortling over something most likely ridiculous. Carefully, Mor blanked her face. Time to play her part. She could feel her soul wither a little bit as she put a vapid smile on her face and followed her mother into the drawing room. Yes, drawing room. Who the fuck has a drawing room? Assholes, that's who.

"Ah, there's my precious girl!" Her father's voice was boisterous. 'Precious girl' indeed. He only called her that in front of people he wanted to impress.

"Daddy." Mor kept the smile on her face.

"Come greet our guest!"

Mor's steps were small and precise as she walked over to the despicable John. She gave a breathless giggle as he took her hand and kissed it. It took everything in her to keep from yanking her hand back and gagging. "Moreen, how lovely to see you." His breath smelled like sour onions. Ugh.

"John." She tried but couldn't add anything to it. This may be harder than she expected it to be now that she had experienced nice men.

"I am so glad that my dear fiancé has come to her senses and abandoned her silly notions of independence." She gritted her teeth to keep from snapping back at him. "And this dress. Very appropriate. When we are married I expect you to continue to dress in a manner that reflects my ideals." He dragged his gaze down her. "You will at all times act in a polite and reserved manner. I expect hair and makeup to be done every day. You will not speak out of turn."

Mor almost threw up at that. Actually tasted bile in her mouth before forcing it down. This was going to be an interminable night. No way would Mor ever marry this guy, no matter what her parents thought. She kept her mouth shut and followed them into the dining room. John, her father, and brother immediately sat down and left Mor and her mother to seat themselves. Suppressing what would probably be one of many sighs, she sat where her mother pointed. Next to John.

The rest of dinner she spent being ignored except when called upon to make agreeable noises. The men spent the time talking politics and business while her mother simpered and agreed. Dinner dragged on and on and on. Dessert was eventually served (she was not given any, as per usual) and John looked at her like he was judging a particularly impressive race horse.

"She'll do for my heirs. And when we are married, I will ensure that our - ah - companies work very well together." He looked her up and down again. "I won't take it personally that she isn't a virgin. At least I won't have to break her in." He smirked, "Not like she'll be bothered by me other than to get those heirs." Her father and brother laughed while her mother smiled politely. "I assume the wedding can take place quickly?"

"Absolutely. I was able to book the club for next Saturday."

"What?" Mor spat it out before she could stop herself.

"You will need to watch that mouth of yours once you belong to me." He gripped her arm, twisting slightly. At her grimace of pain he leaned in and said, "Best remember what happens when I'm not happy." Squeezing her arm one last time before dropping it.

Shooting her a look to shut her mouth, her mother continued, "Yes, next Saturday. I have the vendors set up and a dress picked out for Moreen to your specifications."

She was too stunned to say anything. She wasn't even going to let Mor pick her own wedding dress. Ridiculous. Insane. She had just a few days to get out of here. Fuck. She let the conversation flow around her, vapid smile pasted on her face as she nodded at the right times. Why was he so insistent on her? Surely he could get any one of a dozen girls to be his breeder. What would make him and her parents so set on this wedding? It didn't make sense.

Eventually, Mor was allowed to go up to bed with the admonishment to get her beauty sleep. That way she would be sure to look as pretty as she was 'capable' of according to John. That little weasel. A few days. Just a few days to find a way out of this mess. As the door locked behind her, she realized something else. They had kidnapped her and were keeping her locked in. Getting out was going to be harder than she thought.

* * *

THE NEXT MORNING she woke up without a headache at least. Sighing, she pulled herself out of bed and found another dress waiting for her. She tried really hard to ignore that someone came into her room while she was sleeping to lay it out. What she wouldn't do for jeans and t-shirt. Or yoga pants. She got herself dressed then sat and waited for her mother to come and get her again. After reading one of the super boring books left in her room about proper presentation for ladies for at least an hour, her mother finally came in.

"Good! I am happy to see you trying to improve yourself. Come along. We have a dress fitting." Gag. The book was literally written in the fifties and was all about making sure your husband was happy. It included fun snippets like "never raise your voice, he's had a hard day" and "make sure dinner is on the table when he gets home".

"Breakfast?"

"Don't be silly. You need to lose at least five pounds before you walk down the aisle next Saturday."

Mor gapped at her. She was going to starve her into shape. She really shouldn't be surprised by the hateful and insane things she says, but it was hard to avoid. She had raised Mor as her daughter. She may not have been a very nice mother, but she was the only one Mor had ever known. And it hurt every time she said crap like that. Pressing her lips into a thin line to keep from saying what was on her mind Mor followed her to the car.

The drive into town was slow and silent. Mor clearly didn't rate even basic courtesy anymore. After parking, her mother ushered her into a small dress shop. Immediately accepting a cup of coffee from the saleswoman, her mother made a shooing motion with her hands. With little other choice at this point, Mor followed the woman to the back and stripped off her dress. The woman pulled out a hideous, long sleeved lace thing out of a garment bag. It literally went up her neck turtle neck style and had a ridiculous number of buttons in the back. She grimaced when she looked in the mirror. John seriously must get off on the fifties housewife thing. It made her want to throw up. At least she wasn't hungry anymore.

Resigning herself to this charade, she went back out to her mother. "Don't you just look precious! Oh! My baby girl is getting married!"

Mor couldn't help the incredulous look on her face. Again with the dramatic darling daughter routine. "Please don't, Mother. We both know that's not how you feel about me. Don't bother faking it." She turned around and froze. On the other side of the glass were the four hottest men she had ever seen. They found her? Within five seconds of her seeing them, they piled into the room. "What are you guys doing here?" Fuck, they were seeing her in this monstrosity. Why was she worried about that right now? Stupid thing to worry about.

Atreyu immediately wrapped her in his arms. "We found your car on the side of the road with a cloth smelling like chloroform in the front seat. We were so worried about you."

Another set of arms slipped around her waist. "We are so sorry, darling." Sebastian pressed a kiss on to the top of her head.

One more set of arms. "Please come back to us." Max buried his nose in her neck and took a deep breath in. And then sneezed. "This dress is awful, sweetie."

She couldn't help the snort of laughter that came out. "Way to understate, Max."

Over their shoulders, Mor looked at Ben. "Please, Mor. I know our first meeting was - bad - but I should have talked to the guys and you before passing judgment."

Just then she heard a sharp intake of breath. Mother's shock must have worn off. "Get your hands off my daughter!" Mor turned in their arms to look at her mother. "I am calling the police. You better get out of here!"

They looked down at Mor. "Why are you in a wedding dress, Mor?" Max's breath was soft against her ear.

"They had me kidnapped. I woke up in my old room, locked in, and was informed that I would be paying them back for their years of clothing and feeding me by marrying John who graciously decided to accept me even though I am not a virgin because I am not pregnant. They had a doctor check for those things while I was passed out from the chloroform the kidnapper used."

The silence was deadly in the room. Ben stomped forward, taking her chin in his hand. "Have they always treated you this way?"

"Yes." He held her gaze, waiting. "They have made sure that I knew my place."

He swung around to her mother and stalked toward her. She stumbled back, dropping the phone. He gestured for the saleswomen to hold still. When Mother hit a wall he leaned down until his face was in hers. "You will leave Mor alone. As it stands, I'm having a very hard time not killing you, your husband and son for what you've done to her. You have violated her in terrible ways. If you ever come near her again then I won't hold back. Do you understand?" He waited for her nod. "Good."

He pushed away from her and turned back to Mor. "Get dressed. We're taking you home."

She was frozen until Sebastian nudged her. She rushed to the back, dragging one of the ladies with her. "Please help me with these awful buttons."

"I'm so sorry about this." The girl whispered as she worked on the buttons. "I had always known they weren't the nicest, but I never imagined..."

"Do I know you?" Mor turned to look at the woman.

"I was a few years behind you in school." She blushed.

"So everyone knew, huh?"

"Yes. Well, we all knew that your brother was an ass and that your parents were very, um, particular about their status. At least you have someone sticking up for you now. Super hot someones." Now she gave a breathless giggle as she pulled the hideous dress off her shoulders.

As fast as she could, Mor pulled on the awful dress she came in. All these awful dresses. She wondered what the guys would think of the stupid thing. Hurrying to the front of the shop, she tripped only to be caught by Ben. He smirked down at her and settled Mor on her feet. He leaned down and whispered, "Nice dress," before stepping back.

Blushing, she followed behind him. The guys surrounded her as they walked out the door. They were silent as they piled into a large SUV with Ben driving. That made sense. He seemed like a control freak may be hidden not so deep down in him. "How did you guys find me?"

"Um. We're really good guessers?" Atreyu said. "I knew where your old place was, so we just kind of looked around,"

"Yeah, I'm not stupid." She rolled her eyes at them. "That doesn't even make sense. You had no idea who had taken me. So try again."

Silence reigned in the car. Finally, Ben broke it. "We can't show you here." The silence in the car was heavy.

"Show me what?"

"How we found you. But when we get home, we will."

Mor stared at him blankly for a second before noticing the looks on the faces of the other guys. They were shocked. Max recovered first. "You good with that?"

"I wouldn't have said it if I wasn't. She needs to know if she stays with us. We would be no better than her shit family if we weren't honest with her."

Ben clearly had dealt with shitty families. He'd come home in a bad mood because of family business, Mor remembered. Had it only been two days ago? This was insane. Less than a week and she'd lost her home, told off her family, met four gorgeous guys and moved in with them, and then been kidnapped and rescued. She started breathing hard and her head started spinning. Her vision darkened and her head tipped back.

"Oh look, stars." It slipped out.

"Oh shit!" Atreyu held her up as she wobbled in her seat.

"Get her head between her knees." Sebastian ordered from the front seat. He had turned around.

"You have stars around your head." He really needed to know. "They're pretty."

Atreyu and Max helped her to lean forward and guided her head down. "It's okay, Mor. Breathe. We've got you. You're okay."

"What's wrong with her?" Ben's voice was tight.

"I think everything is catching up to her. She's had a rough couple of days." Max's voice was soothing as he rubbed circles on her back. "Slow breaths, sweetie, slow breaths."

Eventually Mor was able to sit up. "What happened?" Sebastian was turned around in his seat, hand resting on her knee.

"I was just thinking about everything that has happened in the last few days and I panicked a little bit. Thank you for helping me. Again. I seem to be a problem child for you, too."

"Don't you ever say that again. You are not a problem child, you were never that. Your asshole parents were the problem." Atreyu pulled her head into his shoulder.

"Helping you isn't a problem." Ben growled.

She swallowed past the lump in her throat, crying. "Thank you. I'm sorry I'm crying again."

"It's okay. Just let it out."

With that permission, Mor cried the rest of the way home into Atreyu's shoulder while Max gently held their hands laced together and rubbed his thumb across the back of her hand. Sebastian stayed turned around, hand resting on her knee. Ben kept checking on her in the rear view mirror. She felt surrounded. Safe. Taken care of. By four guys who were essentially strangers.

When they pulled into the driveway, she stopped the guys. "I don't understand why you are doing this."

Sebastian smiled. "We told you. You're family."

"But how can you know that when you don't really know me?"

Ben grunted. "We can answer that once we show you how we found you." He walked off toward the back of the house.

"Do we follow?" Mor looked at the others tentatively. The guys had tensed up.

"Yeah, come on." Max took her hand again and tugged her forward. She followed them to the backyard.

"I ask that you don't scream." Ben stated.

"Scream at what?" Mor stared at them in confusion as they all lined up.

Ben nodded at Max who closed his eyes and raised a hand. He started tracing something in - oh shit. He was writing *glowing letters* in the air! What the actual fuck? Mor stepped back. Max was still going, glowing symbols hanging in the air. With a wave the symbols puffed out. The guys shook their heads. Their ears were pointy? And when they opened their eyes they were glowing.

They were exuding a power of some kind and it drew her in. Felt like home. "I don't understand." She took an unsteady step toward them. "You have glowy eyes. You're taller. You're leaking light! What the fuck?"

Ben grunted. "At least you aren't screaming."

"Why is NO ONE answering my question! Why do you have glowy eyes and light leaking from you!" Now she was screeching. Not attractive, but she really didn't care.

"We're Fae, Mor." Sebastian grinned at her.

"Fuck me sideways." She whispered before sinking down to the ground and passing out.

CHAPTER 5

*M*or could hear voices around her that sounded like they were echoing. She tried to force her eyes open but couldn't do it. The voices got closer and closer. Or maybe she woke up more? Either way, she began to understand the chatter. The guys were arguing about if she was alright. There was a damp cloth brushing over her forehead. It felt so good she turned into it with a groan.

The voices cut off. This time when Mor forced her eyes open she was able to get them open a crack. There were blurry shapes and the light stabbed in. "Turn the fucking lights off!" Her voice was a croak.

"Och, hush now lass." A woman's voice. "Boyos, leave now." She had never heard an Irish accent in person so that ruled out anyone she knew.

"Wha - ?"

"Those daft boys showed ye their true selves without preparing ye properly." A work roughened hand brushed hair out of her face. "Can ye open yer eyes for me, lass?" Concentrating, she managed to open her eyes. The woman leaning over Mor grinned. She had dark brown hair and weather roughened brown skin. "There's a good lass. Ye had the boyos losing their damn minds. Not like there was much fer them to lose." She winked.

"What happened?" Mor tried to sit up but her arms wouldn't hold her up.

"Ye saw them as they really are, lass." She gave her an appraising look. "And then ye fainted. Can't say that impresses me, but the boyos assure me ye've been through a lot these past few days." Her brogue was soothing as it washed over her.

"Fuuuck. I can't believe I fainted on them. They must think I'm scared or something. Shit. I don't want to hurt their feelings." Mor tried to force herself up but fell back with a wince. "I need to get to them." When she lay back down she noticed she wasn't in that awful dress anymore.

"Wait, lass. I sent them to get ye a snack. I can hear them trippin' over themselves in the kitchen."

"Who are you? And why am I not in that dress?" She finally was awake enough to realize she should have asked this much sooner than she did.

"Trisha. I've been takin' care of these boyos since they broke out on their own. I've cared for Atreyu's family for well over a century now. Better I be askin' who ye are. As for the dress, the boyos felt ye'd be more comfortable like this so I changed ye." She pinned Mor with a glare.

"A century? What?" She couldn't have heard that right.

"Och, lass. Don't be gettin' off track. I'm a Brownie. We live a long time. Now. Who. Are. Ye?"

"I'm nobody. Atreyu met me and somewhat messed up my life but it was really one big disappointing disaster anyway. And then he and the guys pulled me out of it. I can't believe I fainted. I really need to make sure they are okay."

Trisha looked thoughtful at her response. Before either of them could say anything else, a gruff voice sounded from across the room. "Don't think about getting up." She forced herself to focus and saw Ben striding into the room. His voice and face softened as he reached her side. "Let me help you." He slipped an arm around her back and eased her into a sitting position leaning against him.

Trisha watched with a small smile on her face. "Right then. She'll be fine. Make sure she doesn't exert herself, understand me?"

"Yes ma'am." Ben didn't take his eyes from Mor as he answered Trisha. He tucked her into his side, making sure she didn't fall.

Shadows fell across them and she looked up to see Atreyu, Max and Sebastian setting down a plate with snacks and a glass of orange juice. The room was filled with tension. "I'm so sorry."

"What are you sorry for?" Max's face snapped toward her.

"I can't believe I reacted that way. I am so sorry."

Sebastian sighed and settled next to her on the couch, taking her hand. "You've had an awful few days and then we surprised you with what we are." He looked so sad Mor reached over and squeezed his hand. Before she could move it, he flipped his hand over and laced his fingers with hers.

"Why do you look like you did before?"

Atreyu knelt at her feet. "What do you mean, beautiful?"

"I did see you with pointy ears, glowing eyes and leaking light, right?" Her eyes bounced between them. "Why are you back like this?" They all shifted uncomfortably. No one would meet her gaze. "Guys?"

"We didn't want to make you feel uncomfortable." Max finally rushed out.

"So you hide yourself from me? Do you usually hide at home?" When no one answered she knew what that meant. "If I am making you need to hide in your own home, then this won't work." She tried to pull away from the guys.

"We don't want you to go, Mor." Ben wrapped his arm around her more firmly, keeping her from moving.

"Then you can't hide here." She glared at them. "Max, do your thing." When he hesitated, Mor growled out, "I will not stay here and make you hide!"

He sighed and started drawing the glowing letter things again, but faster this time. When he was done and sent the magic out over them she was staring at four insanely hot guys. They were bigger, more primal. Their ears poked through their hair and their eyes did glow. "Woah." She tried to form more words but couldn't. Without thinking

44

she reached out to Atreyu and traced the tip of his ear. He closed his eyes and a little moan escaped him. "I'm so sorry. Did I hurt you?"

The guys all chuckled. The sound wrapped around her and went straight to her core. They were hotter now than before. Their faces were slightly more angular but the hard planes only made her want to touch them more. She wondered if everything got bigger and harder. She felt Ben lean forward, pressing his mouth against her ear, "Believe me, it isn't pain he is feeling right now."

"Oh. Oh! Um." She couldn't think of anything to say. "So ears are good."

Atreyu leaned forward so his mouth was a breath from hers. He held her gaze, his ice blue eyes almost hypnotic. Because what other explanation could there be for her to not want to pull away? "Ears are real good, beautiful."

A moan escaped before she could pull it back in. Atreyu's wicked grin spread across his face and he leaned in. She didn't think, just closed the distance and pressed her mouth to his. His hand dropped to her waist, holding her still as his tongue demanded entrance. She opened without a thought and moaned as his tongue invaded her mouth. She felt another set of hands drifting across her back and then lips on her neck and then more hands skirting the bottom of her shirt. She ground herself forward onto Atreyu's leg. She couldn't think, only feel.

"Och, really boyos. She was just passed out." Trisha's voice cut across their lust like a bucket of ice water. Sheepishly they pulled back. Only then did she realize all four had their hands on her. Fuck. What was up with that? "What were ye thinkin'? S'cues me, ye were thinkin' with yer dicks instead of yer brains." The tiny woman had her hands on her hips and was tapping her foot.

"Sorry, Trisha. We haven't been around her in this form yet." Max looked somewhat bashful standing behind her. He hadn't taken his hands off of her yet. Actually, they were all still touching her.

"She touched my ears." Atreyu looked as if that was enough of an explanation.

"And who let her, ye wee fool?" Trisha shook her head. "If yer gonna be in yer Fae form around the lass ye need to explain what that means." She stomped out of the room, muttering to herself about idiot boys.

"Ooookay. I'm guessing that means you all have some explaining to do." They were all staring at her, still touching her. Mor slowly started to melt back into them and felt their hands slowly moving over her. When she felt the lust start to rise, Mor jumped up. "I think if I want an explanation I better go sit over there. By myself. Alone. So you can't touch me and overwhelm my brain with your hotness." She stumbled over to a chair, sinking into it. "Stay over there. I can't think if you touch me."

The guys smirked but didn't move. "I rather like that we make you not think." Sebastian had on the expression of a supremely self satisfied male. Mor rolled her eyes.

"What I wouldn't love to do to you after that eye roll." Dark promise was in Ben's voice.

"Shit, stop. I think I need to know what is happening before we all get swept up and then I cause more problems for y'all." She shook her head, trying to clear it of all the dirty images her brain was insisting on. "Start at the beginning."

Max ran a hand through his hair, settling on the floor and leaning back against a chair. "We're Fae. Specifically High Fae from the different elements." He pointed to each of them. "Atreyu is from Earth, Ben Fire, Sebastian Air, and I'm Water."

Sebastian started talking next. "When we are in our true forms, everything is enhanced. All senses, feelings, thoughts. It's as if everything is magnified."

"So that's why we were all making out."

They guys glanced at each other but didn't say anything. "We each have control over our elements no matter what form we are in, but it's a stronger connection when we are in our real form."

"Primal form." Ben grunted.

"We are not having that argument right now." Sebastian rolled his eyes at Ben's statement.

"Primal? And why did Max change you?" It slipped out before she could stop it. Her filtering abilities had really disappeared since meeting Atreyu.

"It makes sense. Everything is more intense. Our responses are baser, instincts stronger." Ben shrugged.

"Ben insists that our natural form is 'primal'." Sebastian's air quotes made it clear what he thought of that. "Max does the changing because he is the best at glamour. We can do it, but not as easily as him."

Max added, "It's because I'm Water."

"I'm ignoring that for now. I have too much to process." She closed her eyes and pinched the bridge of her nose. "So basically, you are stronger in these forms. Your natural forms." They all nodded. "And you can do magic?"

Grins spread across the room. "We can do magic." Max said. "But our magic is specific to our element."

"Mostly, anyway. There is some overlap." Sebastian tapped his chin thoughtfully. "It's hard to explain. We've never had to before."

Mor just stared at them. When no one said anything, she asked, "Can I see it? Your magic, I mean. I mean I'd like to see it, if you'll let me?"

Atreyu grinned. "I'll let you see it any time you ask." Yep, the innuendo was pretty clear. And there was that heat hitting between her legs again. She was going to have to take care of that tonight.

Ben unfolded from where he was on the couch and stalked over to her. He bent over and swept her into his arms. "You're so big." She clapped a hand over her mouth as the room erupted into laughter. "Ugh, why does everything sound dirty? I just meant that you are bigger now than you were." They guys laughed harder. "You know what I mean!"

"Maybe you should stop while you can." Ben's voice wavered with laughter. "Otherwise I may have to show you just how much bigger I am."

Fuck. Every other word was making her horny. Bad enough to have all these hot guys who turn out to have *magic* but they all seem to want her too. Too bad. She wouldn't be able to pick one and drive a wedge between the guys. She'd just have to make sure to keep all her delicious fantasies to herself. She was going to spend a lot of time working off excess energy.

Mor blinked at the setting sun as Ben pushed outside. "How long was I out?"

"Just a couple of hours. You've been through a lot." Ben settled her on a chair on the patio. "Ready to see some magic?" He wiggled his eyebrows at her, startling a laugh from her.

"Definitely!"

He held up a hand and flame appeared in the middle of it. Bringing his other hand up, he tilted the flame so it was suspended between his hands. With a wink to Mor, the flame expanded into a ball that he started tossing between his hands. "That's so cool!" With a grin he flicked the fire ball to a fire pit over on the edge of the patio.

"We can make s'mores." He grinned. It was the first time she had seen him really relaxed.

"My turn!" Atreyu bounded over to the edge of the patio and sank his hands into the dirt. Closing his eyes with a blissful sigh, he sat down. A moment later flowers were pushing their way up through the grass. Then a squirrel ran up his arm to sit on his shoulder. He pulled his hands out of the earth and walked over to Mor, squirrel hanging out like a parrot on his shoulder. He knelt in front of her. "Hold out your hand."

Without hesitation Mor lifted her hand to him. Gently catching it with his he kissed the back before holding it up to the squirrel. The squirrel chittered for a moment before running down her arm to sit on her shoulder. It pet her cheek and then jumped down. "Holy shit. That squirrel just pet me!" She couldn't stop grinning.

Sebastian grinned and sat next to her. "I'm next." He closed his eyes briefly and when he opened them she felt a gentle breeze caressing her face. Then the breeze caressed her legs, smoothed over her breasts and lightly touched between her thighs before disappearing. A moan left her before she could reign it in. Sebastian winked at her.

"Of course you had to do something like that." Max sounded more amused than anything else. "I'm up." He set a glass of water on the table next to her. With a flick of his finger, the water rose from the glass. Another flick and it started weaving around itself in a hypnotic pattern. Final flick and it flowed back into the glass.

She stared at her guys. No. Not her guys. The guys. These amazing, talented, super hot Fae men. "Y'all are amazing." She couldn't think of anything else to say. "Just amazing." Mor couldn't wipe the smile from her face. "Magic is real!" She almost shouted it she was so excited. "Sorry. My nerd side is having a mind-gasm right now"

"Mind-gasm?" Sebastian smirked at her.

"Yep! Like an orgasm in my brain. Because this is blowing my mind." She jumped a little in her seat. "Fuckin' magic!"

"Oh boy, our girl's a nerd." Atreyu laughed.

"I believe I promised our nerd-girl some s'mores." Ben smirked at her. "I'll go get the stuff." He looked at her thoughtfully for a second. "Stay there." He disappeared inside.

"Nerd-girl? That shouldn't be a thing."

"Darling, you should have thought about that before you had a 'mind-gasm' over our magic." Sebastian had a point.

Ben was back pretty quickly. After setting down the stuff for s'mores he came and swept her out of the chair. He carried her to one of the chairs near surrounding the fire. "If you wanted closer to the fire I could have walked over."

"You just fainted a couple hours ago." He sat down with her in his lap. "Besides, I like carrying you." His voice was soft, barely there.

Before Mor could ask him what he meant, the guys came and joined them. They laughed and joked as they passed out the skewers with marshmallows. They all had their's hovering over the fire, barely getting warm. She watched for a moment, not to sure what to do. With a shrug, she put her marshmallow into the flames.

"What are you doing?!" Max sounded appalled when she pulled the flaming marshmallow out.

Mor panicked, trying to blow it out. "I've never done this before! I was trying to copy you." Her voice was quiet and she blushed with shame.

"Why haven't you ever done this?" Sebastian was clearly affronted.

"My parents never let me eat sweets." She couldn't help the sad tone in her voice as she stared at the now black marshmallow.

"Mor." Ben just shook his head. "You can tell us these things." He gently took the skewer from her and removed the charred marshmallow before replacing it with a new one. "Let me teach you how."

Slowly, conversation picked up again and soon Mor had relaxed again. Ben showed her how to roast the marshmallow into a golden brown and then to squish it between two graham crackers and chocolate. Taking a bite, Mor moaned. "Oh my gosh, this is so good. It's better than sex!"

The guys laughed. "Mor, if that's your standard then you haven't been having good sex." Atreyu laughed.

"You may be right, but either way this is so. Damn. Good." She sighed contentedly and snuggled back into Ben's arms. He was gently flicking his fingers at the fire, making it turn different colors and weave into patterns.

Well after the sun set, Mor felt her eyes drift closed. The next time she opened her eyes she was tucked into her bed. Her shoes and jeans had been taken off, but other than that she was covered. She felt vaguely disappointed that she wasn't more undressed. But then she had fallen asleep, so it would have been super creepy for one of them to do that. Maybe she was just disappointed they weren't here with her. Nope, she had not had coffee yet and did not want to unravel that thought.

The thought of coffee drove her out of bed. Mor pulled on some sweats and a clean tank top and headed to the kitchen. The moment she opened her door she smelled coffee. She could have sworn it was calling her name. She headed downstairs in a coffee seeking fog. When she walked in, Trisha was standing on a stool at the stove scrambling some eggs. "Good morning, Trisha."

"Good morrow to ye lass. Ye hungry?"

"Definitely. And I definitely need some coffee. Can you point me to the mugs?"

Trisha pointed to them and she went over and helped herself. She found some milk in the fridge to cut the coffee with and then sat on a stool. A few minutes later, Trisha slid a plate full of eggs and bacon toward Mor. "You are amazing." Barely managing to get the words out before shoveling food into her face. Trisha watched her with a satisfied smile on her face before turning to start the dishes.

"Where are the guys?" She asked between bites.

"They've headed to the shop. "Tis Sunday, so they doo'na usually work, but they want to make up for missin' last Friday."

"My fault." She hung her head.

"Och, lass. Quit yer bellyaching. "Tis no one's fault but Atreyu for messin' yer life up. But I think they all agree "twas worth it." She winked at her. Winked.

Mor blinked at her. "I'm really not worth all this trouble."

"Lass. I'll no be tellin' ye this again. Yer worth it." She glared at her until she nodded her agreement. "Now. Would ye like to be goin' to the shop?"

"Yes, um, yes I'd like that." She nodded.

"Good. Now finish yer breakfast and then go get dressed. When yer ready I'll take ye over." She hesitated a moment before continuing. "Lass. Ye know ye cannae be tellin' others about what the boyos are."

"I understand." There were many reasons to keep this to herself. First and foremost to protect the guys. Trisha watched her for a moment before she turned back to the dishes and ignored her.

Taking that as a sign, Mor worked her way through the rest of her breakfast and coffee. She tried to do her own dishes, but Trisha slapped her hands away and ordered her to go get dressed. She hurried up the stairs, excited to see where the guys worked. When she got in the shower, thoughts of the guys working took over her mind. How would they look, bent over a car with a look of concentration on their faces? Tight jeans, stretched white t-shirt, sweat dripping off them.

Mor's mind bounced between them, unable to pick just one to focus on. Since it was just her she thought, *to hell with it*. Might as well enjoy the images her brain was throwing at her of being surrounded by them. Four super hot mountains of men. Fae. Glowing eyes focusing in on her while eight hands roamed over her body holding her in place for their mouths and teasing her nipples...slipping between her legs to stroke her slit. She shuddered at the thought and slipped her hand down.

"Oy! Lass! We need to get goin'!"

Damn. Trisha had the worst timing. With a sigh, she rinsed off and got out of the shower. Mor towel dried her hair before pulling on a clean pair of jeans and a purple tank top. Hesitating only for a moment, she decided to just put on a little eye liner and mascara. She'd be in a shop all day, so really no point in the full face. No one was here to make her today. She grinned and went to put her shoes on before heading down the stairs to meet Trisha. Today was amazing.

CHAPTER 6

*T*risha ushered her to a car and hopped in. The car had been modified to fit her small frame with extended pedals and a raised seat. The steering wheel had multiple controls on it so she wouldn't have to reach over to the console for much. "Did the guys modify your car?"

"Aye, that they did, lass. I didna get out much 'til those boys got hold of my car." Trisha beamed with pride.

She smiled back at her. Her guys - the guys - were pretty amazing. Taking in strays like her, helping out Trisha. Probably without saying anything, just doing it because it needed to be done to make life better for someone. Mor turned and looked back out the window, smiling as she watched the hill country roll by. How lucky could she be to have been pulled out of the shit show that had been her life? And by guys who wanted her to get better. They didn't pull her out to make her their toy.

After about ten minutes they pulled up to a rather fancy looking shop called Magic Mechanics. She snorted trying to hold in her laugh, but nope! Mor had to wonder which came first? Magic Mechanics or Magic Mike? And why not change the name? They were absolutely hot enough and maybe that was why the name? Maybe she'd get a show. She would not say no to that. In fact, please please please let it be that.

"Go on, girl. I hae to get back. The boyos will bring ye home." When Trisha shooed her off it didn't feel as cutting as when her mother did. Probably because there wasn't a hateful bone in Trisha's body.

"Thank you for the ride, Trisha!" Mor hopped out to the cheerful "Yer welcome" and hurried inside. No one was at the desk in the front but she heard music in the back. May as well let herself in then. Atreyu did say she could come in whenever she wanted. She walked around the desk and opened the door. "Holy shit!" She had walked into hot rod heaven. Mor had no idea what any of these crazy beautiful cars were, but they made her want to do really bad things. Preferably after going really fucking fast.

Atreyu popped up from under the closest car. "Hey beautiful!" He was in his human form, which made sense.

She couldn't help but admire him as he sauntered over to her. And yes, work stained jeans and a white t-shirt straining over all those muscles was super sexy. He bent over and kissed the corner of her mouth. Remembering the name of the shop she started laughing. And then laughed harder as the other guys walked up, looking just a delicious as Atreyu.

"Care to share with the class?" Sebastian crosses his arms and lifted an eyebrow.

"Magic Mechanics?" She gestured to all of them standing in a super sexy line in front of her.

"What of it?" Ben scowled.

She laughed harder, unable to get it out. Finally, after several false starts, Mor gave up trying to talk and googled Magic Mike. When she showed them Max blushed, Ben rolled his eyes and walked away, Atreyu laughed with her, and Sebastian leaned in to her. "Darling, if you want a show all you have to do is ask." He nipped her neck making her laugh slip into a breathless moan. He grinned and tugged her hand. "Come sit with me while I work on this old Ferrari."

"I know that name!" Mor grinned. "No clue which one it is, but at least I know that name!" She did a fist pump.

Sebastian rolled his eyes at her. "That is a travesty, darling. If you are going to be staying with us then you need to start learning your cars."

He lifted the bottom of his shirt to wipe his face off. Mor's eyes strayed down to the perfect six pack of abs that was exposed. A drop of sweat ran down his abs and she followed it's path. She really wished she could be following it with her tongue. He had a perfect V leading into his low riding jeans and Mor couldn't help but wonder at what it pointed to.

"Enjoy the show, darling?" Her gaze snapped up to see Sebastian holding his shirt up and watching her watch him.

"Yep. I definitely was." No point in pretending otherwise. He knew he was hot. And he knew that she knew.

Sebastian snorted and then motioned for her to come over. He had the hood popped up on a red car. "This beautiful little ride is nineteen sixty-two Ferrari 250 GTO. I'm working on the engine so she purrs like she should." He winked and leaned in.

She stood next to him and leaned into the car. "I have no idea what I'm looking at."

He looked over at her. "Do you want to learn?"

"Honestly, not really. Hanging with y'all while you work, sure! Learning to work on the car, nope."

"I appreciate the honesty, darling." He snagged a stool and pulled it up next to him. "Have a seat, we can chat while I work."

Perching on the stool next to him she watched him quietly for a little while. His gaze was focused and intense as he worked on the car. "How long have you been working on cars?"

"Atreyu got me into this. He and his dad were always tinkering on things and when I was able to get away from my oh so superior family I loved joining them. When we all decided to leave I thought this would be something for us to pass our time."

"You mean as a job?" She was confused.

"No, I don't actually need to work. I bought the house and the shop for us."

"Wow, that's amazing."

He glanced around. "Max's family cut him off and Atreyu's family didn't have a bunch of extra. Ben didn't need the extra tie to his." He shrugged. "I wanted to do something nice for once."

"Seems like there's a story there." She didn't say anything else. If he wanted to tell her that would be fine. If not, that would be okay too. She really hoped he opened up

"My family is high born. As in higher than most High Fae born." He glanced at her for a reaction.

"So I have no idea what that means, but the way you say it makes it seem like it sucks."

A relieved smile crossed his face. "I suppose you would react differently than most. Every woman I've revealed that to has been far too interested in my family."

"Have there been many?" She didn't really want to know, but the question popped out before Mor could stop it.

"Well, I'm a little over two hundred years old. So yes."

"Waaaaiiiit." Her eyes bugged out of her head. "Two. Hundred."

"Actually, I'm two hundred and thirteen years old." He kept working. When she didn't respond he finally looked over at her. "Shit! Are you okay?" He dropped his tool and came over to her.

"I don't think I understand." Her brain couldn't wrap around it.

"Well, Fae live longer than the average human." He looked at her like she might burst and was gently rubbing circles on her back.

"Care to explain that a little more?" Mor was trying really hard to not hyperventilate.

"We don't really...die...unless some thing extremely traumatic like beheading or being stabbed directly in the heart happens."

"Shit." She blinked at him and swallowed hard. "I need to leave that for another time. Let's go back to your family before I have a meltdown." She gently pushed him back toward the car. "Work and talk, distract me from my breakdown."

"Right. My family." He went back to the Ferrari, shooting her careful glances as he got back to work. "Think highborn, as in second to the throne. My parents, older brother and sister all believe they are above the other Fae. So I grew up with a bunch of snobby assholes who really didn't understand why I wanted to spend time with Atreyu and Max. Ben was mostly acceptable since he is very high born as well, but they considered the other two peasants." He was focused on the car, talking as he worked. "To be fair, both Atreyu and Max are also high born and High Fae but...frankly, Atreyu's family gives a damn about those in their realm. Max will have to tell you his story when he's ready." He shrugged. "Not to mention they were from other Elements, so that was a big strike against all of them."

"So how did you break away from that? I assume they had a plan for you just like my family had a plan for me?"

"That they did. But when they tried to force me into it I told them to sod off and moved here with the others." He winked at her. "Thankfully, they have decided it's just a phase and eventually I'll return to the fold and the 'life of luxury' I truly deserve."

She could hear the eye roll in his voice and giggled at the thought of this man dressed up like a fancy CEO and sitting in a sterile office. While he was always dressed nice (except here) Sebastian was in his element here, smudged and torso deep in a car surrounded by rock music and friends. "They don't really know you, do they?"

"Absolutely not!" He gave her a fake offended look. "I worked very hard at them not knowing me, I'll thank you very much to remember that." When she laughed out loud at that he threw her a sexy grin. "You're in good company here, darling. All of us are running from something, even Atreyu."

"At least you have a place to fall." She almost sounded wistful.

"Darling, don't you know?" He stood to his full height and leaned into her. When Mor shook her head he lowered his forehead to hers. "Now you do too. We'll always catch you."

Her breath caught in her throat. Before she was physically able to respond Max cut in. "Stop hogging Mor!" He slipped up next to her. "Want to see what I'm working on?"

She looked at Sebastian, wanting to make sure it would be alright.

He kissed her forehead and then pulled her from her stool. He thrust the stool at Max. "Go see, darling. He's working on a lovely little Porsche."

"Thank you." She tried to put deeper meaning in to it. To thank him for catching her.

"You're welcome."

She felt his eyes on her as Max led her to his area. "Do you each have your own spot?"

"We do. We only take on one car each at a time. Since we're a speciality shop, we can do that."

"As in you only work on fancy old cars?"

"Exactly!" He set the stool next to the car. "I'm working on the undercarriage of this one. You can either get under her with me or sit up here. Just don't sit on the edge. If something happened and the car fell…" He winced but didn't finish the sentence.

"Does that happen often?" She shuddered at the thought.

"Definitely not. But I wouldn't ever risk you." He slipped under the car.

After a moment of hesitation she joined him underneath. He pointed to a safe spot for Mor to sit and got to work. "What were you and Sebastian talking about?"

"Families and their stupid expectations." A second later she added, "And having people who will catch you."

"That is more important than family." His voice was soft.

"I'm learning that. Chosen family."

He looked back at her and she could see him weighing whether or not to tell her about his. "Have you had enough sob stories today?"

"I don't know that Sebastian has a sob story. It seemed more like an annoyed story."

Max chuckled, and the sound of it surrounded her in the tight space. "True. They are definitely too formal to sob, ever." He worked on in silence. She didn't say anything. Mor could feel him leaning toward telling her, but his story would be a gift. "My family cut me out of their lives."

"Why would anyone do that? You're so kind and gentle and good."

She shook her head. "I don't know you well, yet, but I know you are probably the nicest person I have ever met."

He hung his head for a moment before going back to work. "That is literally why they cut me off. I wasn't brutal enough for them and I didn't fall in line like a good little Fae."

"What did they want?" She could feel something horrible coming.

"They wanted me to torture a Fae male that was caught stealing. And then publicly execute him."

"What the fuck." She stood as much as she could in the tight space. She went over to him and wrapped her arms around him. He hung his head and then slowly turned in her arms.

"The thing was, we already knew why he was stealing. His little girl was sick and needed medicine and decent food. So instead of torturing him, I bought the medicine and made sure she got it."

Mor's eyes were squeezed shut and her arms were tight around him. "That is why you are so wonderful."

"My brother tortured him instead. And then when he found out I had helped the family he made them watch the execution." Mor was crying now, unable to speak. "My parents gave me a choice at that point. Marry the brutal piece of work they had picked out and give them grandbabies while letting her take over my role in the family - since I was too weak for it - or be cut off like I had never existed in their family." His cheek leaned against the top of her head. "I chose option two."

She just held him, wanting to take his pain away. After several minutes Mor looked up at him. She pulled one of her arms from around him and cupped his face with her hand, "That makes you the bravest person I know." And then she kissed him, because holy fuck.

The kiss was soft, gentle. He swept his tongue across her lips and she opened without a thought. He surrounded her, making her forget where they were as his tongue danced with her's. When he finally pulled away, some of the pain had faded from his face. "Thank you."

"For what?" Her voice was barely above a whisper.

"For being you." He smiled and then kissed her softly one more time before letting her go.

When he turned back to the car, they kept the conversation light. Favorite bands, food, and movies. Anything not heavy. Eventually Atreyu stuck his head down were they could see him. "Come on, you two. Lunch time! We ordered burgers. Didn't know what you wanted, so we got a selection, beautiful."

She smiled as he reached in and helped her up, pulling her in for a hug. Quick as a heartbeat he whispered, "Thank you for taking care of him," before releasing all but her hand to lead her to their lunch room. When she tried to say something, he just shook his head. Mor guessed Max really didn't like talking about it so she let it go for now. The guys all washed up in the sink in the break room and then waited for her to pick which burger she wanted before digging in.

Lunch was fun with the guys going out of their way to include her. She loved every second of it. They teased her like she was one of their own and one of them was always touching her. Like they couldn't help it. Not that she was complaining. There was something so empowering about having these four, hot Fae men doting on her. She'd never had anyone do that, much less one hot guy.

Toward the end of lunch a bell rang in the break room. The guys groaned. Ben stood up, "I guess it's my turn." He trudged out of the room.

"What was that?" She asked around fry.

"Our last receptionist quit. So now we take turns in the front when we have too. We hate it." Atreyu actually sounded whiney.

She choked on a laugh, but before she could say anything Ben walked back through the door carrying a large vase of roses. "This just showed up. No note, no delivery guy."

"Did you check it?" Sebastian was on alert.

"Of course I did! I wouldn't let anything back here that could hurt Mor." Ben rolled his eyes.

"Who would send you guys flowers?" She looked around the shop. "This doesn't seem like the type of shop that would get that."

"Every once in a while we do. Usually it's from a bored housewife that got a look at us when their husband dragged them in to look at their real love."

"I mean, what woman wouldn't appreciate y'all." She smirked, running playful eyes over them while they preened.

"I rather thought you could have them." Ben says almost shyly.

"I'm allergic to roses, actually. And sloppy seconds isn't really my thing." She winked at him to take the sting out of her words.

"Fuck! Why didn't you say something right away, Mor?" He dashed out with the flowers as if they had caught on fire.

He came back in and went straight to the sink and washed his hands and arms. "Okay, I'm not that allergic Ben. No anaphylactic shock. I just get really bad sinus infections if I'm in the same room as them for an hour or more."

"Good." He stalked over to her and caged her into the table with his arms. "Next time you tell us right away. I don't care of it's mild. I don't want anything near you that could hurt you."

Mor narrowed her eyes at him. "That's going a little far, don't you think?"

"No." The word was snapped out and he still hadn't backed up.

So Mor grabbed a fork from the table where it sat next to her and poked herself in the arm with it. "Oh no! I'm in the room with something sharp and pointy."

Ben growled, and she swore it sent a pulse straight to her clit but she studiously ignored the little ho. "Mor. You know damn well what I meant."

"Just making sure you weren't going to far with it, Ben." She smirked at him.

He just gripped her chin in his hand, holding her still as he leaned in and pressed a kiss to her lips. Just one, chaste kiss that had her panting. "You're precious to us, Mor. I just want you safe. Do you understand?"

Mor could only nod.

"I need to hear you say that you understand." He hadn't let go of her chin.

"I understand."

"Good girl." He held her for a second more before letting her go and heading back out to the garage.

She looked around at the other guys. They were just sitting and grinning at her. "How can you all sit there so calmly?"

"Whatever do you mean, darling?" Sebastian tried - and failed - to look innocent.

"Y'all have *all* been kissing me! Doesn't that bother you?!"

Atreyu rolled his eyes. "Didn't Sebastian tell you we were fine with sharing?"

She spluttered. "Well, but, I didn't think he meant it!"

"Huh." Was all Atreyu said before he walked back out.

Max and Sebastian followed him out. She sat there in stunned silence, totally unsure what to make of all that. Muttering to herself about idiotic males, Mor got up and put the food away. When she was done, she turned to see Ben leaning in the doorframe watching her.

"Shit! You scared me!"

"I've been here pretty much the whole time, Mor." He shook his head and walked over to her. "You need to be more observant."

"I'll, um, work on that?" Why was that a question? Oh, yes, because her brain didn't fully function around them.

"Good." He took her hand and led her to the door.

"Where are we going?" She asked as he pulled her into the garage.

"Since you already worked with Sebastian and Max I thought you might want to come sit with me?" His voice had gone soft and hesitant, like he wasn't sure of her answer.

"Of course I'd love to sit with you." She smiled and squeezed his hand. This big, sexy Fae was worried about if she wanted to spend time with him. He clearly hadn't looked in the mirror lately. He was well worth the time even without the hotness.

"What are you working on ? I actually knew the names of the cars Sebastian and Max are working on!" She said it proudly.

He snorted. "Of course you knew those. They're insanely famous car brands." He rolled his eyes. "I'm working on a Model-T. It was one of the first cars made by Ford."

"That is so cool!" She was excited to see a little bit of history right in front of her where she could touch it. His grin was infectious as he launched into the history of the car and what he was doing. The rest of the day passed quickly, listening to Ben's passion for this car. He didn't bring up anything heavy, which she was honestly grateful for. She'd had enough with learning about Max's fucked up family.

When they got home, Trisha had been cooking. They sat around the kitchen table stuffing themselves silly on home made spaghetti and meatballs. She had never had so much fun at a meal. The guys joked around with each other and her, like she had always been a part of their family. By the time they all went to bed Mor felt relaxed and happy, finally feeling like she had a place in the world.

CHAPTER 7

*T*he next day she got up with the guys. They had a quick breakfast together before heading to the shop. The day went by quickly and by the time they headed out they were all pleasantly tired. When they pulled in to the drive Ben abruptly stopped talking. "Fuck."

The guys all swung to follow his gaze. When she looked over she saw a super fancy car sitting in the front of the drive. "Who's that?" Her voice was loud in the car and she winced.

"That is Ben's family." Max's voice was soft. "What do you want to do, Ben?"

He heaved a sigh. "I thought they would give me time to consider." He shook his head. "Let's go in and deal with them. The sooner we deal with it, the sooner they will leave."

Mor wanted to ask what was going on but Ben was already out of the car. The guys hurried out, but Atreyu waited for her and took her hand as they walked in. His face was set in serious lines. "Maybe I should wait out back?" She didn't want to intrude on whatever was happening.

Ben stopped at the door and turned around. "I'd rather you were with me."

Giving him a tentative smile she stopped by his side. He grabbed her hand, took a deep breath and then opened the door. Mor watched a cold mask fall into place as he looked to the left. He squeezed her hand and then led her into the formal living room where a regal looking man and woman were sitting. Neither of the them got up which she found to be very offensive since this was not their home. She hated the formalities drilled into her by her parents, but she had a feeling they would be useful when dealing with these two. Her face fell into a polite mask as Ben led her into the room.

He didn't bother addressing them, instead leading Mor to a seat and assisting her into it for all the world as if she was dressed as the lady of the house instead of in a dirty t-shirt and jeans. He then perched on the arm rest next to her, all the while keeping his hold on her hand. He finally looked at the couple staring at them with a look on their faces like they had smelled something bad. Ben didn't say anything, just stared at them, waiting.

After several minutes the woman finally caved. "Are you not going to introduce us, Benjamin?" She looked like she had eaten a lemon.

"Of course. Mother. Father. Allow me to introduce Mor Williamson. Mor, these are my parents Sylvia and Michael."

She nodded, "So nice to meet you both."

"And how long are you visiting this - house?" Michael's hesitation made it clear what he thought of it.

Ben answered before she could draw breath. "Mor lives here with us."

"Well, that is hardly appropriate for a young lady to be living unsupervised with four men." Sylvia's nose went even further in the air.

"The guys have taken extremely good care of me. Better than my own family, in fact."

"Fascinating." Immediately dismissing Mor, Sylvia turned back to Ben. "Why don't you have your - friend - step out so we may conduct our business in private?"

Ben placed his arm around her shoulders. "I have no secrets from anyone living in this house."

Mor really didn't want to sit through this. But Ben was there through one of her worst moments. Being a buffer for him would not be fun, but it would be worth it. This was a man who stood up for others without hesitation. So she would be here for him.

After an uneasy silence where his parents clearly hoped Ben would cave, his father finally said, "When will you be returning home to marry Marissa?"

It was only through years of training to keep her face straight that she was able to hold the mask. He was engaged? Her heart broke a little. Mor subtly tried to pull her hand from his grip but he tightened his hold. "I told you when I was home. There is nothing that could induce me to marry that woman." Ben looked down at Mor and smiled softly before turning the mask back to his parents. "She was a bitch growing up and is a bitch now. I do not intend to spend the rest of my long life miserable."

"She would provide you with suitable heirs and would be socially acceptable." Michael stated it as if that was that. "In addition, we came to an agreement with her parents when you were both babes. If you do not honor this betrothal then you have dishonored your family."

Ben looked down at Mor. "Now you see."

And she did. He knew exactly how she felt. His family was doing the same thing to him. At least they didn't kidnap him. Looking over at his parents, Mor shook her head. "You dishonor him by trying to force a bad marriage on him."

"Stupid girl! You have no idea what you are speaking of!"

"Actually, I do. My parents just literally kidnapped me to try and force me into a marriage."

They stared at her blankly then chose to ignore her. "Benjamin, with the heir to the throne missing our family stands to gain prominence with an alliance to the House of Durandus." Sylvia stood and was pacing.

"Come now, son. We both know that our family should be leading the - community - with the royal house in disarray." The misstep almost made by Michael would have been amusing in any other circumstance. There was no way for him to know that they had told her what they were. Really, they shouldn't be talking about royal anything.

Ben's face started to turn red. "I - "

"Dinner will be served in fifteen minutes, sir. Perhaps you would like some time to clean up?" Trisha stood in the doorway, formally dressed. Mor blinked at her.

"Thank you, Trisha. Mor?" Ben stood and held his hand out for her. He tucked her hand into his elbow as he looked at his parents. "Please join us for dinner?"

Michael's eyes narrowed at Mor. She was pretty sure that he was really upset that Ben had put us on a first name basis. "We would love to have you join us, Michael, Sylvia." She managed to say it with a genuinely fake smile.

They were silent a moment longer than necessary. "Very well. It has been a long trip, after all."

Trisha spoke up, "Shall I ready the guest suite?"

"What about the Master? Surely we should be there." Sylvia flipped - flipped! - her hair back.

"We gave the Master to Mor." Ben smiled sweetly at his mother. "I'm sure you'll be exceedingly comfortable in the guest suite. Please excuse us, we need to freshen up before dinner." With that, he guided Mor out of the room and up the stairs, every bit the Lord of the Manor. When they got to the top of the stairs he picked her up, swung her around and then kissed her. "Thank you!" He had a huge grin on his face as he let her slide down his front. "That was so much easier with you there."

Laughing breathlessly, she looked up at him, still snug in his arms with her hands resting on his chest. His rock hard chest. "I assume you'll tell me all about this once they leave?" He glanced at her hands before quirking an eyebrow at her. She was petting him. Forcing her hands to stillness she waited for his answer.

"Absolutely. It's too long to get into now, but I wish I could."

"That's okay. We better hurry and get ready so they have less to complain about and we can get through dinner faster. They are exhausting."

Ben's laugh boomed through the hall. "You are right about that. Go on, I'll be here to walk you down to dinner."

She untangled herself and darted into her room. Mor wondered if she could get ready faster than him. Probably not. She intended to go for the works as fast as she could. After a quick shower, Mor fishtailed her hair before doing her makeup in record time. She dug through the few clothes she had with her since everything else was in boxes and pulled on a shiny blue tank top with a pair of dark skinny jeans. No shoes, though, because fuck 'em.

She stepped out of her room to find all four guys waiting for her. "Damn! I thought for sure I was fast."

"Beautiful, you were fast. We just did a hell of a lot less than you." Atreyu grinned at her. "But I must say you are stunning."

Ben grabbed her and tucked her under his arm. "Come on. The sooner we get down there the sooner we're finished with them. And then they can leave tomorrow morning."

"Are they ever nice?" It slipped out before she could think.

"Honestly, no. At least Sebastian's family begrudgingly accepts his life choices. And, I'm sorry Max, but I would love for my family to cut me off. I'm sick of this."

Max clapped a hand on his shoulder. "Watching this makes me grateful for it too!" He winked at Mor and went ahead of them.

Sebastian, Atreyu and Ben stopped in surprise. Ben looked down at her wrapped in his arms. "That's the first time he's been easy about his family. You are somethin' else, Mor." He smiled and kissed her on the head.

"You done good, Mor." Atreyu said while Sebastian just took her free hand and kissed it before lacing his fingers with hers.

"Guys, what are Ben's parents going to say?" She tried to pull away from them but they held her tight.

"Who gives a shit? Plus it'll freak them out." A grin came back over Ben's face. "This is going to be awesome."

They walked into the dining room just as he said that, making her stuff all her questions down for another day. Trisha had set a formal table. Ben and Sebastian led Mor to the head of the table and installed her in it before Ben's father could get to it. The guys then sat on either side of her, with Atreyu and Max next to them, forcing Michael and Sylvia to the end of the table. Trisha began serving the steaks. Mashed potatoes, green beans, and homemade mac and cheese were already on the table. Ben grabbed her plate and served Mor first, filling her plate up and then setting it in front of her. He turned a pointed look to his parents and then gestured to the table.

"Well, go ahead." The guys were already digging in while his parents stared at them like they were aliens.

Eventually, they caved and put small amounts on their plates and nibbled. Mor rolled her eyes and stuffed herself. The rest of dinner was spent trying to get Ben's parents to engage in even basic conversation. They gave them one to two word answers throughout the dinner, so eventually they ignored them and talked with each other. They talked about upcoming projects the guys had and what they wanted to do the next weekend. When they were talking about weekend plans, Mor realized her birthday was a week from Sunday. She didn't say anything, but it gave her a weird feeling to be some place with people who might actually want to celebrate with her.

By the time dinner ended, she was feeling so much. Ben's parents finally excused themselves to the guest suite before dessert was served. Trisha brought out two strawberry pies and they dug in. Trisha set out spray cans of whip cream since Ben's parents were gone and they ended up in a whip cream fight. When the whip cream was gone and they were all a mess, she decided to call it a night and headed upstairs. She was going to have to shower again since she had whipped cream in her hair and she wasn't sure if her shirt was going to make it.

"Heathens." She whipped around at the spiteful word. Sylvia was staring at her with a look like she was a piece of shit that she had stepped in.

"Excuse me?"

"You all are not worthy of my son. With the exception of Sebastian, none of you are worthy of his time."

"Wow. I don't know how to respond to that."

"Don't bother. I know you aren't able to think of anything with that peasant brain of yours."

She looked at her for a moment before responding. She was really stooping low, trying to attack her without Ben around. "What are you trying to do?"

"I have no idea what you are talking about." She huffed.

"Clearly, you have an agenda. I assume that's to make Ben fall into line with the plan you and Michael have for him?" Mor didn't give her a chance to respond. "If you were smarter, you would have thought to make me an ally. Maybe promised me something stupid in return for my help in getting him to return to the fold." She advanced toward her, loving the look of anger and fear on her face. "If you were smart you would have seen how much he cares for me and tried to use it to your advantage. Or you would have tried to find something that I needed in exchange for my cooperation." Now she was in her face and Sylvia was frozen. "But you aren't that smart. You think your family name, which I don't even know, and your money make you better and smarter." Mor shook her head. "So now that I've made you understand what you should have done, please understand this." She paused to make sure she had her attention. "I will never betray Ben. There is nothing you could do that would make me betray him. Not money, not station, not favors. Good luck being miserable the rest of your long existence. I hope you learn to love. Or at least grow some logic."

She turned the corner and ran into Trisha. She nodded once to Mor before continuing down the hall, a small smile playing at her lips. Taking a breath Mor went on to her room to get cleaned up for bed. That night she had crazy dreams of her parents working with Ben's parents and them turning into snakes. Which was super strange because she liked snakes. By the time she got up, she was exhausted from all the bad sleep. She threw her hair into a messy bun, pulled on her favorite pair of jeans and a Rolling Stones t-shirt and headed down stairs.

The guys were all there eating pancakes with ridiculous amounts of syrup. By the time she made it to the table, they had loaded a plate for her. "You guys feed me so well." She grinned at them.

"We just want to take care of you." Max smiled and kissed her hand.

Just then, Ben's parents walked through the doors of the dining room. She groaned out loud - whoops - and then blushed. And then thought, fuck it, and glared at them. After what had happened with Ben's mom, Mor really didn't give a shit anymore. They sat down and waited to be served. When no one put food on their plates, they stared around like they didn't know what to do. Finally, Mor stood up, stalked over to them and forked a load of pancakes on their plates then doused them in syrup. "Eat or leave."

She was sick of it. Sick of people trying to lord it over others just because they have more money. When she sat back down again, Ben picked up her hand and kissed it while Max reached under the table and put his hand on her leg. The contact with them grounded her. She had never had big emotions and had always stuffed it down. But for some reason these two really got under her skin. When they didn't start eating, she growled. What the fuck? It startled her so much she stopped and the guys got confused looks on their faces. Thankfully, Sylvia and Michael had started eating so she didn't need to say anything.

Breakfast was awkward as fuck after that, but at least they were all able to eat. There wasn't much conversation but that was good. Mor really didn't think she could handle speaking politely to them anymore. As soon as they were done, Ben and the guys stood up. "We have to get to work. What time will you be leaving?"

"Oh, we thought we'd spend a few days with you. Perhaps spend some time with your new friend Mor. She could show us - town?" Michael forced a pleasant smile on his face. Too bad he looked constipated.

"No, Mor will be coming with us." Sebastian's accent sounded cultured and smooth next to their posturing. He stood and walked to stand behind her. "We do so love having her keep us company." His smile was positively wicked as he caressed the back of her neck.

"Well, perhaps we should come to the shop for a little while. See

what it is that has our son so conflicted over his duties to his family."
Sylvia sniffed.

Plastering a vapid smile on her face on she said, "Well that would
just be so much fun! I do suggest changing. Stilettos don't really work
well in a mechanic shop." Mor made sure to be very serious when she
said it.

Sylvia grimaced. "I'm sure I'll be able handle it." Her voice dripped
condescension and Mor rolled her eyes.

"Alright. Whatever you want."

Mor walked out with the guys and they started to pile into the
SUV. Before Ben could get behind the driver's seat his father called
out to him. "Ben! Why don't you ride with us, son. We see so little of
you now." His father was better at playing the caring parent than his
mother was, clearly.

Ben looked at Mor with desperation. "I'll go with you, if you
want?" When he let out a sigh of relief and held out a hand to help her
out she smiled.

Tossing the keys to Max, Ben led the way to his parent's car. "I'd be
happy to join you, as long as you allow Mor to come as well."

"Wouldn't she be more comfortable with the others?" There was
the constipated look back on Sylvia's face.

"Oh no, Mor has been learning about classic cars from us. I insist
that she take the opportunity to ride in the Bentley. It is, after all, the
shining example of classic sophistication."

She almost snorted at how overbearingly obnoxious Ben sounded,
but she managed to hold it in. "What an opportunity for me to expand
my knowledge!" She gushed like any other vapid social climber.

Sebastian smirked at her from across the yard as Max gave her a
thumbs up and Atreyu laughed in the closed car. They knew what she
was up to. You didn't have to be a Mensa candidate to get it. Mor's
mission was to annoy the fuck out of Ben's parents until they left. Win
win for all involved. She got to have a shit ton of fun fucking around
with them and then they would leave. She allowed Ben to help her
into the fancy as fuck car and slid over so he had room. He followed
her and then put his arm around her, pulling her hand into his lap

with his free hand. He was definitely staking his claim in front of his parents and making sure they understood her place in his life.

Ben's parents stared at her distastefully the entire car ride, not bothering to speak at all. Mor kept her smirk at disrupting their plans to harass Ben internal. When they arrived, Ben helped her out of the car and then stood tapping his foot while he waited for his parents to exit the car. His father told the driver to keep the car running. Thank God for small favors. They clearly did not plan to spend a long time at the shop. Ben led them through a brief tour, during which his mother tripped four times in those dumb stilettos that Mor had told her to change out of. After that, they claimed fatigue and decided to return to the house and 'just see you all for dinner.'

When they left, the music went up and everyone relaxed. The guys were back to teasing each other and Mor. She bounced around from station to station, learning tools and car parts while the guys had her 'help'. They were about to break from lunch when they got a group text from Trisha to get home right then. She didn't elaborate and wouldn't answer her phone when Atreyu tried calling. What the fuck could be going on now?

CHAPTER 8

The drive home was tense. No one was sure what would be there when they arrived. Would it be fire? Had Ben's parents tried to pack his things? Was the Council there? They kept coming up with wilder stories until Mor made them stop. It was seriously doubtful that there was a secret government agency that had shown up and kidnapped Trisha. That one was the one that had forced Mor into action.

When they pulled up there was a new car parked next to the Bentley. A shiny convertible in Barbie pink. Ben actually stopped the car to look because who the fuck has a car like that? Max poked him in the shoulder until he pulled the car up enough to park it so they could get out and stare at it.

"Is this an actual thing? Like, people want cars that look like they are real life replicas of Barbie's Dream Car?" Mor looked at them in confusion.

"Yeah, we'd never approve this shit." Atreyu scoffed.

"Better question." Max looked at them. "Who's car is this and why would they park this travesty in front of our house? We better pray that none of our customers sees this crap. We'd never live it down."

Before anyone else could say anything, Trisha burst out of the house. "Best come quick, boyos. Ben, yer parents are trying to clean out Mor's room."

"What the fuck?" His face turned red and he stomped into the house with the other guys close on his heels.

Looking at Trisha Mor said, "Please tell me more before I go in there. I'd like to have a clear idea of what and who before I storm off."

"Och, lass, this is why the boyos need ye!" She chuckled for just a moment before a serious look fell across her face. "Ben's parents brought the woman they want ta see him wed. Decided she needed yer room since it's the nicest one in the house."

She stared at her in shock. "No shit." When Trisha held her hands up in the universal sign for 'who the fuck knows' Mor sighed. "They have no idea what's in store for them." She took a few steps and then paused. "Did they actually get into the room and start messing with things?"

"Aye, lass. They were throwin' yer belongin's inta a box when I caught them."

"Oh fuck." She started laughing and then couldn't stop. Trisha started laughing with her. They laughed so hard tears were running down their faces and they were doubled over. As soon as they were able to control themselves, Mor straightened up. "Okay. I'm going to deal with the fallout. Because I'm sure the boys are threatening things." She could hear yelling from the house from where they were standing in the driveway.

She was still chuckling when she made it up the stairs. Sure enough, Ben and his father were toe to toe screaming in each other's faces. Ben's mother Sylvia was having hysterics in the hall with Max standing in front of her like a wall. Mor skirted past them and made it into her room where she found Atreyu and Sebastian blocking a woman from her bathroom.

She was shorter than Mor - which was pretty typical - and had black hair flowing down her back to her ass. She was dressed like she had just come from Fashion Week in a tight black dress with red soled shoes. Mor was not typically a jealous woman, but fuck if she wasn't jealous of those shoes. She took a moment to admire them before heaving a sigh at the unfairness of it and slipping around her to stand between Atreyu and Sebastian.

"May I ask what you are doing in my room?" Her Southern politeness was coming out. But it wasn't the 'you deserve my respect' kind. It was the 'well, bless your heart' type where it really meant 'fuck off'.

"Who are you?" Fabulous shoe girl tried to stare down her nose at Mor. Which didn't work, because even in those heels Mor was taller than her.

Mor leaned forward and lowered her voice, "Might want to lower that nose. None of us want to look up it and you aren't tall enough to look down it."

She gasped in outrage. "How dare you speak to me that way! I am Marissa of House Durandus!"

"Cool. I'm Mor of the House Williamson. But you still haven't answered my question. What. Are. You. Doing. In. My. Room." She enunciated each word. Mor knew she could understand her, but she'd fought with bitches like her before in college. Her parents had made her pledge to a sorority of girls they thought were worthy of their name. Same kind of attitude. Mor knew you had mark your territory right away or you'd never catch back up. This girl had clearly never had anyone stand up to her before. Her guess was that her 'station in life' had protected her from ever having to lift one of those perfectly manicured fingers. A failure on her parent's part. Life is full of people trying to bulldoze you over and if you never learn to stand on your own two feet you'll get plowed over.

"This is not your room! As the highest ranking female in this house I am entitled to the nicest room! You shall be relegated to the servants quarters as you deserve, human."

Atreyu and Sebastian froze. They all knew she should not have used the 'human' word. Not because it wasn't true and not because it was an insult (although she definitely meant it as one), but because Mor shouldn't know about them. She was past caring about this, though. This bitch thought she could waltz in, steal Ben from her and kick her out of her own room? Fuck this shit.

Mor moved a step forward. Marissa took a step back and Mor

barely suppressed her grin. She had her now. She gave over territory without a fight. She pressed forward, keeping her moving. She backed up slowly at first, but then picking up speed as Mor advanced. Marissa tripped and would have fallen if Mor hadn't snapped out a hand and latched onto her arm.

Holding her in a vice like grip, Mor got in her face. "This is not your house. You do not live here. You are not an invited guest."

Marissa paled and tried to pull out of her grasp. "Let go of me!"

Mor tilted her head and looked at her. This was the only time she was grateful for the training her parents had provided. She could literally produce any feeling on her face whenever she wanted. Mor let disdain fill her face as she looked down at Marissa. "Why would you think this was your place?"

Mor still didn't let go, keeping Marissa from trying to get away. Marissa floundered as silence fell around them. Ben and Michael had stopped yelling at each other and Sylvia had stopped her wailing. All eyes were on them. "Ben is my betrothed!" She slapped Mor.

Mor laughed and held on tighter. Rage was filling her at the audacity these people had. It was one thing when her parents pulled this crap against her. No one was going to hurt her guys. No. One. "You will leave this house. You will leave Ben alone. He. Is. Not. Yours." She paused and considered. Everyone should have a choice, even if that choice could potentially break her heart. "Unless he chooses you." Mor looked over at where Ben and his father stood, jaws hanging slack. "Ben." He snapped to attention. "Do you choose her?"

He didn't hesitate. "Never. I would never choose her."

Mor looked back down at Marissa. "I found it funny that you would attempt to take my room from me." She let go and Marissa fell on her ass. Waving her hand around at the room, she continued, "This is just stuff. I don't give a rat's ass about stuff." Her eyes narrowed. Pinning first Marissa, then Michael, and finally Sylvia with her gaze she finished, "Attempting to steal someone's free will, to suppress their very being should be criminal."

Returning her attention to Marissa, she leaned down and said, "Get out now before I make you leave. You will not like my methods."

Marissa scrambled back, stumbling to her feet at the door. "How dare you speak to me this way!"

Mor snarled and lunged. Two sets of hands grabbed her and she started fighting. How dare they keep her from her prey?! This bitch had threatened her guys! *Mine!* Marissa gasped and ran out of the room with Michael and Sylvia following her. Mor struggled for a minute longer until Ben was standing in front of her holding her face.

"Mor. Mor! It's okay, she's gone. They're gone."

It took a minute to process what he had said. Once she did, Mor immediately stopped fighting. "Oh shit! I'm so sorry!" She looked around wildly at the guys. "Are you okay? I'm so sorry!"

All four were standing around her with huge smiles on their faces. Ben cleared his throat, bringing her attention back to him. "These guys have been by my side supporting me since I was twelve years old. We've been through some crazy shit. But never have I had someone fight for me like you did."

"How is that possible? Surely they stood up for you?" She trailed off, her mouth dropping at the shaking heads around her.

He looked down at the confusion on her face. "I know you don't understand. Our society....frowns on disagreeing with females. We tend to be more matriarchal than anything. So the guys have always been a support but couldn't do what you just did." He frowned at his feet while the guys stood shamefaced around us. "Thank you."

Max cut in. "By 'frown on' he means you will be beaten in most cases." He looked at Ben with a considering look on his face. "Well, he probably wouldn't have been. I was." His frown deepened and he walked out of the room with Atreyu following him.

"No." Her voice was clipped, angry. "Just no. These assholes come in here and try to dictate your life. And now you are telling me that because your society 'tends to be' matriarchal you have all been pigeon holed?" She met their eyes. "That stops now. No one fucks with my guys"

"Your guys?" Sebastian looked at her slyly.

78

"Fuck off, Sebastian, you know damn well what I meant." She was so mad she wasn't able to censor what she was saying. These wonderful men - Fae - who had helped her when she had no one and nothing else. They helped even when they didn't have to. No one would treat them as less.

"I'd rather fuck you." He grinned cheekily at her. She couldn't help the snort of laugher that came out. "There she is!" He grinned at her.

"Whatever, Sebastian." Mor gasped when Ben pulled her into his arms. "What are you doing?"

"I just need to kiss you." Before she could say anything else, Ben slipped one hand into her hair and another around her hips before taking her lips in a bruising kiss making her gasp. As soon as her mouth opened he groaned and thrust his tongue in her mouth. When he caressed her tongue with his, Mor moaned and pressed herself into him. A moment later she felt another body pressed up against her back and another set of hands caressing her waist before slipping up to her breasts and tweaking her nipples. Mor's back arched forward pressing into the hands and Ben's chest as lips trailed up her neck. She couldn't help tilting her head back. As her body arched, two masculine groans rumbled through the room as they pressed into her harder. She could feel the hard roll of Ben's cock pressing into her belly while Sebastians ground into her back. Her head landed on Sebastian's shoulder and he took her lips in a kiss as Ben continued on her neck.

"Benjamin!" Sylvia's voice snapped across the room, pulling them out of their lust induced haze. "What are you doing rutting with that...thing?!" She stormed into Mor's room. What was with these bitches thinking they could be in her space?

Mor glared at her. "Did you miss the part where I threw Marissa out?"

She ignored her completely. "You're betrothed is downstairs crying. You will go to her and reassure her that you will be most pleased to marry her."

Ben seemed to shrink in on himself a little and Sebastian's face shut down. With a huff, she stepped in front of Ben. "What is your point in all of this?"

Sylvia continued to ignore her. "Benjamin, if you do not do this then you will be cut off. You will no longer be my son." She lifted her nose in the air.

"You would disown your son because he will not marry as you choose?" Mor shook her head. "You're as bad as my parents." She looked at Ben. "What do you choose?"

"I choose you, Sebastian, Atreyu, and Max." His voice was firm and his back straightened. Sebastian put a hand on his shoulder.

She just nodded and walked over to Sylvia. Without a word, Mor grabbed her arm and pulled her out of the room. "What are you doing? Get your filthy human hands off me!"

"Human, huh? Aren't you supposed to be human?" Mor looked at her thoughtfully as Sylvia's mouth snapped shut. "I always find that to be a funny word. The guys are more human than my own biologically human family. But the definition of humanity is so varied." She hadn't stopped dragging her. They reached the stairs and Mor pulled her down them, thankful Sylvia didn't try to test her on the stairs. "Fortunately, spotting a monster can be quite easy when they are so quick to show their hand." They reached the entry way Michael and Marissa gasped from the formal living room. She opened the front door and shoved Sylvia out of it. Without hesitating Mor went and grabbed Michael and Marissa and drug them out. They seemed too shocked to do anything other than follow her.

Mor pushed them out of the door. "You are a disgrace. Allowing your ambition to cost you your family." She stood in the doorway, hands on hips as she surveyed their shocked faces. "*You* are the disgrace. Not Ben." She felt the guys line up behind her. "You will leave. You will not bother Ben again unless it's to sincerely apologize to him."

Michael opened his mouth to say something but Sylvia slashed her hand down. "We have no reason to be here anymore." Her gaze never left Mor's face. "We have no family here." She turned to the Bentley and snapped at the driver to open the door. Marissa sniffed and followed Sylvia without question, getting into her awful Barbie Dream Car. Michael hesitated eyes focused behind Mor, his face sad.

Huh. Well, at least one of them had a conscience. Maybe he would be able to have a relationship with Ben.

Mor opened her mouth to invite him in when Sylvia snapped at him. "Michael! Let's get out of this disgusting place." He closed his eyes briefly. When he opened them again his face had settled into a blank mask. He turned from them and followed Sylvia into the car.

When the car was out of sight, Mor turned around, tears in her eyes, to look up at Ben. "I'm so sorry, Ben. I don't know what came over me."

"Not a word, Mor." His face held some extreme emotion that she couldn't quite place. "What you just did..."

Mor stepped back from him. "I'll go pack." Stepping to the side she tried to go around him.

"Now why would you go and do something that stupid?" His arm had appeared in front of her, blocking her way.

"Because I just got you disowned." She tried ducking under his arm, only to be swept into Atreyu's arms. He turned her around and held her so she was facing Ben.

"Mor, what you just did went beyond anything I could hope for. I have been trying to fight my family off but couldn't break away." He stepped closer to her. "Maybe it's because it's ingrained in us to do what our Head of House tells us to do. Maybe it was fear. I don't know. But you came in here and set me free." Pulling her from Atreyu's arms he wrapped her up in a hug. "I can never say thank you enough." He didn't do anything else, just held her with his cheek pressed into her hair, body shaking.

After a moment, Mor led him over to the couch and sat down on it. He followed her down and she pulled his head into her shoulder. She was pretty sure he was crying but she was also sure he would hate to admit that. Pretty soon Sebastian came to sit on his other side and Max sat next to Mor. Atreyu pushed the fancy coffee table out of the way and folded himself at their feet. They sat in silence while they waited for Ben to gather himself. After a while he sat up and blinked at all of them. "Sorry guys."

Max cleared his throat. "Don't worry about it. I know how it feels. You feel free and sad all at the same time."

"Exactly." Ben nodded. "But I'd rather be free and with my real family than miserable and tied to them." He shook his head. "I need a drink. Like, I need to get really drunk." He stood up a little unsteadily and made his way into the kitchen.

Mor tried to stand up but was suddenly swamped by hot Fae. They latched on to her an held tight before peppering her with kisses. "What's this for?"

"Just for being you." Max whispered in her ear.

Atreyu pulled her upright. "Let's go get drunk with Ben!" He grinned at her.

"I feel like I really don't understand what I did or your culture." She grumbled. She felt like she had done something terrible but her guys - yes, hers - seemed to be happy.

"We can give you lessons if you want." Max said.

"Nae, lass, I'll give ye lessons. Best they come from an unbiased source." Trisha smiled as she handed her a tumbler of whiskey.

"Bringing out the good stuff, huh, Trisha?"

"Aye! Tis a celebration, no?"

"That it is, Trisha! Our girl here has staked her claim in this house." Sebastian winked and raised his glass to her before taking a sip.

"That wasn't what I was trying to do."

"Doesn't matter! That's what happened. You marked your territory."

"Oh my gosh, you make it sound so weird. Not like I peed on the carpet."

"I was talking about you claiming us, but I would prefer it if you do not pee on me." Sebastian paused. "But I can't speak for the others. We've never discussed our kinks." He winked.

A chorus of 'no' answered that pretty quickly. "I'm glad none of y'all want that, because there is no chance that would be happening."

They kept drinking and eventually Trisha made them eat something. Max, Sebastian and Atreyu stopped after one. Mor figured out why when she started to sway in her seat and Ben tried to help her up only for them both to lose their balance. Atreyu swept her up in his arms and carried her up to her room while Sebastian and Max helped Ben up the stairs. When they tried to take Ben past Mor's room he reached out and grabbed the doorframe. "Noooooo." He was shaking his head. "Don't take her from me. Or me from her?" He started laughing and leaned against the frame.

In her drunken state that was so fuckin' funny! Mor started laughing so hard that she fell over. Sebastian caught her and shook his head. "Okay. New plan. Ben go get ready for bed and then you can come back. Darling, let's get you ready for bed." He took her to the bathroom and steadied her on her feet. Mor just stood there, smiling at him. He was such a nice guy. And super sexy.

"Thank you, darling."

"Wait, what?"

"You said I was nice and super sexy." He grinned.

"Huh."

"You need to get ready for bed."

"Okay!" She smiled at him. So sexy.

"I see I have overwhelmed you with my sexiness." He sighed. "Well, I guess it's up to me." He sauntered over to her, took her by her arms and led her to - the toilet? Sebastian rolled his eyes and then yanked her pants down before setting her on the toilet. "Do your thing," he said gruffly before turning his back on her and walking in to the closet to snag pajamas.

"If you wanted to get my pants off you could have just asked!" Her voice was sing song. As soon as she was done, he knelt at her feet and slipped some sleep shorts up her legs. He then pulled her off the toilet and efficiently stripped her shirt and bra off before getting a tank top on her. He led Mor to the sink and sat her on the counter. Sebastian got out her toothbrush and brushed her teeth for her. When he was done he made her drink some water and take two Tylenol before carrying her to the bed. Ben was already on the bed spread eagle.

"There's my girl!" He crowed and held his arms out to her.

Sebastian set her down into Ben's arms. He bent down and whispered, "Sleep well, darling. And remember - next time I take your clothes off I won't be putting them back on you." He nipped her ear and sauntered out of the room.

"Waaaiiiit." She tried to sit up, but sleep was pulling her down with Ben's arms warm around her. She'd figure it out tomorrow. She snuggled down into Ben's arms and fell fast asleep.

CHAPTER 9

*T*he next morning she woke with Ben wrapped around her.
At some point they had turned on their side. One arm was
a pillow for her and the other was wrapped around her waist. His
hand was splayed across her stomach holding her tight to him. He had
one leg draped over hers. She started to move, but he growled and
pulled her closer to him. His hips flexed forward and pushed into her
ass. Oh. *Good morning, Ben.* She figured he was still asleep and she
wasn't sure if he would appreciate his reaction. He had seemed really
interested yesterday, but that was before she chased off his family.

She tried to pull away again. "Where are you going?" His voice was
a rumble in her ear.

"Oh, um, I thought you were still sleeping?"

"I haven't been sleeping for a while." He nuzzled her neck. "It's
hard to sleep when I'm all wrapped up around you."

She laughed breathlessly. "Ben!" He started kissing her neck. Mor
pushed back into him but then realized she had to go to the bathroom.
"Ben, I need to use the restroom."

"Fine, I guess you can get up for that." He kissed her one more time
and then let go with a sigh.

She sat up with a groan. "There's the hangover." She held her head for a second and then stumbled into the bathroom.

A few minutes later she finished up brushing her teeth and went into the closet to change. She struggled to get into her regular jeans and t-shirt and went back into her room. Ben was still laying on the bed, his shirt off and a pair pajama pants laying low across his hips. The perfect V had her wanting to lick a path across him.

"Want to come back to bed and join me?" He waggled his eyebrows at her.

"Don't you have work?" She walked over to the side of the bed and tugged on his hand.

With a smirk he yanked on her hand and pulled her down on top of him. "I don't know. I feel like maybe we should take the day to process." He winked at her. He reached up to kiss her when the door burst open.

"Come on, lazy bones. Time fer breakfast." Trisha tapped her foot in the doorway.

Mor pushed off Ben with a smile. He pouted for a second and the followed her. "Are you going to get ready first?"

"No, I have a feeling you rather like me like this."

"Can't say that isn't a true statement." She grinned at him.

When they walked into the kitchen, she was met with three other shirtless men. That gave her a thought. "I thought we went over this. You don't have to pretend around me."

They all paused with forks of eggs halfway to their mouths. Max answered first. "Well, yeah. We just didn't want you to feel uncomfortable."

"Why would I feel uncomfortable?"

"Because, well, we're Fae."

She rolled her eyes. "Really guys. This is your home. Be yourselves. Don't make me say this shit again."

They looked a little surprised for a moment, then Max shrugged and did his magic thing. A second later she was looking at four super hot Fae males. They definitely got hotter in this form. She took a second to appreciate them in their shirtless wonder before focusing on her food. It was only Wednesday. One week since she had met Atreyu. She never realized things could change so quickly. A happy, contented feeling wafted over her. This was where she should be. She belonged somewhere, finally.

The doorbell rang, startling them from their comfortable breakfast. Trisha gestured for them to stay where they were and she went to the door. When she came back, she was holding another large vase of roses.

"What the fuck?" Ben's voice was sharp. "Who are these for? Is there a note?"

"Calm down, Ben. You'll no be speakin' ta me that way." Trisha huffed as she put them down.

Max leaned over them and plucked a note from the middle of the flowers. Sebastian grabbed them and took them right back out the door. Max was staring at the envelope. "This is really strange. Mor, they're for you."

He handed her the envelope. She didn't recognize the handwriting, but that could be because the workers wrote it. "Well, might as well see what it says." She shrugged, broke it open and pulled out the card. It had one line on it. *Wait for me*. She shivered and passed it back to Max. "That's creepy. Wait for who? And who knows I'm here?" They all stared at the note like it would suddenly start spouting answers. "Fuck! My family knows I live here. They had tracked my car."

"Damn!" Ben scowled. "How could you be so stupid?"

"Woah, Ben. I didn't know they were doing that."

Ben looked like he was going to say something else but Atreyu stepped in. "Look, the flower shop could have had our address. And even if it was sent by her creepy ass family we know they can't get through us. Let them waste money and be creepy fucks." He clapped Ben on the back and steered him out the door. "Come on, man, we gotta get ready for work."

Max shook his head at their retreating backs. "He's going to be all over the place for a while." He looked up at Mor and took her hand. "I know it will be hard, but try not to take it personally. It's hard being disowned."

She smiled at Max. "I'll do my best."

Sebastian kissed her cheek, "And we'll be there to help you remember. Let's go, Max. We gotta get work done at some point."

She stayed where she was, finishing up breakfast. She tried to help Trisha with the dishes but she sent her out of the kitchen. With nothing else to do, Mor went to the living room to check out the books on the shelves. They had a huge variety. Everything from 'how to' books to high fantasy and space dramas. These guys kept surprising her. She was trying to decide which to start when someone cleared their throat behind her. She turned to see Ben, hanging his head.

"I'm sorry, Mor. I shouldn't have lashed out at you like that. I know that you had no control over them tracking your car."

"It's alright. I'd prefer you don't, but I understand you're going through a big change. And it's my fault." She stayed were she was, unsure if he would want to be around her.

She heaved a sigh of relief when he came over to her and hugged her. He really had the best hugs. Ben was so big it felt like she was completely surrounded by him. After dropping a kiss on the top of her head he said, "Not your fault. You're a blessing. I'm just struggling to come to terms with their choices."

"I know that feeling." Mor's voice was muffled against his chest.

"I know you do. I'll work at keeping it to myself."

"Ben, I don't want you to keep it to yourself. I want you to be able to tell me if you are upset or need an ear. Just remember we're here for you."

He didn't say anything for a while, just kept holding her. When they heard the guys coming down the stairs, he let her go. "I'll try." He laced his fingers through her hand and tugged her to the door. "Do you want to come with us?"

"Of course! I wouldn't miss it."

Max grinned and waved his hand. The illusion fell back over her guys and they all piled into the car. They insisted on her riding with them and rotated who 'got to' sit in the back with her like it was a prize. She had tried to insist that either she could drive herself or they could just take two cars. But no, they kept saying it was better for the environment. Maybe Fae had a greater connection to the Earth? She really needed to pin Trisha down for those lessons. Either way, she wasn't about to argue with being squished between two of them.

The trip to the shop was uneventful. When they got there, the guys got to work and she went to start the day with Atreyu. He was like the light, cheerful and excited about every alteration he was making on the car. She got lost talking to him about movies in between exclamations about the car. By the time lunch rolled around, she was feeling relaxed again. Yesterday had really sucked, but today was so much better.

Ben stomped into the room and glared at all of them. "We need a receptionist, I'm tired of answering the fucking phone."

Sebastian pinched the bridge of his nose before responding. "Ben. You wanted to wait for a while. That was your request."

"I changed my fucking mind."

Max held up his hands. "No problem, Ben. We'll find someone."

Mor hesitated just a moment. "I could do it." Four heads whipped around to her. "I mean, I have no experience in that but I do have a bachelors in teaching. And I have literally nothing else going on...." They still didn't say anything. "I mean, it's the least I could do for y'all saving me from my family?"

"Mor, that would be perfect." Atreyu breathed.

"You'll be here every day, anyway, if I have anything to say about it, darling."

Max simply nodded. Mor held her breath, waiting for Ben's response. "Yes. That will definitely work. We can start training you tomorrow."

She grinned at him. "Thank you!"

They ate lunch without any further problems. Ben seemed to have bounced back to feeling good and joked around with all of them. He asked Mor to come sit with him while he worked on his car. Ben stayed mostly silent but occasionally pointed out things he was doing. Whenever she had a question he had no problem answering, even if he was a bit short. When they wrapped up for the day he laced his hand through hers and led her to the car while Sebastian locked up.

As soon as they passed the gate at home the human illusion dropped. She could feel their relief at being themselves again and she smiled to herself. After a slightly rowdy dinner, Mor decided to call it an early night. So much had happened and it had only been a week - just one week! - after Atreyu had accidentally lost her job. She hummed to herself as she got ready for bed. After turning off the lights, she climbed in to bed exhaustion hitting her harder that she expected. When she was on the edge of sleep she felt the bed dip and hands pull her over. Ben kissed her forehead lightly as he arranged her with her head resting on his chest. "Good night, Mor."

Early the next morning she woke up wrapped around Ben again. She was really loving this. There wasn't anything much better than waking up in the arms of a super hot Fae. Ben was still sleeping so she snuck downstairs and got a bowl of cereal. The sun hadn't come up yet it was so early. She loved being around her guys, but she missed having 'me time ' so this was perfect.

She had only been downstairs for a few minutes when Ben came storming into the kitchen. "What the fuck are you doing?"

She didn't bother to answer him, just raised her bowl in silent salute. He glared at her, waiting for further answer. Finally, she caved with a sigh. "I woke up early and wanted some cereal - so - cereal." She shrugged and kept eating.

"I was worried you left or had been taken! When you weren't in the bathroom, I was terrified." His face did not show terrified. It showed 'pissed off and wanting to hit something'.

"I don't know how you want me to respond to that."

"Why didn't you tell me where you were going!" He yelled. It wasn't a question.

"Last I checked, Ben, you are not my father. And you were sleeping. Why would I wake you up just because I wanted some cereal?" She rolled her eyes at him.

His face changed in an instant to something unreadable and he stalked over to her. When he spoke his voice was soft, sending a shiver down her spine. "Did you roll your eyes at me?"

"Uh yeah. You're being a dick about fucking cereal." She munched some more.

His body slid behind hers and his arms came down on either side of her, caging her in. "I love your spirit. I love your defiance. It makes me want to fuck you blind."

She gasped, almost chocking on her cereal. Fucking cereal. Fucking Ben. Well, *that* would not be a bad thing. His nose drew a line from her shoulder to her neck. When he reached her ear, his lips were a soft caress against her. "Tell me, Mor. Would you like that?"

She swallowed hard and set her almost empty bowl down. "I think I would."

He nibbled on her ear. "Good." Ben's hands slide up her arms and then down her sides. When they reached the bottom of her tank top he slipped his hands underneath. "Lift your arms." As soon as they were up he pulled her shirt off, leaving her breasts free. Her nipples were hard little points, from anticipation and cold. When he filled his hands with her breasts she gasped and arched into them. "Look at how responsive you are."

He continued his assault on her neck with his lips while his fingers plucked and rolled her nipples. Suddenly he pulled back. He spun her around before she could say anything and just stared at her. "So beautiful." Ben gently pecked her lips but when she tried to kiss him he held her still and kissed his way down her neck. This time, he didn't stop until he got to her breast. He latched on to one, alternating between sucking and tugging with his teeth while one of his hands tugged on the neglected nipple.

The onslaught of his mouth and hand was overwhelming, Her hands came up to his head and tugged on his short hair. Mor wasn't sure if it was to urge him on or pull him away. He came off her nipple with a pop and frowned at her. "Hands down." He grabbed them and placed them by her sides. "Keep them there or I'll have make you." Heat flashed in her core and she could feel herself get wetter.

"Make me?" Mor's voice was low and husky.

He held her eyes as he nodded. "I don't want to do that tonight, but I will if you push me. Tonight," a hand slid up her thigh and up the leg of her shorts where he pushed a finger under her shorts and into her, pumping it in a few times before pulling it out. Never breaking eye contact he brought the finger to his mouth and sucked off her juices. She had never seen anything hotter. "Tonight I want to taste you and feel you come on my face."

A moan escaped her lips when he said that. Smirking, Ben leaned back into her body and began to kiss his way down. When he reached the waistband of her shorts, she thought he would pull them off and dive right in. He didn't, making her whine in frustration. He took her right leg and kissed and licked his way up to the hem of her shorts. When he reached that, he did the same on her left leg. By the time he reached the hem again, Mor was beyond thought. Ben gripped the bottom of her shorts and tugged, pulling them off of her in one quick move.

Without any other delay he dove in, pulling one leg over his shoulder and forcing the other one out further. He blew softly on her folds before taking a long lick of her slit. Looking up at her with hooded eyes he whispered, "Delicious," before circling her clit with his tongue and then thrusting his tongue into her. Mor's hips flexed toward him as he fucked her with his tongue. She couldn't stop the sounds coming out of her mouth. He replaced his tongue with his fingers and started thrusting into her while he watched her unravel. "You're so fucking tight. I can't wait to feel you come on my cock." Then he sucked on her clit, hard, and her orgasm crashed through her body. She screamed out as his fingers kept up their pace until he had wrung the last aftershock from her body.

He stood, licking his fingers clean before leaning in to kiss her with her juices still gleaming on his chin. That was so fucking hot. The whole thing was so fucking hot. They hadn't even had sex and it still topped her list of sexual experiences. Although, to be fair, the ones she had had before could be described as mediocre at best. He slipped her tank and shorts back on her before swinging her into his arms and carrying Mor back to her room.

"What about you?"

"Don't worry about me, Mor. Watching you and feeling you come on my face definitely did it for me." He chuckled down at her. "I haven't come in my pants like that since I was a teenager. You have magic pussy." He growled and nipped at her bottom lip playfully. When they got to the room, he laid her down before crawling in next to her. "Next time you want cereal, let me know so I don't wake up to you missing?"

She snuggled into him, already falling asleep, feeling wrung out and satisfied from their little escapade in the kitchen. "I will."

"Thank you." He whispered. When she was on the edge of sleep, she thought she heard him say, "I don't know what I would do without you." But surely not. They had only known each other a week. That thought chased her into a dreamless sleep.

CHAPTER 10

The next morning she woke up feeling boneless and relaxed. She was still tucked against Ben. When she moved his eyes opened. "Good morning." Her voice was soft.

"Good morning, Mor." The way he said her name sent shivers down her spine. He leaned forward and kissed her softly.

"Ack, no!" She tried to pull away from him.

"You don't want to kiss me?"

"I have morning breath!"

He laughed and pulled her to him. Mor tried to pull away again but he wrapped her in his strong arms and held her still. "You really think you can get away from me?"

Laughing, she finally stopped struggling. "Nope! I know some martial arts, but it was more for show. My parents never let me do competitions or anything." She paused thoughtfully. "And yoga definitely wouldn't help,"

"Hmmmm." He paused thoughtfully. "We can definitely find some use for your yoga skills but I think we should get you up to date on your self defense skills."

"Why? I have you four muscley hunks to take care of me."

Ben rolled his eyes at her. "I think we'd all feel better if you had some practical knowledge in self defense." His face was a little intense. "Your previous knowledge in martial arts will be a good basis to start from."

She chose to ignore it in hopes that he would forget. "Should we go down for breakfast?"

"Hungry?" His voice came out with a growl.

"For actual food, Ben."

"I don't know, my favorite food is right here." His grin was cocky as his hand slid inside her shorts to cup her sex.

Just as he slid a finger along her slit there was a pounding on the door. Not a knock. A pounding. "Come ON. We have things to do!" Atreyu sounded grumpy.

Ben sighed and pulled his hand back. With another wicked smile he brought the finger to his mouth and sucked it clean. "Delicious. Come on, love. It's time to start the day." He smacked her ass and helped her stand up.

With a grin he followed Mor into the bathroom and they got ready together. There was something nice about having someone to get ready with. He continuously found reasons to touch her - brushing her hand, kissing her head, pinching her ass. She laughed every time he did the last. When they were finally ready they headed downstairs together, hand in hand. Before they walked into the kitchen, Ben stopped her. "I need to cover your eyes, love."

Mor gave him a confused look but nodded at him. He stepped behind her and put his hands over her eyes. He gently pressed her forward, guiding her into the kitchen. When they were a few paces into the kitchen he whispered, "Close your eyes." A moment later he moved his hands and she felt his presence leave her. Just a few seconds later she head, "Surprise!"

Startled, her eyes flashed open. Her guys and Trisha were standing behind the island. There were balloons and a stupid amount of food. "What is this?"

Atreyu bounced around the island and pulled her into his arms. "Happy One Week Anniversary! We were going to do it yesterday, but with everything that happened it got pushed back."

"What?"

"I thought we should celebrate since it's been a whole week since I lost you your job and your apartment and you got us!" His grin was unrepentant.

"We're celebrating that you fucked up my life?" She grinned back at him.

"Pretty much!" He bent down and kissed her softly. "I'm so glad I fucked up your life."

Mor leaned up and kissed him back. "I'm glad you fucked up my life too. This is waaay better."

"Come, beautiful! Your breakfast awaits!" He kept his arm around her shoulders and led her to a seat at the island. The guys had already fixed her a plate. She grinned at them and cleared her throat. "Thank you all for picking up the pieces of my messy life and holding on to them so I could put myself back together." She looked each of them in the eyes. "I am so grateful to you all."

The rest of breakfast was a loud and fun affair. Mor ate way to much food for the start of the day. There were pancakes and sticky buns and cinnamon rolls and fruit and donuts. She had to try them all. When they had all eaten way more than they should, she sat back with a groan. "I'm going to need to cut back. Y'all are feeding me way too much, my jeans aren't going to fit!"

"Oh no! More of Mor to love." Sebastian dripped sarcasm.

"Mor, you're parents forced you to be skinny. We want you to just be you. If that's a size six or a size twelve we really couldn't care. As long as we have you." Max smiled as he picked up her hand and kissed it. Her cheeks flamed up. Damn, these guys knew just what to say to her.

Sebastian pulled her out of her seat and swung her into his arms. "Come on, darling, it's time for us to go to work!" She grinned at him, happy to be part of their routine. "Just kidding! We are taking the day to celebrate!"

"Wait, what?"

"You seem to be saying that a lot, beautiful." Atreyu grinned again. He had spent most of the morning with a ridiculous grin on his face.

"That's the benefit of owning a specialty shop. If we want to take a day, we can." Ben had a confident smirk on his face. She really loved it.

"So what are we going to do today?" Sebastian still held her in his arms.

"We thought we could go play for the day. Maybe go to the zoo?"

"Seriously?" she hadn't realized it was possible for her smile to get bigger at this point. "I love the zoo! I never really got to go, though."

"You're parents did not seem like the zoo-going type." Max said as he walked beside them.

"Nope! Not enough people to impress." She wiggled in Sebastian's arms. "I am so excited!"

The guys laughed at Mor's antics and installed her in the SUV. Forty-five minutes later they were in line to get in. She was almost bouncing with excitement. Atreyu had slung his arm over her shoulders and Max was holding one of her hands. At first it was fine, but as they stood there, Mor noticed a lot of dirty looks being thrown their way. As they made their way up the line, she tried to discretely pull away from her guys. Her cheeks were hot again, but with shame this time. Atreyu frowned and Max looked confused when she stepped away from them.

After buying the tickets, they went up to the gates to make their way inside. As they walked through a woman brushed past her, pushing her out of the way with her shoulder. "Whore." Mor stopped and gasped as she shot a glare at her over her shoulder.

"Ah." Max nodded as he caught what happened. He pulled her into his arms and rested his cheek on her head for a moment before pulling her into an out of the way corner. The guys surrounded her. "Want to tell us what's going on?"

"There were just some people giving us dirty looks."

"When were they giving us dirty looks, love?" Ben's voice was soft but demanding.

She hung her head. "When Atreyu had his arm around me and Max was holding my hand."

"Beautiful, you can't let assholes get you down!"

Max shook his head. "There was a woman who pushed her and called her a whore."

All of their faces took on a sheen of anger. Mor could see the air simmering around them. "Hold, guys. Don't lose the human."

With an effort, she saw them force down their anger. "Mor, you can't let them change who you are. That's what your parents and brother tried to do to you for your whole life." Max was always the reasonable one.

"I guess you're right. I just - I hated them staring at you that way! Like you're all a bunch of freaks."

Now Atreyu broke into a laugh. "I thought you were upset about how they were treating you!" His shoulders shook as he laughed. "Beautiful, I love that you are so protective of us. But I can tell you now that no amount of dirty looks or name calling will ever stop us from wanting you."

Lacing his fingers with hers, Ben tugged her forward. "Fuck what anyone else thinks. We're here to spend time with our girl."

Atreyu slung his arm around her shoulders and they moved out to see the zoo. At all times that day, at least two of them were touching her. They fed giraffes and got a picture of the five of them. They played with the animals in the petting zoo, taking goofy pictures of each other feeding fat little goats and pigs. By the end of the day, she was so happy. Mor was pretty sure they had gotten a lot of strange looks, but the guys were right. Fuck 'em.

Sebastian suggested heading out to find someplace for dinner when the woman from the beginning of the day appeared in front of Mor. "You are a whore and a sinner!" Her face was red and spotted as she yelled.

"What is your problem?" Mor snapped it out before she could think better of it.

"You shouldn't be coming out here, whore, and making all these nice families see your shame! God will rain fire down on you for your whoring ways! You disgust me, you vile cunt!"

Mor's mouth dropped open. She glanced around and saw looks of horror on all the faces of the people surrounding them. But they weren't directed at Mor and her guys. They were directed at the crazy lady in front of them. She leaned in. "Take a look around you. You are the one yelling. You are the one using vile names and words in front of children. It's not me and my guys they are disgusted by. It's you." Mor was so proud her voice didn't waiver.

The next thing she knew the woman took a drink and threw it in her face. She gasped at the shock of the cold, sticky drink hitting her. Max sprang forward and pushed the woman back. One of the bystanders, a tall man with a biker look grabbed the woman and hauled her back before forcing her to sit on a wall.

Sebastian appeared at Mor's side with a stack of napkins and started gently wiping her face off. "They're calling security to escort that woman out. We'll need to give a statement and then we are going to get you a new shirt."

She grimaced down at what she was wearing. "I'm so sorry."

"Darling. You have nothing to apologize for." He started to say something else, but broke off when another woman approached.

She held out a package of wipes. "These may help you better than the napkins. I can't believe that woman did that to you!" She shook her head in disgust. Her baby laughed up at Mor from her stroller.

"Thank you." Mor took them from her but before she could start using them, Atreyu grabbed them and started helping Sebastian clean her up.

The woman looked at the four guys with a thoughtful look on her face. "Are they all yours?"

Mor started to respond but was cut off by the chorus of 'yeses' from her guys. "We have differing opinions on that." She said with a sigh.

The woman sighed too. "Damn, you are one lucky bitch." She lifted her hand for a high five.

Mor laughed and hit her raised hand. "Thank you. For the wipes and for, you know...."

"Not being an asshole because someone has a different lifestyle? Girl, it's sad that you have to thank me for that. One day, I pray that isn't the case. Until then, you do you. And them. Please, do them for the sake of all women out there." She winked and walked back to her family.

"Wait! Your wipes!"

"Keep them, I bet things get messy for you and I have like eight billion wipes." She grinned and waved.

Security showed up, finally, and took their statements and the statements of several witnesses. The woman was escorted out and banned from the zoo. When they asked if Mor wanted to press charges, she decided not to. She was glad they asked where the woman could hear them. Her face had blanched and she put her head in her hands. Mor hoped that by showing her grace she would learn some herself. Either way, not her fucking problem anymore. The zoo gave her a free t-shirt so she wouldn't have to leave sticky.

By the time they made their way to the car, she was exhausted. All she wanted to do was to get food and go to sleep. Between the walking all day and the confrontation, Mor was worn out. Seriously, this week had kind of been a mind fuck. When Max suggested drive-thru on the way home, she was totally in. They stopped for burgers and then ate their food at home.

The guys followed her up to her room but they all went to their own rooms to get ready for bed. When she was done, she went into her room to see four guys crowded on her bed. "What the fuck is going on?"

"Well, we were all pretty upset that Ben has gotten to sleep in here two nights in a row. We want cuddles too!" Atreyu pouted at Mor.

"There isn't even room for me to lay down!" She laughed at him.

"You could use us for your bed." Sebastian waggled his eyebrows at her.

Mor pretended to consider it for a moment and tapped her chin with a finger. "No. I think y'all would be too lumpy."

Atreyu pouted again. It was really adorable and she wanted to kiss it. Or suck on it. Whatever seemed to work at the moment. "Fiiiiine, Mor. BUT! We get turns too."

"How are you going to decide who gets to sleep in here?" Mor laughed at their antics as they shoved each other on the bed.

"We will go by age. Ben is the oldest, so that would make me next." Sebastian said primly. "All of you, out. It's my cuddle time." His face had a possessive smile on it as he looked at her. When they didn't move he yelled, "Out, heathens! It's my turn to cuddle." There was a lot of grumbling as the guys piled out of the bed. One by one they gave her a kiss on their way out. Atreyu grinned and pulled her into a dip before kissing her. Laughing, he spun her out of his arms and into Ben's. Ben gripped her chin and kissed her softly. Max was the last and he swept Mor into sweet hug before kissing her.

"Yes, yes, it's my turn." Sebastian was pouting.

She was still giggling as she crawled into his open arms. "Sebastian, you get cuddles the whole night. Stop pouting!"

"I will pout if I want to, darling. But you're right. I get you. All. Night. Long." He punctuated each word with a kiss. The last one he deepened, pulling her tight against his body.

Just as it started to get good, Mor yawned. "Oh, shit! I'm so sorry!"

A deep chuckle rumbled through Sebastian. "It's fine, darling. Sleep. We have all the time in the world."

She settled into his arms, letting his hand soothe her with soft circles on her back. As she drifted into sleep a thought struck her. All the time in the world? The guys had that, but not her. It woke her up and she tried to move away from Sebastian. He had fallen asleep already and just pulled her in closer to him. Mor laid there for a long time before finally being able to fall into an uneasy sleep.

* * *

THE NEXT MORNING she woke up bleary-eyed and exhausted. You know how you feel when you've had such vivid dreams you wake still feeling awful? That was her. The night had been spent with super fun dreams of her as an old lady still living with her guys. Only they barely looked at her anymore. Mor kept trying to get their attention but they walked away. And she was too old to chase them so they just kept getting further and further away.

"Good morning, my darling." Sebastian looked ruffled and sexy this morning with his hair out of place. When he kissed her softly Mor burst into tears. "Woah, darling, what's wrong?"

She just shook her head, unable to say anything through her tears. Eventually she calmed down enough to say, "It's nothing, just a stupid dream."

"Must have been a powerful dream to leave you in such a state." His hand came up to cup her face. "Tell me about it."

"You'll think it's dumb." She tried to pull away but he didn't let her.

"Nothing that could make you cry like that is dumb."

Hesitating only a moment longer she finally burst out, "I had a dream that I was really old and y'all were ignoring me and I was trying to chase you but I was too old and y'all just got farther and farther away!" Tears started falling again.

Sebastian was quiet for a moment. "What are you worried about?"

"You said we have all the time in the world, but I don't. I'm human, we are finite."

He pulled her into his arms and just held her head to his chest. As she listened to his heartbeat she was able to slow her breathing and calm down. When she had stopped shaking his voice whispered over her, "We will figure something out. But even if we can't, there is nothing that could make us ignore you. Do you understand?" Mor nodded against his chest feeling worn out physically and mentally. "Go back to sleep for a little while. I'm guessing you didn't sleep much at all last night." When she tried to get up, he pulled her back down. "Sleep, darling." He kept on rubbing her back and then started - singing? Sebastian had a low tenor and it washed over her. She couldn't understand the words but it didn't matter. It relaxed her enough that she was able to fall asleep to what she was pretty sure was a love song.

The next time Mor woke up she was alone in the bed. The sun was streaming into her room, bathing it in a soft warmth. With a stretch she got up and wandered into the bathroom. Sebastian was in there brushing his teeth. With her toothbrush. He smiled as she walked up to him. When she snatched the toothbrush from his mouth he laughed.

"Ew! That's my toothbrush!"

"You do realize that I've been in your mouth too?" He smirked at her. "So I really don't see why it's 'ew'."

"It just is, Sebastian!" She grumbled as she cleaned it off so she could use it. "Personal boundaries."

"I'm sorry, I do not understand what those words mean." He pressed up against her back, wrapped his arms around her waist, and then kissed her neck. Resting his chin on her shoulder he watched her brush her teeth in the mirror.

Rolling her eyes as she finished up, she turned in his arms. "So, are we going to the shop today?"

A thoughtful look crossed Sebastian's face. "Actually, I thought it might be more beneficial for you to spend the day with Trisha."

"Are you going to have her explain the - everything?"

Sebastian laughed again. He was always handsome, but relaxed like this? Holy shit. "I don't believe she can answer everything, darling, but about our culture? Probably most of it." He turned her toward her closet and gently pushed her toward it. "Get ready for the day love! And be prepared to return to school!"

She grinned. Mor had a feeling Trisha would be very thorough. She put on some yoga pants and a t-shirt figuring she would want to be comfortable if she was going to be sitting and learning. Throwing her hair in a ponytail, she ran down the stairs and into the kitchen. Her guys were eating breakfast at the island. She went to her usual spot to find a plate already made up for her. Smiling to herself, she dug in. Listening to them talk about their plans for the cars was soothing.

"Well, sweetie, it looks like we will be missing you today." Max nudged her.

"I'm excited to learn from Trisha today, but I'm definitely going to miss you." The pancakes melted in her mouth and she groaned. "How does she make perfect pancakes?"

"I've been cooking fer well over five hundred years, lass. I best be able to make pancakes." Mor's eyes bugged out. "Doona bother askin' yet, lass. I'll be answering yer questions shortly anyway."

She nodded and focused on her breakfast. When they were done, the guys stood and kissed her on the way out. They were little kisses to the top of her head and her cheek, but something about them was so much more intimate than a make out session. Once they had all left, Mor turned to look expectantly at Trish. "Come on, lass. These lessons will best be done outside."

CHAPTER 11

*M*or followed Trisha out into the yard. She didn't stop there but went into the trees beyond the yard. She wasn't sure what to make of it, but whatever. They hiked for a few minutes before coming to a clearing with a circle of flowers in the middle. Trisha waved her hand and a blanket and pillows appeared outside of the circle.

"Holy shit." Mor stared at her wide-eyed. "Magic. Like, I knew the guys did the elements thing, but that was straight up fucking magic!"

"I'm Fae, lass. Of course it's magic." She plopped herself down on the blankets. "Well, lass, are ye going to stand and stare?"

Mor jumped forward, settling herself on the blanket with Trisha. She just stared at her. Finally, Mor couldn't take the silence anymore. "Soooo....what is this place?"

"'Tis a fairy circle. An entrance into the Fae realms." She gestured at the circle.

"You just walk into it?"

She rolled her eyes. "And say the correct spell to trigger the realm jump. Alright, lass, I'm going ta give ye the general run down of Fae society and the boyos place in it." She took a breath and launched into it. "Fae society consists of four main states. Fire, Water, Earth, and Air.

Each has several high born families that are charged with caring for the Fae in their element and the lands associated with it." She looked at Mor to make sure she was following.

"So the guys are from different states?"

"Yes. Now, what is different is that most Fae doona fraternize with the other states. Most High Fae only associate with other High Fae and even then they have business dealings only outside of their own Element."

"So the friendship of the guys is frowned on? That's stupid."

"Aye, lass, it is mighty stupid as ye say. And 'twas not always like that." She looked sad for a moment before continuing. "That the boyos also come from the highest families in their elements is almost secondary to that. To associate outside of yer Element when ye are High Fae...."

"That's fucked up. Anyone can see they're like brothers."

"Aye, that's true lass. Atreyu's family helped them to stay in contact when it became clear to them that the boyos were close."

That drew her up short. "When you say close..."

Trisha burst out laughing. "Och, lass, I see where yer headed with that question. Nae, the boyos are not 'close' in the way yer thinking. That may have been easier, truth be told. Nae, the boyos just always felt they needed to be together." She shrugged. "When they came of age at thirty-five Atreyu's family allowed the boyos to live in a house in their lands."

"Where do they live?" Mor wondered if they would ever let her meet Atreyu's family. They sounded like good people.

"The Fae lands, lass. The boyos came here about thirty years ago when the pressure from their families started to increase."

"What were they wanting? Wait, marriages, right? And Max told me they moved in together five years ago!"

"Correct. Marriage alliances are important. 'Tis somewhat of a feudal system right now." She gave Mor a significant look. "And it's no like Max could have told ye how long the boyos have lived together. Ye didn't know what they are then."

"I guess that's true." She paused, thinking. "Was marriage like that for the Fae before?"

Now Trisha did look sad. "Nae, lass. We had a ruling family who held the Elements together. They disappeared three hundred years ago. We doona know where they went or what happened." She leaned back. "Before they disappeared, Fae were matched through magic." She held up a hand to stop Mor's question. "We doona know how, so dinnae ask."

Something popped into her head then, triggered by talking about things that happened over hundreds of years ago. "Wait a second! Atreyu said his mother loved the book and that's why he was named that, but that book came out in the seventies!"

"His mother does love that book. When they moved to Earth, the boyos changed their names to fit their new lives."

"What were there names, before?"

"That'll be up to them to be tellin' ye. I doona know if they want to remember them."

They were silent for a little while. "Trisha? I need to ask a question but it's...personal."

"Go ahead." Her face was neutral.

"Well, it seems, that, um..." Mor blushed and couldn't finish. "Never mind."

"Lass, my guess is that yer asking why all four boyos are pursuing ye but no one seems mad about it?"

"Basically? Sebastian made some statements when I first got here...."

"That they share."

"Yessss..." Her face was flaming by this point.

"Fae society is not as... reserved as human society." Trisha chuckled. "Most Fae are in multiple arrangements. The exception is unions arranged for heirs such as Ben and Max's parents wanted." She chuckled again. "Lass, Sebastian has three fathers and a mother while Atreyu has two mothers and a father."

"Oh?" She felt herself perk up for a moment but then she remembered - human.

"I doona understand why the long face, lass."

Mor pointed to herself. "Human. Short life."

"Lass. If that's all that's bothering ye..." She laughed. "Magic is quite powerful in the Fae realms. I'm sure there is something that could be figured out."

"If you say so." She couldn't shake the feeling that they were missing something. She didn't believe that it would be possible to find something to extend her life to forever. "What is the Fae realm like? Is it a parallel universe or a separate planet or what?"

Trisha shrugged. "My guess is the realm is a reflection of this world but there are others who believe it is a separate world. There are entrances all over the world. They're like moveable doors. Ye enter the circle, say a specific spell and it brings ye to yer destination. Ye best be knowing the spell to the door ye want to meet with, though, or no tellin' where ye may end up."

"Wow."

"'Tis a beautiful realm. Each Elemental State shows it's affinity through the land. Earth has endless forests, Water has oceans and lakes and rivers every other step, Air is high in the mountains, and Fire has controlled volcanoes. I'm not a huge fan of Fire or Air." Trisha shuddered.

"Which are you from?"

"The Brownies hail from Earth." She said it proudly. "There are many types of Fae in the States, but the High Fae will have ye believing they're no important."

"The guys don't feel that way."

"Nae. They are good boyos." She grinned at Mor. "Would ye care to join me fer lunch in the Fae realm?"

"Seriously? Fuck yes!"

"Lass, yer language is nearly as bad as the boyos."

"I can't seem to help it. It's getting worse. Maybe all those years my parents spent trying to make me the perfect American Princess." She rolled her eyes. "Fuck that."

"Aye lass, fuck that." Trisha winked at her. "Come on, I'll introduce ye to the Earth realm and Atreyu's brother."

"Wait, what?'

"He'll be wantin' ta meet the lass who stole his brother's heart." She nodded and took Mor by the hand.

"What are you talking about? I can't meet his family! I'm in yoga pants! I have no makeup on!"

"Lass, that's yer parents speakin', no ye." She looked at her sternly. "The boyos know I was planning to take ye to the Fae side."

"Y'all planned this? Why?" She wasn't sure how she felt about that.

"They want ta know if ye may have a chance to be comfortable over there." Her face took on an annoyed look. "They didna want to be present for fear they would 'unduly influence' yer decisions. Ridiculous. No like ye'll be making decisions anytime soon. The boyos have obligations here fer now."

"Their shop? Are they wanting to go back home?"

"I think that has more to do with ye and what will be best for ye. But they're Fae and their word is their bond. They cannae break their word without consequences."

"Oh shit." Mor let her pull her into the circle.

"Brace yerself lass, the transition can be a wee bit hard on ye the first time." With that she started speaking and the world swirled. Or she swirled? Either way, it was spinning and everything was bleeding together. Suddenly it was a solid color and there was a *pop!* and they were someplace with trees. She was looking up at trees, their trunks stretching endlessly above her. She was lying down? How did that happen? Mor chose not to move because the world still felt like it was spinning around her.

"This her? Doesn't seem to be made of very stern stuff." A voice sounded over to her right.

"Hush yer mouth, ye devil! 'Tis her first travel and she's had a week of big changes."

"It can't be that bad." She could hear the disdain in the voice.

Mor forced herself to sit up and look over at the speaker. The world spun, but at least she didn't throw up. "My family kidnapped me and tried to force me to marry an awful man. That's not all that happened, but that was the worst."

"Oh shit. Okay, that is a terrible week. I'm Adair, older brother to Atreyu." He offered his hand to her and pulled her up when she put her hand in his. "Welcome to Earth State." He grinned. "I didn't tell my parents you were coming today. Figured this would be enough. They are going to rip me a new one when they find out you were here, though!" He grinned.

She could see the resemblance between Atreyu and Adair. They both had black hair but Adair's flowed all the way down his back. They both had the same full lips and ice blue eyes. Adair was thicker than Atreyu with rippling muscles. Definitely hot, but Mor had scored the hotter brother. She smirked to herself. Wait. There she was doing it again. Being around the guys had really turned her into a ho. And she was loving every minute of it.

"You can see every thought on her face, can't you? I bet she's thinking about sex and my brother right now."

Mor gasped and her eyes flew up to him. "What the fuck?"

"You checked me out and then I could see your face change as you dismissed me and then thought of something else that gave you happy thoughts. Which I know were about sex because I could smell your arousal."

"Oh my fuck." Her face flamed up again. "I just can't."

Adair and Trisha laughed. "Lass, magic is strong in this realm and the Fae have heightened senses. Ye'll be wantin' to learn to control yer thoughts." She looked thoughtfully at Adair. "I do think the boyos can smell her even in the human realm."

"Probably. You can learn to focus your thoughts, Mor. Or just let them flow. We're more in tune with our desires than humans are." Adair winked at her. "Let's get you two fed. And then we can explore for a little while before you have to go back."

He led them to a small house. Inside was a simple meal of fruit, meat, and vegetables. They ate and kept conversation light by unspoken agreement. After finishing, Adair led them outside to explore. Trisha decided to stay behind saying she wanted a break from young ones. They hiked in silence but Mor didn't care. The forest was beautiful and ethereal. Strange birds flew among the trees and she caught glimpses of huge deer like creatures in the distance. When they reached a small pond, Adair sat on the edge and gestured for Mor to join him.

"Trisha wanted me to meet you." He said.

"That's what she said to me." She didn't add why but that didn't matter because he did.

"She said she wanted me to meet the girl who had stolen my little brother's heart."

Mor gulped. "We haven't known each long. Literally nine days."

Adair gave her a small smile. "And yet he brought you to live with them. Then they rescued you from your shitty family - although, truly that should have been done regardless - and they exposed who they are to you."

"Well, when you put it that way…" She stared into the clear water. "There is…something…I can't put my finger on. It fits, all of us. Somehow, we fit."

"It's hard, trusting you to hold my brother's heart. I was already grown when he was born and I've protected him ever since." He paused, "He thought he had found someone, once." Adair held her eyes when she looked up. "That's what drove them to the human world. She chose someone else."

Tears crept into Mor's eyes. "I don't know how she could have done that. Atreyu is…wonderful."

"I'm glad you see that, too." Adair hesitated again and then whistled. A moment later a huge wolf trotted out of the woods and came to sit between them. She held her breath, heart going nuts in her chest. *Holy fuck.*

Mor whisper screamed, "There's a wolf!"

Adair just chuckled and scratched the wolf's ears. "This is Faelan. He isn't exactly a wolf, he's…well, he's the Fae version, I guess. He was Atreyu's constant companion growing up. I thought you might want to meet him."

She forced herself to relax, watching Adair interact with Faelan. Okay, it wasn't trying to attack them and Adair was petting it - him. As soon as she relaxed, Faelan laid down and put his head in her lap, looking up at her with huge golden eyes. Hesitantly, she reached her hand out to pet him. Faelan sighed and snuggled in to her. His fur was softer than she thought it would be and she buried her fingers in it.

"He's amazing." Mor grinned up at Adair.

"For what it's worth, I think you're a good choice." He gave Mor a serious look. "Don't fuck it up."

She nodded. "I will definitely do my best."

Adair hesitated but Mor could see he wanted to ask something else. She waited him out, petting Faelan and enjoying the moment. "What about the others?"

"What about them?" She wasn't going to make it easy on him.

"Are you attracted to them too?" He rushed it out.

"For someone who had such a good time commenting on my arousal smell you're certainly seeming rather prudish now."

Adair threw back his head and laughed. "You're right of course. It's weird talking about this to someone with dirty thoughts about my baby brother." When she didn't say anything else, he said, "Well? Is it a fit for everyone?"

"Ben was disowned by his family for refusing to marry their choice and stay with me." She hung her head. "And yes, I feel it with Sebastian and Max too."

"Good. I want him happy and I know living with those guys helps." He stood up and brushed off his pants. "Come on, it's time to get back. Your guys will be home soon and they will want to know how your day went." He winked and pulled her to her feet. Faelan whined when he was dislodged from Mor's lap.

The hike back was much quicker. When they reached the Fairy Ring, Trisha was already waiting in the middle. "Thank you for everything, Adair. It was nice to meet you."

"It was nice to meet you too, Mor. I'm sure I'll see you soon."

She stepped into the circle and was more prepared for the swirling but still opened her eyes while she was lying flat on the ground. The sun was low in the sky and the sky was painted with blues, yellows, and reds. "Our girl is back." Atreyu's voice sounded just before his face popped over her. "Have a nice trip?" He pulled her up from the ground and they started walking back toward the house. Trisha was no where in sight.

He was trying to sound cool but she could see the anxiousness in his face. "I had a great time! I got to meet your brother and your wolf."

"What? You got to see Faelan?" His face lit up and then shut down. "How'd it go?"

"He laid his head in my lap after I stopped freaking out - because he is as tall as me when I sit down - and then we cuddled." She grinned at him.

"He let you? Damn." A real smile slowly spread across Atreyu's face. "That really makes me happy. He hasn't let anyone except my brother near him since I left."

"Why didn't you bring him with you?"

"I don't think he would be happy here. Not enough space or freedom." Atreyu shrugged. "I miss him but I didn't want him to be miserable just so I could have him here."

Mor leaned into him and he put his arm around her. "You're a good Fae, Atreyu."

"What did you think of my brother? Did he keep his promise and not tell our parents? Because they would freak out."

"He did keep that promise. I rather liked him. He seems more reserved than you and he definitely has a protective streak where you are concerned."

"He is one hundred and fifty years older than me, so I can see where that would make him more reserved. He's an old man."

She laughed at that. "He doesn't look like an old man!"

"Oh, so you like how he looks? Going to go for the older brother?" He was teasing, but there was a tense tone to his voice.

"Nah, I don't like old dudes. Plus, you are definitely hotter."

Atreyu burst out laughing. "Old dudes." He shook his head, still laughing. "You realize that *we* are old dudes compared to you."

"I'm ignoring that." She said it severely but couldn't stop her smile. "Where is everyone?"

"Getting dinner ready. Friday and Saturday are usually Trisha's days off."

"She wasted her day off on me?" Mor frowned, upset she had given up her personal time for her.

"She didn't think it was a waste. She thinks you're special too." He kissed the top of her head.

"It's so strange."

"What is, beautiful?"

"Having people care about me."

"Beautiful, you will never have to worry about that again." He grinned down at her.

"I'm beginning to see that." Mor smiled up at him as they walked into the door. Dinner was fast and then they all hung out in Atreyu's room, playing Smash Bros. Sebastian, Max, and Atreyu did not tell Ben about her con job on them so she had fun pulling it on him too. Just as she had him defeated the doorbell rang.

Ben huffed, "I'll get it."

The rest of them burst out laughing. "He didn't want to have to face his defeat!" Max crowed.

"That is way more fun watching you do that to someone else, darling." Sebastian held up his hand for a high five.

A moment later, Ben came back in holding an envelope. It was addressed to Mor. She shrank back from it. It felt bad even though it was just an envelope. "Courier mail for you, Mor. I checked it by magic, because it's weird but there is nothing dangerous about it." He handed it to her.

Mor's hands shook as she opened it. She pulled out a short letter and read it over, gasping in surprise and anger. Looking up at the guys she read it out loud to them,

Mor,

If you do not return to us and seal your marriage you will force our hand. You will not like what happens.

114

. . .

Mr. Williamson

THEY WERE ALL SILENT, letting the words sink in. "He referred to himself as 'Mr. Williamson'?" Sebastian shook his head. "He is *clearly* a prick."

"What do you think they will do? Should I go back?"

"Absolutely not!" Ben growled.

"Mor, sweetie, nothing they could do would be worth you going back." Max's face was deadly serious.

"But what if they come after you? They could drag your names through the mud or try to take your shop or - "

Sebastian cut her off. "Mor, darling, if they try any of that we will simply outspend them. The secret to success in the human world is money. And quite frankly, we have more than your - parents - could ever possibly amass."

Her eyes popped open at that. "I don't know what to say to that. You don't seem like the type of people to care about that."

Atreyu grinned. "We don't! But it's like a game and we are very good at it. Plus, it helps us smooth over any strangeness that comes from our long lives." He winked at her and added, "Also, it means we can buy new toys whenever we want."

"I'm not surprised you would want that. You do have every gaming system."

"You haven't even seen our outdoor toys!" He clapped his hands in excitement. "Maybe that's what we should do this weekend!" He did a fist pump. "Jet skis here we come!"

The guys all started planning what they would all do this week-end. It sounded like it was going to be a lot of fun. Jet skis, boats, beer? Fuck yes, count her in! She grinned but then realized she didn't have a swimsuit. "Guys." They were so excited they didn't hear her. "GUYS!"

"What?" They all stopped to look at her like she was crazy.

"I don't have a swimsuit. So all this talking about swimming is cool, but I can't go."

"Huh."

"Well, I guess we just add shopping to the list." Max smiled.

"I think I'll like watching our darling try on different suits." Sebastian's smile was wicked.

"Easily solved, Mor." Ben grinned.

"I've never been on a boat. My parents didn't deem it to be a place that business could be conducted. And if there was no business that could be conducted then...." She shrugged.

"Well, we shall remedy that tomorrow!" Sebastian stood up. "But for now, it's time for sleep. Come on darling, I get my second night now." He grinned and swept her into his arms carrying her from the room.

CHAPTER 12

*A*fter a glorious weekend on the lake drinking way too much and definitely getting a sun burn, Monday rolled around. Mor was actually excited for this Monday because her guys were going to start training her to take over the office job. She hadn't ever run an office before, but surely it wouldn't be that hard since it was such a small shop? Answer phones, schedule appointments, provide updates. Mor figured eventually they would have her work on some billing, but it wouldn't be too bad since they were a specialty shop and rarely worked with insurance.

She hopped out of bed and nudged Max. The last two nights had been spent cuddled up with the sweet Fae. He never did anything beyond a few sweet kisses, but somehow their conversations had created a deeper level of intimacy than she had expected. They had talked about everything. He had touched briefly on his family, but they didn't get into it too much. Mor was confident he would let her in to that side of him eventually.

She grinned at him. "Come on! It's Monday!"

He gave her the side eye and pulled a pillow over his face. "You were perfect right up until you were excited about Monday."

She giggled and pulled the pillow off of him. "I'm only excited because today I get to start working with y'all!"

He groaned and pulled her back down. "Ugh. Fine. You can be happy about that. But take it down a notch until we have coffee?" He kissed the top of her head.

"Fine, but I'm going down now to have coffee so you best get on that." She pressed a soft kiss on his mouth and then danced out the door.

Mor made her way down the stairs and into the kitchen. The smell of cooking bacon and omelets greeted her. She took a big breath. Bacon. She loved bacon. A mug was pushed into her hands. "Coffee, beautiful?" Atreyu was grinning at her.

"Yes! Thank you!"

His laugh rumbled over her. "I'm not sure you need coffee this morning. You seem far too awake for a Monday."

"She's excited for work." Max grunted coming up behind her and swiping the coffee out of her hands. "I clearly need this more than you."

"Hey now!" She looked at him indignantly. "Not cool to swipe coffee!"

Atreyu laughed, hard, and started making her a new cup of coffee. "Come sit away from Max, beautiful, you've clearly annoyed him this morning."

She sat next to Atreyu and looked up at him. Mor loved that they had started using their Fae forms at home all the time. "Thank you for coffee, *Atreyu*." She emphasized his name and stuck her tongue out at Max. Max stuck his back out at her before taking a slow drink of his coffee.

Mor giggled as she started drinking her own. "Perfect start to a perfect day."

"It's Monday!" Sebastian walked in just in time to hear that. He sounded as though she had personally affronted him. "No Monday is perfect, darling. How dare you!"

"Everyone is out to rain on my parade. Ugh." She rolled her eyes. "You can't make me be unhappy today."

Ben stomped in to the kitchen. "Please don't tell me that you are a morning person. Or a Monday person. You haven't been like this other mornings."

"Only today, Ben!" Mor paused thoughtfully. "Well, probably for the next several weeks. I'm just so excited to work with y'all! To go to work someplace I won't be miserable or surrounded by my family!"

Max groaned. "I hate that you have a legitimate reason to be happy on a Monday morning. I can't even be mad about it."

She grinned happily. Trisha started putting the breakfast on the table, winking at her as she handed Mor a plate. "The boyos don't understand. They've never really worked in misery."

She nodded while said boyos protested loudly. Trisha didn't say anything else, but Mor figured she would know. She wouldn't wish that on anyone, though, so she was happy that they hadn't. They did continue their grumbling as they worked their way through breakfast. When they had finally finished eating, they went to head out to the car. She was so excited she had trouble getting her seatbelt in place and Sebastian finally had to do it for her with a huff.

"Remind me to start drinking extra coffee." He didn't say it to anyone in particular.

Ben drove them down the drive, slowing for the gate to open. He paused longer than normal, staring at the gate. "Huh."

They all stopped talking and looked at Ben, then at the gate where he was staring. Tied to it was a bunch of roses. "What the fuck is that?" Max sounded grumpier than usual. He got out and stalked toward the roses. He looked at them for a second and then tore them off of the gate before tossing them to the ground. He stomped back to the car. "Let's get out of here."

Mor leaned forward. "Was there a note?"

"No."

At his short answer, Mor sat back in her seat. Clearly, she had done a number on his mojo by waking up cheerful. Mor hadn't noticed this problem before. Maybe it was because they hadn't woken up as early? She wasn't sure, but either way she was going to just back off from Max until he calmed down. She felt Sebastian and Atreyu exchange a look over her head. When she looked up at Sebastian he had a serious look on his face.

The rest of the drive to the shop was silent. When they pulled up to Magic Mechanics, Max pulled her into a hug as soon as they got out. "I'm sorry for being short with you in the car. These random flowers are making me feel on edge."

"I thought you were mad because I woke you up."

Max laughed, "I thought that was cute. And it gave me an excuse to steal your coffee." He winked at her. Max let go of her and grabbed her hand. He led her into the shop office. Mor gasped when she saw it. There were balloons everywhere. The guys were standing behind her with big grins on their faces, "What do you think? We wanted to make your first day special."

"Oh shit!" She gaped at him up at him. "So when you all were being grumpy about me being excited....You had already set this up?" She put her hands on her hips and schooled her face into anger. She was secretly dancing inside, but it was time they got some of their own medicine. "Y'all have some nerve." Mor stood glaring at them as they lost their smiles and started fidgeting.

"Mor - " Ben started.

As soon as he said something she dropped the glare and grinned at them. "This is fucking awesome! Thank you!" They stared at her like she had two heads. "Super fun, isn't it? Thinking you pissed someone off." She winked.

"You sneaky little thing. We should have seen that coming." Sebastian wagged his finger at her, a grin on his face. Smiles grew on the faces of Max, Ben and Atreyu. "Come on, darling, lets get you settled in."

She followed Sebastian behind the desk while the others went to the back. With a flourish he sat her in the desk chair. It looked new and was super comfortable. He settled in a chair next to her and started teaching her their scheduling system. A call came through while they were working and he walked her through setting it up. He showed her how they kept the customer's information stored in the system and loaded it to a cloud. By the time lunch rolled around and they put the closed sign up Mor was feeling pretty confident.

"I think in a few weeks I'll teach you our billing system. Would you want to do that, darling?" Sebastian asked as he held the door for her to walk into the break room.

"That'd be great! I'd really like that!" She couldn't help the smile that had been plastered on her face the whole morning.

They sat down with the other guys. They had ordered Chinese and, unsurprisingly, had already made her a plate. Lunch was nice with the guys talking about their projects and asking her how her training went. By the time lunch ended, she knew that she belonged without a shadow of a doubt. It was like she had been there for years instead of just a week. Mor reached for her water bottle and realized it was empty. She would need another one before she went back to her desk.

"Shit!" Ben jumped up as a water bottle moved across the table. And stopped in front of her.

"Well, that was weird." They all stared at the bottle, waiting for something else to happen. When nothing did Mor reached out and grabbed it. "Which of you did that?" She started to take a drink

"Stop!" Atreyu snatched it out of her hand. "None of us did that. It could be....something."

"Something? What does that even mean?"

"Well none of us did that. And you're human. So then who did that and what was the motivation?" Ben was looking around the room like they were about to be attacked.

"That's just silly. It must have been one of you. Haven't you ever done things accidentally?"

Atreyu snorted. "Not since we were children."

"There's no other explanation." She tried to grab the water from Atreyu but he wouldn't let her have it. "Fine, if you won't let me have that one then can someone else get me a water?"

Sebastian handed her another bottle. "Let's get you back out front." He wrapped his arm around her shoulders and guided Mor out of the room. Sebastian took her back up front and they got to work. He had her review all the procedures and locations for things. They reviewed general policies like payment, return time, what happens if someone has a complaint. That last one was her least favorite in customer services but she had dealt with it a lot at the coffee shop. Sebastian said that didn't usually happen, but when it did it was usually pretty epic. The last one had been because they had been honest that the car couldn't be restored with the budget they had been given. So after calling the owner to pick up the car *and* returning all of the money the man had a meltdown in the shop, screaming at all of them until Ben had finally gotten tired of it and used a bit of magic on him to shut him up and get him to go home.

By the end of the day her head was stuffed full of all the new information. Mor knew it'd be a few days before she got the hang of it, but it wasn't going to be that bad. She hadn't really stopped smiling during the day, except for the water bottle incident, but other than that it had been an excellent day. On their way home, she was just thinking about how good it was going to be to get changed and eat dinner. By the time they got to the gate she was feeling anxious to be there already. Just as Ben reached up to press the button for the gate it swung open on its own.

Her guys froze. "Why aren't we going through?"

"The gate opened." Ben stated, slowly.

"That's what it's supposed to do, right?" Mor was confused.

"He didn't press the button." Atreyu said tightly.

"Well, if the gate opened he must have opened it." She shrugged. "Maybe he brushed it before consciously pushing it?"

"Maybe." Sebastian didn't sound like he really believed that.

Max cleared his throat, "Let's get on in there. It's been a long day."

Mor really thought they were freaking out over nothing. Probably they just needed to relax. After they parked and piled out of the car, they all went their separate ways to get cleaned up. The guys needed a shower after all that work and she just wanted to wear yoga pants. After Mor had cleaned up, she went downstairs and decided to grab a beer from the fridge. She reached for it and it almost jumped into her hand. "Huh."

"What was that, lass?" Trisha was standing behind her, giving her a weird look.

"Oh nothing, Trisha." She smiled at her. "Just a long day."

"Did it no go well? The boyos didna give ye a hard time?"

"Not at all! Best first day ever! There was just a weird thing with a water bottle sliding across the table. They said that none of them did it, but there isn't another explanation." She sat down at the island. She wanted to offer to help, but last time she had tried Trisha had very firmly turned her down.

Trisha opened her mouth to say something, but then Atreyu came in. "Beer is a great idea!" He grinned and grabbed four. "We thought we could sit outside? It's not too bad out this evening."

"That'll be nice!" Mor loved being outside, especially since the 'lesson' with Trisha last week. There was something special about the forest surrounding the house. Or maybe it was just being with people who actually liked her. Whatever it was, Mor loved it.

She settled in next to Atreyu and he held his beer up for a clink. As they sat watching the sun slowly set, the others joined them. They sat in quiet contentment, just enjoying being together. Just as the sun dipped below the trees, Trisha brought out dinner. Conversation flowed and they all slowly unwound. When dinner was done, she stood and took her plate inside. She knew better than to try and actually do the dishes but at least she could bring them to the sink.

Atreyu followed her in and when she turned he was watching her with hooded eyes. "Ready for bed?" His voice was rough, sending a shiver over her.

"Definitely ready." She smiled.

His wicked smile spread slowly across his face and her breath caught. He was definitely sexy. When he held out a hand to her, Mor slipped her hand into his and let him lead her upstairs. When they got to her room he pulled her inside. As soon as she had closed the door he pushed her up against the door and kissed her. It was slow and deep, his tongue playing with her like she was the center of his world.

Atreyu's hands slid down her sides and then hooked under her legs, lifting her up onto him. She wrapped her legs around his hips and groaned as he pushed against her. She could feel every inch of him pressing into her and hitting just right as he ground against her. He left her lips and started kissing down her neck. When he reached her shoulder he turned from the door and carried Mor over to the bed and laid her down in the center of the bed. As soon as she was down, his hands traveled to her shirt and gently pushed it up and over her head, lips breaking contact with her skin for just a moment.

Looking down at Mor, he seemed frozen until he whispered, "Beautiful." He bent over, lips kissing down her chest to the lace edge of her bra. Gently taking the edge between his teeth he pulled it down. As soon as it was out of the way his mouth latched on to her nipple. She moaned and brought her hands up to his head. His teeth tugged while his tongue teased circles around her nipple.

"Atreyu!" She gasped. Mor was past thought and just feeling. He came off of her nipple and went to the other side. Just as he started to pull her bra down with his teeth, she looked over and saw the lamp hovering above the nightstand. "Holy fuck!" She yelped and pulled away from him, shakily pointing at the lamp. It crashed just as soon as he looked, shattering all over the nightstand. Glass shards would have hit her if Atreyu hadn't hunched over her to shield her from the flying pieces of glass.

"What was that?" She sat up. "Atreyu! You're bleeding!"

"Well, flying glass will do that." He winked and then grimaced as he sat up.

"Hold on, let me get help."

"Wait, Mor - " He tried to stop her but she was already out the door.

Sebastian's room was closest and she went in without knocking. "Sebastian, a lam- oh." She looked at him and saw that he was lying naked on the bed with one had wrapped around his impressive cock. "Um."

He took a long slow stroke. "Did you come to help me, darling?" His eyes flicked down to her chest.

"Oh shit!" Mor looked down and saw that her breasts were still out. Quickly, she fixed her bra "So, that would definitely be fun to help you but the lamp in my room just floated and shattered and Atreyu is bleeding and there is glass everywhere."

"Damn." With a groan he sat up and reached down to the side of the bed and grabbed his boxers. Pulling them on he followed her out of the room. "Did you say floated?"

"Yeah, it was just floating above the nightstand."

He was all business going into her room. "Go get the others, Mor, I'll get started on Atreyu and the room." She started to go back down the hall but he reached out and grabbed her. "But first." His head dipped down and caught her mouth. His kiss was hard and fast and left Mor gasping when he suddenly let her go and went into her room.

It took a moment for her to gather herself and then she went to get Ben and Max. This time she knocked. She definitely would not have minded seeing that again, but Atreyu was bleeding and a lamp fucking floated in her room. Floated. In her room. She had to force her focus to that instead of Atreyu and Sebastian's muscles.

By the time she got back to her room, following behind Ben, Trisha had come in too. The glass had somehow already been cleaned up and Sebastian was picking pieces out of Atreyu's back. "Ouch! What are you doing?"

"Calm down. I have to get all of theses pieces out." Sebastian rolled his eyes.

Mor walked up next to Atreyu and sat next to him. Picking up his hand she looked up at him, "I'm so sorry."

"Beautiful, what do you have to be sorry for? Not like you could make a lamp float."

"I'm sorry you got hurt."

"I will never be sorry about getting hurt to keep you safe. So get used to it." He answered gruffly and bent down to kiss her.

"Hey!" Sebastian grabbed him and jerked him back. "You have to stay still so I can get all of this out. Honestly." He sounded annoyed but she could see the lines of worry on his face. "Ben, what do you think?"

Ben had been staring at the nightstand. "I don't sense any outside magic. And we have no breaches…" He looked over at Trisha.

"I don't know, lad. I can't sense anything different." Trisha looked over at Mor, a thoughtful look on her face. "I'd say the lass needs to stay with one of ye at all times. Maybe set up personal wards every night." She looked like she might say something else, but instead she shrugged and walked out of the room.

"You aren't sleeping in here tonight." Atreyu flinched as Sebastian dug another piece of glass out of his back.

"That was the last one." Sebastian sighed and then gestured to Max who laid his hands on Atreyu's back, softly murmuring. A glow surrounded his hands.

"What's he doing?" She whispered.

Sebastian laughed. "You don't have to whisper, Mor." He smiled softly. "He's healing Atreyu's back."

"So why did you have to take the glass out?"

Sebastian's voice took on the air of a lecture. "Magic can do many things, but it cannot do everything. If he had healed him without removing the glass his body would have sealed the glass into him. It would have been very painful."

"That sounds awful." She shuddered.

"Not only that, but then we would have had to slice open his skin to dig out the glass before healing it again." Max's hands stopped glowing. "All set."

Sebastian grinned at Mor. "I'm going back to my room to finish what I had started." He winked at Mor, adjusted himself, and then sauntered out of the room.

"What was he doing?" Atreyu asked. He hadn't seen what Sebastian did.

Mor blushed. Max and Ben laughed at the look on her face. "He was, um, taking care of, um, himself." Her face felt like it was on fire.

Atreyu stared at her for a beat and then started laughing too. When he was finally able to calm down enough to speak, he pulled Mor to her feet. "Come on, beautiful. You'll sleep in my room tonight. I'll ward it so we will be perfectly safe."

She followed him out of the room and settled in. Even after he had warded the room and fallen asleep with her wrapped in his arms, she couldn't sleep. It felt like they were missing something or maybe something was going to happen? Either way, sleep didn't come easily.

CHAPTER 13

The next day, Mor was not nearly as excited to get up. She had spent a restless night, waking up every hour worried that something else might be floating. Nothing else happened, but she was so tired. Max greeted her with a large travel mug of coffee. "Thank you." She took a big drink and then spluttered. "Hot!"

Max laughed, the asshole. "It's coffee. Of course it's hot." He shook his head at her antics.

Still grumbling, she made quick work of breakfast. Her guys had already finished and were just waiting for her. As soon as she was done, they headed out. "I'm sorry to keep you all waiting."

"Don't worry about it, Mor. We know you had a long night." Max squeezed her hand gently.

"How did you know?" She asked.

"Atreyu told us you had a hard time sleeping."

"Oh, no. I didn't mean to keep him up." Mor put her head in her hands as she sat in the car.

"Beautiful, don't worry about it. That was some crazy shit. Of course you would have trouble sleeping." Atreyu pulled her into his side and kissed the top of her head. She snuggled into him as Ben started the car. He really didn't like anyone else driving.

128

Mor dozed on the way to the shop and sighed when she had to get up and go in. She made her way automatically to the front door only to be pulled back by Ben. She looked up at him in confusion and found his handsome human face set in lines of - anger? "What's gong on?"

On the step was a vase of roses and a small box. Ben gestured to the items with his chin and Max went over to them. He hovered for a moment, then looked back and shook his head. "I don't sense anything." He knelt down and opened the box. "What the fuck?" He pulled out a white garter from the box.

"Is there a note?" Ben's voice was sharp, his arms tight around her.

"No note."

"Burn it." Ben waited until Max had taken the flowers and box to the back. "This is getting weirder and weirder."

Sebastian came up next to him. "It feels like something is coming."

"Have y'all every gotten a present like that from one of your admirers?" Mor's voice was small.

"No, but we have gotten some rather risqué pictures before." Sebastian admitted.

"So this could just be that. Some woman that is crushing on y'all." she shrugged.

Atreyu shrugged uncomfortably. "Maybe."

"Well, either way we need to get to work. It's after opening time." She smiled at them and walked up to the door. Ben growled and stopped her from opening the door. He gently nudged Mor back and then opened the door himself. He went inside and slowly looked around. Finally, he nodded and gestured for her to go in. She wanted to roll her eyes and started to tease him, but then she remembered being kidnapped. He was probably just worried about that. "Thank you for looking out for me." Smiling softly at him, she stood on her tiptoes and kissed his cheek.

His face softened as he looked down at her. "One of us will stay up here with you."

"Ben, you don't have to do that."

"We know. It'll make us feel better." He leaned in and kissed her quickly.

Mor went to her desk, settling in and getting to work. Ben sat in one of the two chairs for customers and was reading on his phone. After a couple hours, Max came in to sit with her letting Ben get back to work. By the end of the day, they were all on edge and ready to get home. Just as she turned off her computer the door opened. It was another delivery person. This time he was carrying a large box of chocolate.

"Delivery for Moreen Williamson."

Her mouth fell open in shock. "What?"

Now he looked annoyed. "I have a delivery for Moreen Williamson. Is that you? Can you sign?" Sebastian stood and walked to stand next to her when the man moved toward her.

"Why don't you let me sign for that." His voice was formal, almost bored sounding.

"The delivery is for Moreen Williamson." The delivery guy was looking pissed.

"I heard you the first two times you said that. I will sign for the delivery and you will be on your way." Sebastian held his hand out.

The man reluctantly handed him the clipboard to sign and then gave him the box. "Look - "

"Sir, as you can see we are closing for the day. Please leave."

The man glared at Sebastian, then glanced at Mor before heading out. Sebastian didn't move until they heard the start of the truck. He moved quietly over to a window and looked out, watching until he was gone. When he was gone, Sebastian stuck his head in the back and called for the others to come up front. "I don't sense any magic on it, but he was very insistent on giving the box to Mor."

They all stared at it silently. Finally, Ben said, "Go ahead and open it."

Sebastian nodded once and then gently opened the box. Inside was chocolate. Expensive Godiva chocolate. "OOO!" She reached for one only to have the box pulled away.

"Wait, Mor." Ben held the box up to his nose and took a deep breath. His nose wrinkled in disgust.

"What do you smell?" He asked her and held it up for her to smell.

"I smell some crazy good chocolate. Give me!" Mor tried to snap it from him. She *needed* that chocolate. Now. She needed it now. "Why aren't you giving it to me!" She screeched at them. They were going to eat it all! How dare they! There was a crash from her desk. The guys looked over at the paperweight that had fallen off and shattered. She took the distraction to try and grab the chocolate.

"Shit!" Ben shouted and held it up over his head. She clawed at him, trying to get it. "Hold her back while I get rid of this."

"NO! Give me my chocolate!!" Mor screamed as Sebastian and Atreyu held her. A second later Ben was through the door and she stopped fighting them. Shaking, Mor looked up at them. "What just happened?"

"You went crazy for the chocolate." Sebastian's face was blank.

"I don't even like chocolate." Her head chose that moment to start hurting. She grimaced and closed her eyes.

"What's wrong, Mor?" Atreyu's voice was soft in her ear, but it still sent shooting pains through her head.

"My head is hurting." She started swaying.

"We need to get her home." The voices were bleeding together and Mor couldn't tell who was who.

"I'll get the others."

"Get her to the car?"

"Yes." The sound of keys being thrown and caught made her grip her head in pain. She was pulled up into strong arms. "Don't worry, I've got you."

A few minutes later they were driving. She could barely think from the pain. There was silence in the car and she was so grateful. Every sound was like a knife in the brain. When they got out, she heard a new voice.

"What happened?"

"A delivery guy brought chocolate that made Mor go crazy and then she started with this headache."

"Get the lass inside and in her bed."

She felt them moving again. Mor couldn't tell where they were going from the pounding and swaying in her head. She stopped moving forward and felt herself being lowered down. "She stinks of enchantment."

"Aye, but what enchantment."

"We didn't sense anything. The chocolate did smell like it was rotten but she couldn't tell."

"Must hae been targeted for her then."

The voices kept talking but Mor couldn't pay attention anymore. She drifted in a sea of pain for an unknown length of time. Eventually, the pain ebbed and she slowly started pulling back into herself. When she managed to blink open her eyes and look around, she saw Ben, Max, and Sebastian in chairs around the bed. Turning her head, she saw Atreyu laying next to her with his arm around her waist. Trisha was standing near her head.

"What happened?"

"Ye were spelled, lass. It was a targeted spell. When it didn't get ye to eat the chocolate it caused ye to have the headache." Trisha paused. "The boyos didn't want me to tell ye but if they hadn't gotten ye here behind the wards the pain might hae killed ye."

"No wonder I feel like shit."

"Aye. Best ye get some rest."

"Wait, Trisha. Will you help me wake them? I don't want them to be uncomfortable tonight."

"We're already awake, darling." Sebastian gave her a weary smile.

"I'm so glad you're back with us." Atreyu breathed from behind her.

"I'm so sorry, Mor." Ben hung his head.

"Not your fault." She said and then yawned.

"Mor? Would it be ok if we stayed in here?" Max asked, his face full of anxiety.

"Of course, but won't you be uncomfortable in the chairs?"

"What he's trying to ask is if we can all sleep in the bed with you, darling." He ran a hand over his head, messing up his blonde hair. "We're all feeling the need for connection right now."

"Oh, sure, if you want?"

As soon as the words were out of her mouth, she felt Atreyu pull her to the far side of the bed. With a relieved sigh, Ben crawled in next to Mor and pulled her onto his chest. Sebastian put himself at the bottom of the bed, head resting on her legs. Max laid down next to Ben and held her hand where it rested on Ben's chest. With a deep sigh, she fell back to sleep surrounded by her guys.

* * *

THE NEXT MORNING they all woke at the same time. She expected there to be an awkward moment, but they all just stretched and said good morning to each other. Mor, on the other hand, they all kissed good morning. She felt so much better. "Thank you for saving me. Again." She sighed.

"What's the sigh for?" Max asked, gently stroking her hair.

"You just seem to have to keep saving me."

"Mor, you are not to blame for the actions of a psychopath. You just seem to have more than your fair share of crazies after you." Atreyu winked. "Of course, you have the four of us after you, too."

That made her laugh as she got up to get ready. "Not sure what I did to deserve that good fortune. Four hot Fae? I'm in!"

They all laughed. As soon as she was ready, Trisha appeared at the door and escorted her to breakfast while the guys went to get ready. "I'm guessing they aren't going to leave me alone now, are they?"

"I wouldna count on it, lass." She smiled up at her. "Ye hae the boyos wrapped around yer finger."

"I wasn't trying to do that."

"That's what makes it so endearing." She patted her hand and then pointed to her chair. "Sit, sit. We'll get breakfast in ye and send ye off ta work with the boyos."

Breakfast was over quickly and they were headed to the shop in no time. "We set up wards all the way to the edge of the property last night." Atreyu said.

"When were you able to do that?"

"Once you had fallen asleep, Trisha sat with you while we set wards out to the edges." Ben's voice was tense from where he was in the drivers seat. "We wanted to make sure that if something happens again, then we'll be able to get you to safety faster."

"We'll set wards around the shop, too. So even if someone brings something in, it won't hurt you." Max was the calmest one.

"Do we have any idea who it was?"

"No." Sebastian's voice was clipped. "But when we do find them, they will not like meeting us." His voice took on a dangerous edge.

"I don't want y'all getting hurt because of me."

They all threw her an incredulous looks. "I'm pretty sure you are the most likely out of all of us to get hurt." Atreyu said, laughing. "Go on in the office. We're gonna set the wards and then be in."

She couldn't even argue, considering all that had happened since she had met the guys. Mor shook her head and walked into the office and froze. Sitting on her desk was a box. With a gasp, she turned and backed out. "Um, Max, there's another box on the desk."

Max sprinted to her as the guys came running back so fast they blurred. Max kept her in his arms while Ben, Atreyu and Sebastian went inside. A few minutes later, Sebastian came out with a grim look on his face. "It was a box of dead flowers."

"Like they died overnight?' She asked.

"No, like they were rotten with bugs living in them." Sebastian grimaced. "Ben and Atreyu went around back to destroy them. We'll get into position here and when they're ready, we'll set the wards." He looked at her. "When we start setting the wards, stand in front of Max."

"You don't want me to go inside?"

"No, we need one of us with eyes on you." Sebastian leaned forward to kiss her. "We'd be lost if you were hurt."

Before she could respond to that, Sebastian turned and walked off. Eyes wide, Mor turned to look at Max. "Whaa - ?"

"He's right, you know." Max smiled and held her close while he waited. After a few minutes he gently pushed Mor away. "Stand right there. Please don't move. You're distracting." He winked.

Holy fuck, Max winked. It made him look roguish. All he needed was a pirate hat. Hmm, maybe for Halloween? Her lusty thoughts were pushed to the side when his hands started glowing and he lifted them in the air. Mor saw light pulse out from them. Following the arc of the pulsing light she saw that it met three other arcs. "Wow." She couldn't help the exclamation. It was beautiful. The light pulsed, dripping down to the ground and upward to meet in the middle over the shop. Max let out a contented sigh and lowered his arms as the light faded.

He took the few steps towards her and hugged her close to him. "We'll keep you safe, Mor."

His promise made Mor melt into him and she closed her eyes, drinking in this feeling. Not because of them saving her, but because she was wanted. Mor was lo- nope, she was not going to think that word. Nope. Nope. Nope. After a few moments, she heard footsteps and then she was gently turned into Atreyu's arms. "We've got you, beautiful."

Sebastian was next. He didn't say anything, just rested his cheek on her head, holding her tight. She felt him shudder a little bit and then felt something drip on to her head. Was he crying? She held him tighter. What did she do to deserve these tears? They had only known her a week and all she had done was mess up their lives.

Ben pulled her into his arms last. His grip was tight as he stared down into her eyes. "We will not fail you again." His voice was rough.

Mor shook her head. "You haven't failed me. You barely know me, but y'all have changed your whole lives to include me and keep me safe. Nothing could happen to make me think you failed me."

He gripped her chin in one of his hands, keeping her from shaking her head anymore "We have failed you. You got hurt on our watch. It won't happen again." He hesitated a moment and then kissed her, slowly. He made her knees weak. It was a good thing he had his other arm around Mor's waist holding her up. When he finally let up, he led her into the office. After she was situated, he settled into the chair in the waiting area.

That afternoon, Atreyu was sitting with her. They were smiling and laughing while she tried to get work done when there was a loud bang in the back. "Shit!" He stood up and ran to the door into the garage. He paused and looked back at her, "Beautiful, don't leave the office." As soon as she nodded he ran into the back.

She sat there anxiously staring at the door to the garage. "Excuse me, miss?"

Mor gasped and turned around. There were two police officers standing in front of her desk. They both held up their badges for her to inspect. "May I help you?"

"Are you Moreen Williamson?" The older one asked, a kind look on his face.

"Yes. What can I do for you?"

The younger one walked around to her side of the desk. "You're under arrest. Come with us." He grabbed her arm, his grip so tight it hurt.

"What? What are you arresting me for? Let go!" She started yelling.

The kind looking officer said, "Ma'am, we're going to need you to calm down." The younger was reading her rights. "You don't want to add resisting arrest."

"Add it to what? Sebastian! Ben!" Mor was yelling, but the noises from the back were too loud. "I can't leave without telling my guys. Max! Atreyu!"

Her hands were handcuffed behind her back. "It's okay, Ms. Williamson. You're family is very concerned about you."

"My *family* is in the garage! Let me go!"

They were physically hauling her out the door. She tried to drop her weight, but they just grunted and carried her. When she tried to slam her feet down, they just picked her up completely and then forced her in the back of their car. She pressed her face to the window. "No." Her voice was a whisper as tears started to fall down her cheeks.

Just before they turned out of the drive, Mor saw Ben run out of the back, staring at the police car in horror.

CHAPTER 14

$\mathcal{T}$he next few hours were a blur. Mor was driven to a police station and had her mug shot taken. She was placed in a holding cell. No one else was being held, so Mor crawled into the far corner seat. Pulling her knees up to her chest, she stared blankly ahead. Mor had finally felt safe, even though there had been a bunch of creepy shit going on. At least she had her guys with her. Now...now she didn't know what would happen.

After a couple hours, the kind police officer came back. "Come on, Ms. Williamson. The judge needs to see you before he leaves for the day."

Mor stood up in a daze, well aware that resisting could make things worse. *Fuck.* She followed him down a hallway and into a courtroom. Small towns. At least she didn't have to go to another building. The judge was already seated as she was led in to the defendant's seat. Sebastian was standing there, a frown on his face. He was dressed in what was clearly a custom suit. Any other time, Mor would be drooling over the charcoal suit perfectly molded to him.

She looked over to the prosecutors side and saw a woman in a power suit standing next to - her mother and father? Mor's father smirked where just she could see him before turning back to the judge with a tragic look on his face. She felt her face turning red again, but this time it was anger. The officer led her to Sebastian's side. He looked at her cuffed hands and Mor could see a muscle tick in his jaw.

"Your Honor - " the other lawyer began.

"Is this really necessary? Handcuffs?" Sebastian cut in, his accent made him sound so much more than the twang of the prosecutor.

"Mr. Connor, you will respect the court." The judge frowned.

"I apologize, Your Honor. Is this really necessary? My client has never had a violent episode in her life."

"Actually, Your Honor, these are the defendant's parents. They have brought documentation of a history of self harm and delusionary behavior."

"What?!" Mor burst out.

"You will remain quiet or be held in contempt of court." The judge snapped at her.

"I apologize for the outburst of my client, Your Honor. She is understandably distraught by the false allegations."

"They are not false, Your Honor. These are the medical records provided by a Dr. Mark Robertson. He is the long time personal physician to the Williamson family."

She forced her mouth closed. What was happening?

"As you can see, she has a history of delusions and suicide attempts. We recommend a mental health hold so we can get to the bottom of what is happening. Her parents are very concerned that she is being used by the men she is now living with."

"That is preposterous."

"You would say that, you're one of the ones she is living with."

"Your Honor, Ms. Williamson came to live with us after her brother fired her and kicked her out of her apartment. Her parents subsequently attempted to force a marriage on her. She chose to live with us to escape the machinations of her family."

"You lie! You are nothing but a piece of shi- " Mor's father spluttered.

"Taylor, you better quiet them down before I throw them in jail!"

"Your Honor, may I please speak?" Mor's mom spoke meekly. She nearly snorted at the absurdity of it.

"Fine. But be brief."

Mor watched her in disbelief as tears fell down her mother's face. The audacity of this woman. She was almost impressed with her acting ability. If only she wasn't trying ruin her. "We adopted Moreen when she was just a year old. She was always a troubled child. We suspect..." Her mother's voice dropped to a whisper scream, "she was molested." Her voice went back to a normal volume when she continued. "We've lived in constant fear that she would hurt herself and have spent our lives trying to protect her. I may not have been able to have more children, but I love her like my own. Please protect my baby from these monsters taking advantage of her." She sobbed and Mor's dad pulled her into his arms so she could cry into his shoulder.

Unbelievable. Surely the judge would see through this crap. "Mr. Williamson, do you feel the need to comment as well?" He was clearly exasperated.

"No, Your Honor." Just before the judge could say something Mor's father interrupted, "I'd only want to add that Mor is my baby girl. I think of her as our future and the thought of her being hurt by those animals tears me apart. She is a delicate and trusting soul and can't be trusted to make her own decisions."

The judge looked over at Mor then turned to Sebastian. "Would you like to clarify your earlier comments on her parents?"

"Absolutely, Your Honor. Her parents planned to use marriage to Mor as a bargaining chip for a business deal. They were planning on marrying her to a Mr. John Davis. They even forced her to be checked by Dr. Robertson for virginity and then pregnancy." He didn't bring up the kidnapping, which was probably good since none of them called the police. "Ms. Williamson asked us to grant her sanctuary from her family. We have provided her with a job and her own room with an en-suite. My friends and I have experienced familial persecution as well and are always willing to help out those in need of an escape."

The judge frowned and pinched the bridge of his nose. "This is a mess. It's like something I would expect to see on a soap opera. I hate soap operas. Fine, twenty-four hour mental health hold ordered for evaluation to determine the validity of your parent's claims."

Mor's face paled and she looked at Sebastian in shock. "Your Honor, I request a private meeting with my client before she is taken to the facility." His voice was tight and he didn't look at her.

"Granted. You have twenty minutes."

Sebastian led Mor to the back, his hand on the small of her back as he guided her to the room indicated by the judge. As soon as the door closed he pulled her into his arms. "Mor, I'm so sorry. I got here as fast as I could."

"I don't understand what's happening. I may be in shock." She was shivering and had a detached feeling.

"Not good, we need to snap you out of that. If they see any signs of mental health problems they will extend the hold." He leaned down and kissed her. Mor groaned and leaned into him as warmth leeched into her body. By the time he pulled away, she was feeling much more centered. "Okay, your asshole parents contacted the police and claimed you were delusional and we were taking advantage of you."

"You're a lawyer?"

"I am. Now, I can't get you out of the hold. I need you to hold together for twenty-four hours. I'll get the information to discredit your parents and Dr. Robertson. Don't talk about the kidnapping. Just stick to facts about daily life. You might want to leave out our relationship beyond friendship."

Mor snorted. "Yeah, I don't think they would approve of me dating all four of you." She leaned her forehead against his chest and then pulled away. "How are you going to get information? It's all locked away in my father's office and in the doctor's office."

He winked at her. "Don't you worry about that." He pulled a small brown circle out of his pocket. "I need to stick this behind your ear. It'll allow you to contact us in emergencies and keep you clear headed even if they give you medication." He reached out and stuck it behind her ear.

"Won't people see it?"

"No, it's spelled to cloak itself." He tucked a strand of hair behind her ear. "I promise we'll get you out tomorrow. If we can't make it work though the legal system we'll break you out and return to Fae."

Mor started to say something else but the door opened. It was the nice police officer again. "It's time Ms. Williamson."

"I'll pick you up at the state hospital tomorrow." Sebastian said, holding her gaze but not touching her.

"Oh, she isn't going there. Her family has agreed to pay for a private facility in the hill country. It's called The Retreat."

Sebastian's face hardened. "I'll pick you up there tomorrow."

That wasn't good. She knew that. That meant that the doctors were probably bought off by her parents. Mor trusted Sebastian to get the information in front of the judge tomorrow. He'd take care of it. She had to believe that or she would really go crazy. But her guys would get her, no matter what.

* * *

THE FACILITY they arrived at was swanky. Like, fountains in the drive and lions flanking the stairs. There was a man in a suit waiting for the police car. He opened up the door and assisted Mor out like she was a lady. Impatiently, he gestured for the police officer to undo her handcuffs.

The younger, crankier officer refused. "This one is wild. She'll try to run."

The man looked down at Mor. "She won't run." His voice was arrogant. The officer grumbled but unlocked the handcuffs. She rubbed her wrists and waited. "Come, Ms. Williamson."

Mor followed him inside and was led to a private room. Where her parents, brother, and John were sitting. "What's this?" Anger laced her voice.

"Your family wished to speak with you and I felt it would be... therapeutic." He smirked at her. "As they are generous donors to our facility, we do try to accommodate reasonable requests." He gestured for her to sit across from them and then stood by the door.

"Moreen." Her father's voice was curt. "You have humiliated this family."

"I've done no such thing. All I have done is refused to be used as a pawn." Mor's voice was calm, cool even. Somehow she had slipped her mask back on.

"By refusing John you have made quite a mess for our family. We had a deal!" Tom spat.

"No, Tom, *you* had a deal. I did not." Mor looked at John. "There is no way I would date someone as awful as you, much less marry someone who expects to be able to sleep around."

John gave a nasty laugh. "That's just how men are. You need to get used to it. I'd only have children with you. Your children would inherit, anyway." He smirked and licked his lips while looking her up and down.

Her lip curled in disgust. "You're disgusting." She turned from him, dismissing him.

"Mor. We have a business proposition for you." Her father regained her attention.

"There is nothing that you have that I want."

Her father rolled his eyes. "Come now, Mor. Everyone has a price. If you agree to marry John tomorrow we will deposit one million dollars in an account for you. Each year you are with him and faithful we will add another million. Once you have provided him with two heirs you will obtain an easy divorce and access to your account. None of us will bother you again." He sat back, a satisfied smirk on his face as if the deal was already closed.

Although she knew what the answer would be, she had to ask. "What would happen with the children?"

"The children will remain with John and you will have no contact with them ever again. You are merely a donor."

Mor stared at them. They really meant it. "Y'all are insane. There is no way I would ever agree to this. To be a paid brood mare." She shook her head. "I am no longer your daughter."

With that, she stood and turned away from them staring down the man at the door. He cocked an eyebrow at her while she refused to acknowledge the screaming behind her. Her father grabbed her arm and spun her around, screaming in Mor's face about what an ungrateful bitch she was. Her mother was wailing about how she ruined everything. Her brother was yelling that she was a worthless whore. John was screaming that she would never amount to anything.

Eventually, the man in the suit clapped his hands. "I believe that is enough for tonight." Mor's ex-family stared at him in shock. "Clearly she isn't ready to see reason. Let us...work...with her. Perhaps she will be open to the plan later on." His smile made Mor uncomfortable.

Her father immediately agreed. "Of course, Dr. Smith. We will leave her in your expert care." He turned and smiled at her. "The next time we see you I trust that you will be more agreeable."

She just turned her head, refusing to speak further to him. They spoke briefly with Dr. Smith on the way out. Mor just stood there, trying to maintain her calm and focus. It wouldn't do to have a break-down now. "Well, Ms. Williamson, that wasn't so bad, was it?"

"Excuse me?" She stared at Dr. Smith. He had been in the same room as that shit show.

"Your family obviously cares for you very deeply." He was trying to make his voice soothing, but all it did was give her chills.

"Did you hear the part where they wanted to buy my uterus?" She forced herself to keep the blank look on her face. At least something good was coming from her years of forced formal training.

"Now, now, Ms. Williamson. Business is, after all, business. You cannot expect them to back down from a business deal. That's not how a gentleman's agreement works."

"It was their agreement, not mine." Short and sweet. She had to respond but she wouldn't give too much for them to work with.

"You are their daughter. That makes it their right."

Mor couldn't help the appalled look that crossed her face. What was with these people and not realizing that daughters couldn't be bought and sold anymore in the United States of America in the year two-thousand and nineteen? *What in the actual fuck?*

"Language, Ms. Williamson. Crass language will be punished."

"Oops, did I say that out loud?"

"Yes, you did. This is your only warning." Rage clouded his face for a moment before returning to the smooth mask.

"I apologize." *Fuck head.* "Please understand my shock that you would find it acceptable to buy or sell a daughter in this day and age."

"Ms. Williamson, there is no need for dramatics. You simply need to improve your family's business the only way you can."

"By selling my uterus."

"By making a good match and providing heirs for your family."

"So by selling my uterus and compromising my morals."

Dr. Smith sighed heavily. "Very well, Ms. Williamson. Perhaps you will be more amenable in the morning. I will have food delivered to your room and you will stay there until our morning treatment session."

"What will that consist of?"

"You will see in the morning." He grabbed her arm and forced her out of the room and down the hall. Dr. Smith continued to pull her up some stairs and into a hall with doors at regular intervals. Opening one, he pushed her inside. "This will be your room for as long as is needed."

"You mean for twenty-four hours per the judge."

"Oh no, I mean for as long as necessary. I fully believe that the judge will respect my determination that you really do need more help." He smirked. "I suggest you take the pills that arrive with your tray. If you do not take them, tomorrow will be that much worse."

He slammed the door, leaving her by herself. Mor explored the room. One small twin sized bed and a toilet and sink in the corner. There was a window in her door which meant anyone would be able to look in and watch her use the bathroom. *Fuck.* She sat on the bed and was not shocked to find it hard as a rock.

A few minutes later a cheerful woman in white scrubs opened the door. "Good evening, Ms. Williamson. How are we feeling this evening?"

"I would feel better if this circus was over." She couldn't help the bite to her words, but she did manage to keep the pleasant expression on her face.

"Well, the sooner you fully commit to your treatment, the sooner we can get you out of here!" She was enthusiastic, that was for sure. It made Mor want to hit things. She held up a little cup of pills. "Time for your medicine! Be a good girl and open up!" Ugh. Did she really have to talk to her like a child?

Mor held her hand out for them. "I'll take them."

"Oh no, dear, I have to pour them in your mouth to make sure you actually take them." Her face was serious now.

After a moment, she caved, fighting her panic at taking unknown medications. Only the knowledge of her protection from Sebastian let her calm down enough to take the pills. She opened her mouth and let her pour them in and then took the cup of water she handed her to wash them down.. "I suggest eating quickly, those pills will kick in soon!"

"Can you tell me what I took?"

"Oh no, dear, you aren't allowed to know that. Your parents are taking care of everything while you recover your stability." She patted her head. "Just knock on the door when your are done eating." She skipped out.

Mor stared at the food and decided to eat it. It looked like overly cooked chicken with some sort of soggy vegetable. She managed to force half of it down and then gave up. She knocked on the door and just a minute later perky nurse showed back up. "Oh dear, Ms. Williamson. You'll need to start eating more than that. But since it's your first day, we'll let it slide. Make sure to eat all your breakfast like a good girl!" She patted her head again. "Now get into bed so you can get your beauty rest. You don't want to look haggard!"

This woman really tested her restraint. Look haggard? As if that was what she needed to be worrying about. What the fuck was her problem? Mor prayed she would not be there tomorrow. She couldn't handle perky nurse and Dr. Smith. Something was clearly wrong with this 'facility'. All she could do was trust that Sebastian would get the information he needed to get her out. She stood and quickly made use of the facilities, getting really flustered when a male nurse watched her use the toilet with a smirk on his face. This place really needed to be burned down.

After getting ready for bed and changing into a nightgown that was laid out on the bed for her (thankfully peeping nurse didn't watch), she climbed into the awful bed and settled in. Once she was still she noticed a slight tingle behind her ear and touched the spot. Immediately, the voice of Ben filled her head.

"Mor! Are you okay? Just think your response."

"I'm fine. My family was here when I got here and they offered to buy my uterus, essentially, while 'Dr. Smith' watched. When he finally made them leave he said I should honor the business deal that my father had made because it was my duty as a daughter to do the only thing I could to help my family's business."

"That's disgusting, Mor. Absolutely disgusting. You are worth far more than bearing children."

A tear slipped down her cheek. *"Thank you."*

"I need to apologize again for not protecting you."

"What could you have done, Ben? They were police officers, not creepy stalker/kidnappers. There was nothing you could have done then." Mor tried to force her understanding on him so he would stop blaming himself.

Finally, she felt him relax. *"You're right. Thank you."*

"How is Sebastian's search going?"

"Well he has proof that your family lied including emails to a certain doctor about changing your records. He also has proof that they were trying to sell you to Davis. But the icing on the cake is that he found emails to a Dr. Smith about directing the course of your therapy once they managed to force a mental health hold."

"Oh damn. How is he going to get it to the judge?"

"Well, we might have used our magic for this. We compelled the only detective in the precinct to get a warrant to search the home and computer of your family. And then he compelled the judge to give it...So the officers are there now and Sebastian is staying Unseen to make sure it goes correctly."

"I have so many questions, but I think I will wait and ask them in person."

"How are you? What are they doing? To you?"

"Well, they gave me a shit ton of pills and wouldn't tell me what was in them and informed me I have a 'therapy session' in the morning. Dr. Smith seems to think it will make me change my mind. But if it doesn't then he will lie to the judge and say I'm unstable."

"We won't let that happen. Sebastian says the detective is determined to bring the information to the judge first thing in the morning. He also says that your dad just arrived and is really pissed." Ben chuckled. *"He's going to make sure the evidence stays safe to make sure the judge sees it in the morning."*

Mor yawned. *"I think I need to get some sleep."*

Ben's response was instant. *"Of course. Just press the circle again and it will end the connection."*

"Ben? Do you think you could just stay with me until I fall asleep?"

"Of course, love, of course." She fell asleep with Ben's presence in her mind, reminding her that she wasn't really alone.

CHAPTER 15

*M*or spent the night barely sleeping. She could hear the cries and screams of other patients. Whenever she woke up, Ben reminded her that he was there. At least she had that. If he hadn't been there, Mor thought she would have gone a little crazy. He kept reminding her that even if they couldn't use magic to convince the judge, they wouldn't hesitate to break her out and take her to Fae. She was especially worried about what the 'therapy' was going to be. Mor was one hundred percent sure that it was not going to be pleasant. Every once in a while she would see that creepy male nurse look in the window adding another layer to her fear.

The next morning, a different woman brought her breakfast and more meds. She didn't say anything, just held them to her mouth. Mor went ahead and opened her mouth without complaint. She said nothing, just set down a gown and left her to her breakfast. Mor picked at the breakfast, but then remembered what perky nurse had said about eating all her food. She forced down the chewy eggs and burned bacon.

Mor dressed in the soft, white gown they provided. It had buttons down the front and was sleeveless. The dress only fell to mid thigh which made her super uncomfortable. With a sigh, she sat on the bed to wait. She wasn't sure what time it was when Dr. Smith finally came to get her but it had felt like hours. She kept a pleasant look on her face, hoping to ease her 'treatment'.

"Good morning, Ms. Williamson. Are you ready for your treatment?" Dr. Smith's voice was smooth.

"Good morning, Dr. Smith." She chose not to say anything else, figuring that if she even started to say anything else then what she really thought would come out.

"Please follow me. We have a lot to get done." He turned and walked out of the door.

Mor followed him down the hall to the elevator. She got in and stood quietly next to him. She didn't want to risk talking and giving anything away. As her nerves increased she could feel Ben's reassuring presence in her head. Dr. Smith pressed a button with a LL on it. Basement, shit. When the elevator stopped he walked out. She followed him out and down the hall. He stopped outside a door and glanced back at her before opening it and gesturing her in.

"Come in, Ms. Williamson."

She hesitated before walking into the room. There were two nurses standing around the room working on different equipment. Fear coursed through her when she saw a chair with restraints in the center of the room. "Please have a seat, Ms. Williamson."

"Thank you, but no." She remained polite. *Fuck. Sitting would be a terrible idea.* "My understanding is that I am to undergo an evaluation. I am fully aware that an evaluation does not involve a chair with restraints."

"Well, that may be what the judge ordered. But your parents have ordered something quite different."

"Luckily for me, the judge has a higher authority than my parents."

Dr. Smith smirked at her. "Your parents are generous donors to this facility and personal benefactors of mine. Believe me when I say that I will take their directions over a judge's any day."

"Ah. So you aren't really a doctor." Mor could feel Ben's horror through their link. *"The judge is reviewing the evidence. Stall!"*

"To the contrary, Ms. Williamson. I have a Ph.D."

"So you're not a medical doctor. I'm unsure how you could possibly be licensed to use a restraining chair. I'm pretty sure none of these other creepy people could possibly be qualified."

"Luckily for you, you don't need to worry about that. What you need to worry about is how long it's going to take you to sign these papers." He patted a stack of papers next to him. "Get her in the chair."

The two male nurses turned. One of them was the creepy nurse from the night before. They advanced on her with hungry expressions on their faces. Mor backed up toward the door. It slammed behind her and she flinched but managed to keep her eyes on the nurses. With no warning they lunged forward and grabbed her. She screamed and fought them but they were so much stronger. "Let me go! NO!"

They laughed and creepy nurse grabbed her ass. "Oops."

"Fuck you!" Mor snarled. A piece of a glass flask fell on the floor.

"Fascinating." Dr. Smith looked at her like a particularly interesting experiment.

"NO! You can't do this!" Mor screamed.

"Mor!" Ben's voice screamed in her head.

"Ben! I can't stop them!" She panted hard, fear taking her over.

"Strap her down. We need to make the placement precise so we don't ruin her brain or her uterus." Dr. Smith gave a cruel laugh. "I don't know why they want to keep her brain, but that's what they ordered."

"Stop! You don't have to do this! Please!" She was begging.

"I love it when they beg." Creepy nurse whispered to the other man.

"Me too." His voice was harsh and the look on his face terrified her. They proceeded to strap her down, 'accidently' groping her as they went.

"Remember, boys, you can feel but you can't mark or break." Dr. Smith gave an evil grin. "I may feel too. I bet she will beg for it for a break."

Mor panted harder as he approached her. He held up some electrodes and started applying them to her arms and legs, caressing her as he went. After he was done he connected them to wires that led to a big panel. "Let's start on the lowest level, shall we?" Dr. Smith said. He messed with the panel and then winked at her before pushing a button.

"Hold on, Mor! We're coming. Be strong, we're coming!"

Pain shot through her arms and legs. Mor clenched her teeth. She would not give them the satisfaction. She would be strong. "How was that Ms. Williamson?" Mor didn't respond. She wouldn't give him the satisfaction. "Nothing? Hmm. I guess we'll need to make it more intense." He pressed a few buttons and then...*The pain!* She had never felt anything like this. It was like knives were slicing her body.

She grunted, unable to stop herself. No. Strong. They're coming. Her guys were coming. *"Ben, please hurry. Basement."*

"Such a fun game, isn't it Ms. Williamson?" Dr. Smith smiled and walked over to her. "Lets make some adjustments." He moved the patches on her legs into her inner thighs. He gently caressed her skin. "You are a pretty little thing, aren't you? Pity your parents sold you to John Davis."

"You are a sick fuck." Mor spat out. "The only way you can get any is by tying down helpless women? Pathetic."

"And spunky." He commented to his assistants who chuckled. "I'll be curious how long that spunk lasts. I noted down the time we started, so be sure I'll find out." He walked back over to the box. "Ready or not, Ms. Williamson." He grinned. Mor wanted to vomit. Sick, he was sick. She suppressed a whimper. Dr. Smith pressed a button. Now she did scream. It hurt, it hurt so bad! She clenched her teeth so hard that her jaw was shaking. "Ah, I did so think I'd get a bigger reaction than that. No matter."

He didn't give her any longer to recover, just hit the button. Mor screamed. Her body was being ripped apart by pain. Time stopped. She couldn't think, couldn't breath, could only feel as her body was shredded. Her scream went on and on and on until suddenly the pain stopped. She could hear yells in the room.

"Mor! Mor are you okay?" Sebastian's voice was desperate. "Please, darling, please be okay." She felt tugging as the patches were pulled off of her skin. She whimpered as pain flashed through her and tears started falling. "I've got you. I've got you. I'm taking you home." Mor blinked up at him and then let darkness take her over.

* * *

SHE WOKE UP LATER, surrounded on all sides by her guys. She tried to sit up, but was weighted down. Lifting her head she saw the guys wrapped around her. Trisha was sitting in a chair, watching them. "Trisha." She croaked. Her throat hurt. As soon as she spoke, the guys jumped up.

"Darling!'

"Beautiful are you ok?"

"We were so worried, sweetie."

"Mor." Ben's voice and face were filled with pain. He wrapped around her and started shaking. She looked down and saw tears falling down his face. She wrapped him up tight in her arms.

"You got me." She winced at the pain in her throat.

"When Sebastian followed the officers in, he let us in to watch. We saw you strapped to the chair screaming." He shuddered and pulled her closer. "We should have just grabbed you and taken you to Fae. I'm so sorry."

"Ben, it wasn't your fault. We could never have come back here otherwise." Mor snuggled into him. "What happened?"

"As soon as we got the evidence in front of the judge, he was appalled and ordered your parents, brother, and John arrested and sent officers to come get you. I demanded to go with them, and thankfully he didn't have a problem with that. When we broke in… they tried to stop us, but since you had told Ben you were in the basement I convinced - ah - them to search bottom to top." Sebastian closed his eyes, pain flashing across his face. "When we saw you… Everyone was arrested. That 'doctor' … turns out he has a Ph.D. in philosophy."

Atreyu sat on the foot of the bed and held out a mug. "It's hot tea. Trisha made it for you, said it would help your throat."

"Fuck! I can just heal you!" Max shook his head and reached over to place his hand on her throat. She felt a warmth flood into her throat from Max's hand. "I'm sorry I didn't think of that earlier."

Mor smiled at him, "Thank you for fixing it. And why are you sorry? You saved me. They were….they were planning to torture me until I signed the papers." She shuddered. "They…they…"

Trisha came back in the room. "Did they hurt ye in other ways, lass?" Her voice was soft, her face full of pity.

"No. They had orders to keep my brain and body injury free. But they were very free with their hands." She shuddered. "Thank you for saving me." Reaching out for the mug, she drained it and then coughed. "That's a lot of whiskey."

Trisha winked. "Aye. I figured Max would heal ye and ye would need a strong drink."

"You weren't wrong." Ben's shaking had slowed down. "Ben, you know what helped me while I was stuck there?" He shook his head. "It was you. You kept me sane. Knowing that I could hear you and you could hear me. And knowing that you would never leave me there."

He finally relaxed and softened against her. After a few minutes, she realized he was asleep. Sebastian had fallen asleep in the chair, Atreyu was curled on the end of the bed, and Max was watching her with tired eyes on the other side of her. Trisha nodded once. "Sleep, lass. Ye all need it."

She nodded and relaxed back. Safe. Hopefully for good this time.

* * *

THE NEXT TIME Mor woke the sun was streaming through the window. Ben was still wrapped around her, but he was awake. "Where is everyone?"

"Downstairs eating, making plans. I couldn't bare to leave you." He hugged her tight. "I know you don't want to hear it but I'm - "

Mor put a finger over his lips. "Nope. Don't want to hear it. It wasn't your fault. Place blame where it belongs. Right on my parents."

He signed and buried his face in her hair. "You're right. Thank you." He stood and reached out a hand to her. "Hungry?"

"Starving. The food in that place was worse than the treatments." Mor tried to joke but didn't quite make it. "Too soon." She smiled and laced her hand through his. "Let's go get breakfast."

They went downstairs and found everyone gathered in the kitchen, as usual. The guys immediately stood and wrapped her in a hug. There was something amazing about being wrapped up by four sexy Faes. She sighed in contentment. Suddenly, there was a knock at the door. They broke apart and Mor looked around, confused.

Sebastian looked resigned. "The police need to come and talk with you about what happened. They need a statement."

"Right, that makes sense." She shifted uncomfortably. "Maybe in the formal living room?"

"Sure." He smiled tightly and went to the door while Mor settled on a couch. Ben and Atreyu sat on either side of her while Max stood behind her with a hand on her shoulder. A moment later Sebastian led two detectives into the room.

They sat across from Mor and took out little notebooks while Sebastian came to stand behind her with Max. "Ms. Williamson, I'm Detective Hernandez and this is Detective Reed. Thank you for seeing us so soon."

"I'm guessing I didn't have much of a choice." She shrugged.

"We'd like to wrap up the case against your - family - as soon as possible."

"My family is here, Detective Hernandez." Mor said it firmly so there would be no doubt.

He cleared his throat, uncomfortable, and said, "Please describe what happened."

"My brother fired me from working in his coffee shop and then kicked me out of the apartment above it. Atreyu had accidentally caused that, but now I think Tom was going to find a way to make it happen." Mor patted Atreyu's leg and smiled at him. "Atreyu felt guilty, so he offered me a place to stay. My parents forced a meeting to try to make me marry John Davis and I refused. They threatened to cut me off and told me I owed them for their care my entire life. That I had been adopted - " her voice caught, " - so that I could be useful to them." She paused, trying to force tears back but not being very successful.

"When that didn't work, they claimed I was crazy. But the place they sent me to...my parents were waiting for me when I got there. They asked me to sign an agreement to provide two heirs to John, and they would give me a million dollars per year that I was married to him. After providing two heirs I would be divorced and leave, never to see my children or them again. When I said no they left me to be tortured. I was strapped to a chair and they electrocuted me to try and force me to sign the paperwork."

The detectives had grown pale while Mor was speaking. They just stared at her for a minute. "That's...that's..." Detective Reed swallowed. "I'm sorry that you went through that." He paused, clearly not wanting to ask, "Did anything else happen?" When Mor hesitated, shifting uncomfortably, he said, "Please, anything you tell us will help us put them away for a long time."

"Dr. Smith let me know that my parents were paying him to falsify my paperwork and to force me to sign the agreement. They also touched me inappropriately while strapping me down and while I was in the chair."

"You mean...?"

"They groped me." She said it bluntly and as fast as she could.

The detectives wrote down her statement. "The DA is looking at max sentences for Dr. Smith and those nurses. Your parents are up against those charges as well, but they are very wealthy. I know they already have lawyers fighting the charges." Detective Reed hesitated. "They haven't found your brother or Mr. Davis yet. He isn't at any of the residences held by your family or the Davis'. Right now we're monitoring credit card activity to try and find them."

Mor's face paled. "I - I'm not sure what to say to that. That is scary for me, considering what they were willing to do to force me into a marriage."

"We can place you in protective custody if you would like." Detective Hernandez offered.

Mor looked at Ben. He said, "We have an excellent security system here. And we'll be working to increase it's effectiveness. She will be with one of us at all times."

She shivered at the fierceness of his voice. But it wasn't a fear shiver. It was her lust shiver. She really shouldn't be turned on right now. She'd been literally tortured and now she was giving a statement about it and all she could really think about was getting the guys naked.

"Alright. Let us know if you change your mind. Do you have any questions for us?"

"Will I have to testify?" She didn't want to but she would.

"We hope not, but would you be willing to if we need it?"

Hesitating, Mor looked at her guys. They all nodded. "Yes."

The detectives stood and shook her hand before shaking the hands of her guys. "You're a very lucky young woman to have such fine friends standing with you."

"I most definitely am." Mor smiled at the detectives.

Sebastian came around the couch and led them out of the house. They promised to contact them if there was any change in the case. As soon as the door closed behind them, she sank into the couch. "I'm just so tired."

"Why don't we all go to the movie room and hang out for the day."

She perked up. "Movie room? What the fuck! Why were we in Atreyu's room?"

"He has all the systems set up." Max shrugged. "Downstairs is were we usually go to watch movies."

A movie day sounded perfect. "Snacks?"

Atreyu jumped up. "Max and I'll get 'em. You three head downstairs and pick a movie. No sappy shit!" He wagged a finger at Sebastian.

"Sebastian, are you into sappy movies?" She laughed. "Somehow, I can see that. Maybe a little Love Actually? Or Under the Tuscan Sun?" She laughed harder.

"Those films are highly underrated, I will have you know." He sniffed and sauntered away.

Ben smiled and then swung her into his arms. "Ben!" Mor laughed and tried to wiggle down but he held on tight. "I can walk!"

"I know you can. I just need to hold you right now."

"Okay."

Ben carried Mor over to a door underneath the stairs and followed Sebastian into it. At the bottom it opened into a big room with huge reclining chairs. There were five of them. "Can I go get some pillows?"

"Why do you need pillows?" Ben looked at her with confusion.

"So I can make a nest on the floor."

"Why do you want to do that?" Now he looked well and truly baffled.

"So I don't have to stand." His face was blank, clearly not understanding. "There are five chairs and six people."

He laughed out loud. "Mor, the middle chair is for you. Trisha doesn't watch movies with us. She says we're too rowdy."

"So why do you have five chairs? Not that I'm complaining." She hastily added that, not wanting him to feel upset.

"We bought it the day you came back after I chased you out."

"What? That's - that's - just - " Tears formed in her eyes and she couldn't speak.

"I know." He whispered. He set her down in the chair and then kissed her softly.

Cupping his cheek with her hand she held his gaze. "You will never know how much you mean to me. All of you."

He smiled softly before standing up. Mor had quite the view of him standing over her. Tight shirt, low riding jeans, and just a peak of stomach as he stretched. She licked her lips and he smirked.

Sebastian cleared his throat coming out of a side room. "Did you give Mor the run down?"

"Nope. Mor, there's a bathroom over there and a bar over there. Rundown done!" He grinned and flopped in the chair next to her. "What movie should we watch?"

She thought about it. "What about Captain Marvel?"

"Excellent choice!" Atreyu crowed from the stairs. She turned to see him with an arm full popcorn and candy. Max was right behind him carrying another load. "Get it loaded and we'll be right back!"

"What are they doing?" Mor asked.

"Getting the rest of the snacks." Ben said it off handedly while he scrolled to find the movie.

"The rest? There's enough here for all of us three times over!"

"You haven't been to one of our movie nights. Or days in this case." He winked at her. Sitting up straight, he intoned, "Prepare to eat your weight in snacks!"

Laughter bubbled out of her. "Y'all are nuts."

"Probably." Sebastian said, sitting on the other side of Ben. "At least we're fun!'"

"So true. I wouldn't want to be anywhere else." Atreyu and Max came back in and dumped the rest of their haul on the coffee table in front of them. Ben picked up a controller and pointed it at a wall. When he pushed a button the lights dimmed. After getting drinks for everyone Max sat in the chair next to Mor. She leaned back, nursing her drink, and just took in the moment. She was back where she belonged.

CHAPTER 16

They had watched movies all day. Trisha had brought them lunch and they had ordered pizza for dinner. They were just in their own little world, avoiding everything. Mor hadn't realized that's what she needed. It made her wonder how they had known. She meant to ask, but kept getting swept into the movies. At some point Mor must have fallen asleep because she woke up in her bed with all the guys crowded around her.

Mor gently extricated herself from her guy pile and went into the bathroom. She felt nasty. Shower. Thats what she needed. After using the facilities, she turned on the hot water and slowly undressed while she waited for the water to heat up.

"You know, darling, Ben was serious when he said you weren't to be alone."

Mor gasped and held her shirt up trying to cover herself. When she saw who it was her breathing slowed. She looked up to see Sebastian slowly looking her up and down, face filled with lust. He was dressed in a button down and a tie. She loved it when he was dressed like that. She wished he would turn around because Sebastian's ass in slacks should win awards. "What could possibly happen to me in the bathroom? Why are you dressed up?"

"First, we thought the same thing about the shop. Second, because I was going to go to the courthouse to see what the progress was." He growled, his voice lower than usual. "You know that shirt isn't covering anything."

Suddenly, she was feeling wicked. She dropped her shirt and just stood there. He started - purring? Damn. Who would have thought that was a sexy sound. She could feel herself growing damp between her legs. When she saw his nostrils flare she knew he smelled it. She was starting to like their heightened senses. With a hopefully sexy smile, Mor got into the shower. And promptly slipped.

She braced herself to hit the tiles but instead she fell into hard muscles. Sebastian stared down at her, perfectly mused hair and deep brown eyes sooo close. His voice was a whisper. "Mor, Mor, Mor. This is why we are setting a twenty-four hour watch." He smirked and set her up into the water.

"I thought it was to protect me."

"Apparently you need protection from yourself." He leaned in and she backed to the other side of the spraying water. He ignored it and caged her in with his arms. "Now I'm wet, too, darling." His voice was wickedly low and he bent down to her. Instead of kissing her mouth he kissed down her neck, hands coming to her waist. "Tell me now if you want me to go. Because I really want to taste you."

"No, I think you should stay. But maybe we need to get you out of those wet clothes." Mor was breathless and turned on. She wanted to see and feel him.

He chuckled and moved away from her to the other side of the water. Sebastian loosened his tie without breaking eye contact with her and tossed it to the side. He started on his buttons and she tried to reach out to help. He shook his head. "Stay. If you help me I won't be able to slow down enough to get them all off." His grin was arrogant as he slowly unbuttoned every. Single. Button. And then shrugged off his shirt. Mor literally moaned out loud as she took in his sleek form. He was solid, lean muscle. But it was the tattoos swirling across his body that caught her attention. He had a swirling pattern on his left shoulder and going down his arms. Others started just under his heart with some sort of stylized compass, maybe? From there, they traveled down across the deep V at his hips and disappeared into the tops of his pants.

She licked her lips. "Are you sure you don't want help?" Her voice was low and husky. It was only ever that way around her guys. Sebastian shook his head, slowly unbuckling his pants. He popped the button on them and dragged the zipper down.

"Mor?" Max's voice came to them as he walked in. "Oh." He looked into the bathroom, taking in her wet body with a slow perusal that had her knees shaking. He cleared his throat a couple times before being able to get out words. "You got her, Sebastian?"

"Oh yes." He purred. He looked back at Max. "Want to join us?"

Max's smile became sinful and a rumble started coming from him too. Fuck, she was seriously close just from the sounds they were making. Add it to her list of questions because there was no way in hell she'd be saying anything other than 'please more' and 'don't stop'. Sebastian turned back to her and pushed his pants down. Commando. He went commando. His cock was long and hard, glistening on the tip.

Her eyes caught movement just outside the shower. Max was staring at her as he pulled his shirt over his head with one hand. Fuck, that was sexy. He pushed his sweatpants down and yep. He didn't have boxers either. His skin was clear of tattoos and almost gleamed he was so pale. Sebastian still hadn't come to her. Max stepped in and stood next to him. They both watched Mor, waiting for something. She licked her lips and they both groaned. Max's hand came up to his thick shaft and he stroked it.

"But I want to do that." It popped out of her mouth before she could stop herself. A moment later she was so glad she hadn't been able to stop herself. The guys took the two steps to her and their mouths descended on her. Max claimed her lips while Sebastian kissed his way down her neck with biting kisses to her breasts. She felt one of Max's hands gently knead her breast while Sebastian's mouth locked onto the other one. The contrast had her trying to grind against them until hands pushed her hips to the wall and held her there. Sebastian's mouth was demanding, tongue flicking and teeth pulling. He came off with a pop and moved to the other side. Max held her breast for him while he took her nipple into his mouth. *Holy fuck, why was that so hot?!* She couldn't move, held to the wall by their hands and mouths.

Suddenly they both pulled back. Max sat down on the deep bench in the shower, setting her between his legs. Sebastian stood watching them, slowly stroking himself and making her mouth water. She ground herself back against Max, desperate to feel him. When her ass pressed against his cock he moaned. Then his mouth was on her neck and an arm wrapped around her waist to hold her in place while the other tangled in her hair and pulled her head to the side, giving him better access. "Please." It slipped out. She needed.

At her whispered word, Max slipped his hand between her legs and gently explored her folds. He pushed a finger in and slowly pumped. "You're going to come for us, aren't you, Mor?" His voice purred across her skin and he slipped a finger in. She panted against him, trying to flex her hips forward when he slipped in a second finger, unable to take her eyes from Sebastian standing in front of her. Max pressed in harder, hitting her clit with each stroke and bending his fingers to hit her g-spot. Mor couldn't stop moaning.

"Time to come, Mor." He latched onto her neck giving it just enough of a bite to send her flying over the edge. He kept moving his fingers until her aftershocks stopped and then brought his fingers to his mouth and sucked her juices off. "Delicious. Next time I want a taste from the source." Max kissed her, hard and deep.

"My turn." Sebastian's voice was hard. Max used his legs to push Mor's open. Sebastian knelt between them. "You're beautiful, Mor." He traced a finger across her pussy, gently brushing her sensitive clit. When her hips flexed forward on their own he grinned, leaned in, and took a long lick. He looked at Max. "Definitely delicious." Then he was on her, his tongue taking long licks and then swirling around her clit slowly driving her higher. When Mor's pants turned to moans he dove in and started fucking her with his mouth. Her hips wouldn't stop moving now.

Max moaned as her flexing hips moved his cock between the cheeks of her ass. He pulled her tighter to him with an arm around her waist, pressing himself hard against her. His other hand kept her head positioned to the side and he didn't stop kissing her neck. Sebastian's mouth picked up the pace and now she was loud. Mor was sure everyone could hear her and she really didn't give a shit. It felt so good. But she was close it almost hurt. "Please, I - " She couldn't finish it. Sebastian pulled his tongue back, but before she could complain he replaced it with two fingers and moved his mouth to her clit and sucked hard.

She threw her head back on Max's shoulder and screamed her release. It raced through her, setting her body on fire in a way she had never felt before. She felt Max grinding up against her ass before stiffening. Just as she felt Max's cum hit her back in spurts, Sebastian stood over her, fingers still pumping in her and drawing out her orgasm while he stroked himself to completion. He came on her stomach, eyes glued to Mor's as he groaned his release.

When her aftershocks stopped, Sebastian pulled his fingers out of her and sucked them off. His smile was wicked. "My new favorite dessert." He winked at Mor. "Now that we've made you suitably dirty, the least we can do is clean you up."

He pulled her up and had her lean on him. Max and Sebastian soaped her up, even washing and conditioning her long hair. They took turns holding her up while they cleaned up. When they stepped out of the shower they found towels sitting on the counter waiting for them. "Oh my gosh."

"What?" Max looked at her, confused.

"Someone came in and dropped off towels for us."

"And?" Sebastian looked just as confused as Max.

"Well, that means…you know. They saw."

They started laughing. "Mor, darling, you should know that sharing has it's benefits." He winked at her and chuckled again while toweling himself off. "I'm going to get dressed and head to the courthouse." He pulled her into him and kissed her softly. "I'll see you in a little while." He sauntered out of the bathroom. They heard him say good morning to the guys then head out.

Mor blushed, hard, and went into her closet to find clothes. Max had pulled his sweatpants back on but left the shirt off. She really appreciated his thoughtfulness. As soon she was dressed, Mor frowned down at her yoga pants. "Max? Are we going to the shop today?"

Max shook his head. "We're closing the shop and going 'on vacation' until this is all straightened out. We can't risk you."

"What about your projects?"

Now it was Max's turn to turn a little red. "Atreyu went in last night after you were asleep and used magic to finish the cars."

"What? Why didn't y'all do that before?"

His blush deepened. "We like working on cars."

She snuggled herself into his side. "That makes sense." Mor started to say something else, but she yawned.

"Why don't I get you settled for a nap before breakfast. I think we wore you out." His smile turned lusty as he led her out into the room. It was empty. "Ben and Atreyu went to get ready for the day." Max led her to the bed and crawled in with her. He pulled Mor into his side and whispered, "Sleep."

Sometime later she woke again. Max was reading on his phone next to her. She turned into him, not ready yet to get up and get going. "Morning."

He laughed. "Definitely closer to afternoon. Want some brunch?"

"Brunch?"

"It's too late for me to rightfully call it breakfast but it's breakfast food so - brunch! I think we have the stuff to make mimosas, even." His smile was infectious.

"That sounds amazing." Stretching, she got up and followed him downstairs. Sure enough, there were eggs, waffles with toppings, and bacon. And coffee thank you to whoever the Fae worshipped. She looked out on the porch and saw Ben and Atreyu hanging out there. Mor smiled and made herself a plate before heading out there.

"Good almost afternoon!" Atreyu waggled his eyebrows at her. "How was your shower?"

She choked and blushed but Max came up to save her. "It was climactic." He winked down at her. "Thanks for asking."

Now Atreyu groaned. "I'm jealous. It's official."

Mor couldn't help but laugh. "Which of you brought us towels?"

Ben and Atreyu exchanged a confused look. "Towels? What are you talking about?" Ben asked.

"There were towels on the counter. When we got out of the shower." She moaned as she took a bite of waffle. All three sets of eyes latched on to her mouth as soon as that sound came out. *Hmmmm.* She swiped a dollop of whip cream on her finger and slowly licked it off. Now they all groaned as Mor grinned wickedly at them. "So, towels?"

She could see them all snap their focus back. "Wasn't us, beautiful. You must have set them out before you got in."

"I hadn't thought of that. I guess I could have and just have accidentally grabbed extras."

She settled between them. A minute later, Trisha came out carrying mimosas for all of them. "Really?" Ben looked at the champagne flute like it was rotten.

"Mor wanted mimosas." Max shrugged as if that was the only answer necessary.

"I'll drink anything alcoholic." Atreyu grinned. "Besides, it's mostly juice so don't be a baby, Ben." He held his glass out. "To Mor! Home safe and sound again."

They clinked glasses and drank. "It's so nice to be home."

"Home. I'm glad you feel that, Mor." Ben squeezed her hand.

"I'm sorry you couldn't keep working on the cars."

"Don't apologize for that. It's more important to keep you safe than to fix some old cars." Ben was firm.

"I know, but y'all loved doing that."

"But now we get to hang with you and play video games all day!" Atreyu held up his hand for a high five.

She grinned and hit his hand. "So we gonna go play, then?"

He jumped up. "Yes! But no Smash Brothers. I don't want to lose all day."

"Aww, poor Atreyu." Max leaned over to her, "You know, before you came here he held the Smash Brothers throne in this house."

"So thank you." Ben winked at Mor. "He needed to be taken down."

"What?! I did not! I never -"

"Oh you did." Max chimed in. "Every time we played you were just the worst. 'You cannot beat me! I am undefeated!'," Max's imitation had them all cracking up.

"I do *not* sound like that." Atreyu crossed his arms.

Mor laughed harder. "You just sounded like that!"

He turned a betrayed look on her, "Et tu, Mor?"

"Yes, me too, Atreyu." She smirked at him.

He heaved a dramatic sigh. "Very well, then, let's go play Mario Kart oh Queen of the Brothers Smash."

She laughed and followed him into the house. "Don't be such a baby, Atreyu." She punched his arm. "Ow. Shit." Mor shook her hand as she passed him.

"That should teach you not to hit this solid wall of Fae."

"There's that humble spirit we know and love!" He tried to grab her but Mor ran.

"I'll still get you, my pretty!" He lunged and wrapped an arm around her waist. Atreyu pulled her to him, kissed her neck, and then swung her over his shoulder. "Now this is a view!" He smacked her ass making her squirm. "That won't work, beautiful!" She was still trying to get out of his hold when they got to his room. He threw her on the couch and flopped down beside her. "Ready to be defeated?" He tossed her a switch controller set in a steering wheel.

"You really weren't kidding about all the toys, were you?"

"Uh, no. I take my games seriously, Mor." Atreyu's voice became formal and he bowed to her before cracking up. "Seriously, though, what else are we going to spend money on? Sometimes we travel and we love cars, but we each have our own side hobbies."

"So your hobby is games. What about Ben?"

"Outdoor sports, particularly ones that go fast."

"Max?"

"Max loves movies. Sometimes he even tries to make some, but don't tell him I told you that."

"Sebastian? Wait, let me guess, studying!"

"You aren't totally wrong. He has a massive library and loves reading fiction."

"Like Game of Thrones?"

"Think a little more nerdy." Atreyu started up the game.

"Star Wars?"

"Yep! He has every single book. He also loves fantasy novels. And one time I'm pretty sure I saw him reading a romance novel." He winked at her.

A laugh fell from her at that. It was really hard to picture the formal and put together Fae man reading something so naughty and dirty. On the other hand...maybe he got good ideas from it? This morning had been amazing...

Suddenly, Atreyu's nose flared. "Somebody likes the thought of that." His eyes were hooded and his voice low as he looked at her.

"Fuck. That's super inconvenient that y'all can do that."

He laughed at that. "Okay, Mor. Prepare to be DEFEATED! Pick. Your. Driver."

He did take games seriously. Too bad he was going to be sorely disappointed here, too. Mor may not have been allowed to her own gaming system, but she had regularly played in college. She barely managed to keep her smile to herself as she picked Princess Peach. Atreyu was in for a rude surprise. They started the game and she let him get a little ahead of her. When that got boring, Mor caught up and beat him at the last minute.

"Beginners luck!" He said. "Let's try a harder course!" When she beat him on that one he looked like he might be catching on. "Okay. That's it. Rainbow Road. No one has ever beat me on that one."

She just smiled. "Alright." She decided not to tease him this time and just flat out beat him.

"How did you do that?! And with PEACH! She's the worst! You -

you - you're fucking awesome!" He went from outraged to ecstatic in a heartbeat. "Seriously, Mor! How badass are you?!"

She stood and bowed. "Thank you, thank you! I am the Queen of Mario Kart!"

Atreyu laughed and swooped her up into his arms. He marched her downstairs and then sat her on his shoulders when they got to Ben, Max, and Sebastian. "All hail the Queen of Mario Kart!" He sat her down while they laughed. "Seriously, she beat me with Peach. On Rainbow Road!"

"Shit, Mor, you really are the Queen." Max grinned.

"Hey Sebastian!" She slipped her arms around him in a hug. "How was your day?"

He sighed. "They still haven't caught your brother or Davis. They don't have any leads, either. We'll need to be careful."

"What do you think we should do?" Her voice was quiet.

Ben cleared his throat. "We've called in some reinforcements. They'll be here tomorrow morning first thing, hopefully."

"Do y'all have guest rooms?" She looked around. "I haven't seen any where they might fit."

"Well, we do have one, but we'll need at least two rooms for the people coming. So..." Max trailed off.

"So, what? Do I need to move out of my room? I can do that!" She smiled at them. Surely they knew she wouldn't mind. "I don't want any of y'all giving your space up. I barely got here. I can sleep on a couch or something." She figured that would never happen and she'd be with one of the guys, but you know what the say when you *assume*.

"Actually, darling, we thought perhaps we would just move in with you?"

She gave Sebastian a shocked look. "Of course. But won't we be uncomfortable?"

"Sooooo.....we figured you would be fine with it so we put in a bigger bed."

She snorted. "Y'all just now put a bigger bed in my room so we can cuddle." When they nodded she laughed harder. "And you only did it because we have company coming." Now they were shifting uncomfortably. Just as she thought. This was the excuse. Mor grinned at them.

"Well, see, we like cuddling and we need to make sure someone is with you at all times so really this is just the best way to make sure that happens, right?" Atreyu batted his big blue eyes at her.

"I'm so glad you got me fired." She smiled up at him before looking at the guys. "Of course it's fine. I love cuddling too." They all sighed in relief and went about their dinners. Trisha was off so they were all on their own. She was curious about the people coming. Hopefully they would like her and she would like them. Either way, she was grateful for their help already.

CHAPTER 17

$\mathcal{M}$or woke up refreshed and much less cramped. This morning the help called in by her guys would be here. They had insisted on trying out the new bed and she had slept in the middle of them. It made her feel safe. She nudged Ben so she could get up. With a whispered good morning he helped her to stand up. After getting ready for the day, they headed downstairs.

She sat on the porch with Ben, watching the sun rise. She should be feeling calm, but Mor felt tense. "Ben? Is there somewhere I could do some yoga?"

"You want to go to a studio?" He was already shaking his head.

"No, I know that we can't do that right now. I have an app. I just need some space."

"We can get you a mat if you want to stay out here, or I can take you to our gym."

"It doesn't have to be today, just soon. Out here would be a perfect way to end or start the day." She smiled. It was peaceful out here.

"We can always take time for something you need." Ben picked up her hand and held it laced through his. "Our visitors will be here soon."

"Will you tell me who they are?" She had forgotten to ask last night. She was easily distracted by the guys, because hotness.

"Atreyu's family." Ben smiled. "I haven't seen them for a while, but I know they will love you."

"Is his brother coming too?" She really liked the older Fae. He was more serious, but so sweet about his brother. When Ben nodded she asked, "What are his parent's names?"

"His father is Michael. His mothers are Cassandra and Isabella." Ben smiled. "His family is more traditional than mine. No arranged marriages there. That may be why they are a bit more - stable."

She thought 'nice' might work, but she couldn't say that without sounding like a bitch even if it was true. Leaning in to him she sighed, just soaking in the moment. "What time are they coming?"

"They'll be here sometime this morning. I thought they would be here already, but they haven't made it yet." He kissed the top of her head and pulled her into his lap. Mor laughed when the chair she was sitting in almost fell over. Once Mor was settled against him he said, "That's better."

She opened her mouth to tease him when they felt a vibration in the ground. "What was that?" Mor looked at Ben. He was frowning and staring at the forest when it happened again, stronger. "Ben?"

Suddenly, the ground shook hard enough to knock their chair over. Ben pulled Mor on top of him so she landed on him. "Fuck." He held tight while the ground kept shaking.

When it stopped the other guys ran outside and Ben sat up with her in his arms. She looked at their tense faces, "I assume that wasn't an earthquake."

"No, it was not." Max's voice was hard.

"We're being attacked." Ben stood, taking charge of the situation. "Atreyu, take her inside and fortify. Trisha will be able to help you." He looked at the others. "Let's go hunting."

Atreyu snatched her into his arms and ran into the house, stumbling as the shaking started again. "Wait!" He didn't listen. "Atreyu! Stop! I'll go in, but go help them!" He ignored her and kept going into the house. The ground shook again. Atreyu stumbled, running into a wall with his shoulder.

"Trisha!" He yelled.

"Here. Office, now."

"Why are we going to the office? What's happening?"

"Hush now, lass." Trisha shot her a sharp look as they entered a door Mor hadn't been in before.

Trisha slammed the door shut while Atreyu stood her up. "Sit down, Mor." His face was blank, voice hard. Where was her sweet Fae? He turned to the door and held his hand up to it, palm facing out. His hand started to glow, the light reaching to the door. From there it bled out from the door and into the walls, ceiling and floor until the whole room glowed. The house shook again, but it felt less in this room, even though they could hear things shattering outside of it, nothing else fell in there.

Atreyu dropped his hand and turned around. His face looked feral, fierce. She started to stand up but he growled and pointed. "Stay."

"Atreyu, I don't understand what's happening."

"We're being attacked."

"How do you know that?"

"We can sense the attack on our wards." He started pacing in front of the door. Mor looked around, realizing there were no windows.

"Why aren't there windows?"

"This rooms doubles as our safe room, lass."

Panic was rising. "What the fuck? A safe room? Why do you need a safe room? Everything has gone to shit since I met you!" She was yelling. Apparently she had lost her mind. Mor knew she wasn't being fair, but she couldn't stop talking. "I've been kidnapped, arrested, and literally fucking tortured! And now we're being attacked? BY WHAT?!" Her breath was coming in short pants and her heart rate was going crazy.

Atreyu's face softened and he came over to her. "I'm sorry, Mor." He sat next to her and pulled her into his arms.

"Please explain it to me." She whispered.

He sighed. "I'm not sure. All I know is that we are being attacked by magic." He growled. "It's connected, somehow. It must be connected. All the insanity with you and now this?" He looked over at Trisha. "What do you think?"

"I agree. Somehow, Mor is the key. I'm just not sure how, or why." They both looked at her. "Can you think of anything?"

"I never even knew magic existed until two weeks ago. I'm twenty-four! Well, at least for a few more days, but still!"

"Few more days?" Atreyu asked.

"My birthday is next Sunday. July twenty-first." The house shook again, but it felt weaker.

"Were you going to tell us, lass?" Trisha's gaze pierced her.

"We have a literal magic attack going on and I've been a little distracted, what with kidnap and torture." Sarcasm dripped from her.

"Doona sass *me*, lass." Trisha's face was thunderous. "I cannae believe ye weren't going to tell us!" She started muttering under breath.

"Trisha likes birthdays." Atreyu commented.

"I see that."

The house shook again. "It's getting weaker."

"Why don't you go help the others? I'll be fine here in the glowing safe room."

"Mor, I believe we told you that we were not going to let you be alone until we figured this out?"

"But...this is different?"

"No, Mor. It's serious." He sighed. "You've been hurt twice while we were supposed to be taking care of you. It won't happen again." His face hardened again as he looked down at her. Another rumble, but they barely felt it.

They sat there for at least another half hour before they heard knocking at the door. Atreyu didn't move. The knock pattern was repeated. Then again. With a relieved sigh, Atreyu waved his hand. The glow disappeared and he stood up with Mor still in his arms. Trisha was already at the door opening it. Sebastian stood on the other side.

"Let's go to the kitchen. I need a beer." Sebastian grunted.

"I can walk, you know." She wiggled, trying to get down.

"True, but I like carrying you so tough shit." Atreyu winked at her but his face was harder than usual.

"Y'all say that a lot." Mor leaned her head into him.

"Because it's true." When they got to the kitchen, he sat Mor in a chair. Sebastian went over to the fridge and grabbed five beers. Once he had passed them out and sat down, they all looked at Ben.

Ben didn't say anything right away, but frustration lined his face. Mor reached over and grabbed his hand before she could think better of it and he relaxed fractionally. "We didn't catch whoever it is." He sighed and took a long drink. "I'm not even totally sure what kind of magic it was. Anyone have an idea?" He looked at each of them, waiting for their head shake.

Max spoke up. "We know there were two of them. I saw at least two sets of footprints, but it could have been more. There was too much going on to get a clear picture."

"I couldn't differentiate any smells." Sebastian looked frustrated. "Whoever it was brought in something to cover up their smell."

"So they know who we are."

"How far did the attack get? Did it breach anything?" Atreyu leaned forward.

"It pushed in but didn't crack." Ben shook his head.

"What took you so long to get there?"

Max frowned. "We couldn't pin point it fast enough. It was spread out over a quarter of the wards."

"This is more advanced than we thought." Ben grimaced and looked at Mor.

"I know, it has to be connected. Trisha, Atreyu, and I talked about it while we were in the safe room. I also have no idea where or why."

Now Atreyu grinned. "One good thing that came of this - Mor let it slip that her birthday is next Sunday."

"What?" They all perked up while she tried to brush it off.

"It's no big deal."

"I'd say it's a pretty big deal." Max rolled his eyes.

"No, it's really not." Mor said it sharply and stood up. "I want to go lay down. I know it's early, but I need a break." She turned and marched toward the stairs. She heard footsteps following her but ignored them. She went to her room and left the door open for whoever was following. Without a word to them she collapsed on the bed and closed her eyes.

Sometime later Mor woke up. Apparently, she had needed sleep. When she tried to sit up she found herself held in place by Max. "Have a good nap, sweetie?" It had a distinct feel of 'are you feeling better'.

"I did, actually."

"Good. What do you want to do for your birthday?"

Her crankiness came back immediately. "I don't want to do anything."

"Why?"

She heaved a sigh. "Is there any way I can get you to ignore it?"

"That's definitely not happening."

"Fine. I don't want anything because birthdays have never been fun for me. They were always appointments and workouts. No cake, no party, no fun. Every year it was the same. Physical and mental assessments. And I never did well enough to make them happy."

"That would be miserable." Max said.

"Yeah. So I'd rather ignore it this year."

"Just so you have a heads up, that isn't going to happen." He smiled softly at her. "There will be cake. There will be presents. There is no stopping Trisha. Or us. We want to celebrate you."

Groaning, she buried her face in his chest. "I'm not sure I know how to have fun on a birthday."

"That's just sad. We'll help you learn." His face turned serious. "I never had fun birthdays, either. But when I was with the others they taught me how. We just had to hide it from my family."

"Fine. If you can do it, I guess I can do it too."

"That's the spirit! Ready to get up?"

"Yeah. I'm hungry."

Max led the way out of the room. "Atreyu's family is here. We can get you a snack and introduce you. Trisha is making a big dinner, so I don't think she'll let you eat lunch."

"Oh shit!" They were already out the door, but when she heard they were here she turned to go back in and change. And ran smack into a very handsome Fae who looked like Atreyu. But it wasn't his brother. She cringed. "Heeeeey."

"You must be Mor!" The Fae grabbed her and spun her in a circle.

Max was laughing at Mor's confused face. "Michael, good to see you!" He held out his hand for a shake and was pulled into a back slapping hug.

She started inching away, but Max reached back and grabbed her, pulling her into his side. "Mor, this is Michael. Michael, it was an easy guess for you."

"That it was! She's the only new face in the house." He grinned at Mor. "My older son told me he had met you already, the little brat." There was no venom in his voice when he said it. Just teasing.

"Ah, he did. He made me feel very welcome." She had no idea what to say.

"They're all meeting downstairs. Not sure what they can figure out, but you know Ben, Adair, and Isabella."

Max turned her and she was sandwiched between them as they walked down. "Those three all led in formal military units for both Fae and human armies."

"So they are trying to set up a war room?"

Michael burst out laughing. "War Room. I like that. Yes, they are determined to 'work through the logic' and 'prepare a plan of attack'."

"I take it you don't think that will help?" She looked up at Michael. He had an infectious spirit about him. It made you want to have fun.

"No, I don't think it will. It's going to take a sneak attack, probably. Or luring our enemies into the open." His eyes took on a deadly glint.

Just then, they walked into the formal dining room. It had definitely been turned into a war room. There were maps all over the table and Ben was leaning over them pointing at something while Adair and two women leaned over it. The others were sitting in chairs around the table. As soon as they walked in, Adair and the two women looked up at Mor.

"Hey, Mor!" Adair came over and gave her a big hug.

The woman sitting at the table squealed and jumped up. "Mor! I'm so happy to meet you!" She pulled her into a big hug. "I was so mad that Adair didn't share you when you were in Fae." She pushed her long, black hair out of her face as she stepped back. She was small and soft looking with a kind smile lighting up her face.

"It's nice to meet you." Mor smiled. It was impossible not to.

The other woman walked up to her. She was intimidatingly tall and had her red hair pulled back into a tight braid. She looked Mor up and down, and then walked around her in a circle. "Mom. Cut the shit out." Atreyu grumbled.

"I reserve the right to assess any woman you are interested in." Her tone was formal, clipped. "She looks soft. But from what you've told me she has an iron will." She paused in front of Mor, searching her eyes. "You'll do." She held her hand out and shook Mor's hand. "You may call me Isabella for now." She nodded once, let go of her hand and went back to the table. "Let us continue, boys."

The other woman, who must be Cassandra, smiled and wrapped an arm around Mor's shoulders. "She must like you."

"I would hate to see dislike." It definitely came out louder than she planned. Everyone in the room started laughing, except Isabella who at least cracked a smile for half a second. She felt her face flame up again. One day, she would love to have just a little tiny bit of control over that.

"Oh my dear, you most definitely would not like that!" Cassandra giggled. "It usually involves knives." She smiled affectionately at Isabella.

It was disconcerting that Michael, Cassandra, and Isabella were parents. Not one of them looked much older than her. "My head hurts." She mumbled it and went to find a corner to sit in. Atreyu came over, picked her up and then sat back down again.

"You just really like holding me, huh?" Mor rested her head against his chest.

"I do! But really, you look like you're in pain. So what's up?"

"There's just so much going on. And your parents don't look like parents. And we have a War Room now. And it's all my fault."

She felt his hand slip into her hair. He gripped it and tilted her head back to look at him. "Mor, if you try to blame yourself one more time for any of this then I will take you over my knee and spank you."

Mor gasped in outrage. "What? Fuck you very much, that's never happening." she glared.

"Not sure how else to get it into that beautiful thick skull of yours." His other hand came up and tweaked her nose. "In all seriousness, beautiful, none of this is your fault. It is the fault of the psychos behind this. Don't blame yourself again."

She huffed and tried to pull away, but his hand was firm in her hair. "Fine. But if I wasn't here then you wouldn't have to deal with it."

"You are right about that. The alternative would be you with no support and probably being forced to marry Davis so I'd say that's a win." He smiled. "Now, the other. You're freaking out because my parents don't look like parents?" He chuckled. "They've always looked the same. But that's Fae. Our bodies just sort of freeze and then that's it."

"I'm just going to have to get used to it. All the other parents I know look old."

"Dear, why would you want to look old?" Cassandra wandered over, smiling affectionately at Atreyu.

"I don't think anyone wants to. It's just what we humans have to figure out." She shrugged.

She shuddered. "It must be awful." She looked at Mor. "I'm sorry, sometimes I don't think before I speak." Cassandra looked down, shamefaced.

"It's alright, Cassandra. Nothing to be done about it." She smiled. "I just know that I'll leave before I start to look the guy's grandma." She was joking but Mor felt Atreyu stiffen underneath her, and not in a fun way.

"Let's not talk about leaving." He growled and tugged her closer.

She just nodded, knowing that is what she would do whether they liked it or not. She let him hold her for a minute longer. "I'm going to go get a snack from the kitchen."

"Okay, beautiful. Trisha is in there and I can watch you from the door." Mor rolled her eyes and walked out of the War Room. Maybe she could make some popcorn for everyone. Trisha was humming while she cooked. She pointed her in the direction of popcorn and Reese's Pieces and Mor got to making one of her favorite snacks.

She got a big mixing bowl, poured all the popcorn in and stirred in the candy. Then she grabbed enough bowls for everyone if they wanted some and started back toward the War Room. She paused, seeing Atreyu talking with Michael and Cassandra.

"But your mate?" Cassandra's voice was sad as she looked up at Atreyu.

"I know. But it doesn't matter. She's the one we want."

"You can't fight the mating bond, son." Michael put his hand on Atreyu's shoulder.

"I - " He stopped and looked over his shoulder and saw Mor. He smiled but she was frozen to the spot.

"Mate? You have a mate out there waiting for you and y'all are wasting time on me?" Anger laced her voice. They were wasting time on her, a human with a million problems. The War Room had gone silent and everyone was staring at her. "How dare you? And to pull me in with talks of family and safety and really fun sex?! When your mate could just appear one day and then you all would abandon me! I. Am. Not. A. Toy! I am tired of being used!!"

She started to throw the popcorn, thought better of it and threw the bowls at Atreyu before turning and fleeing to her room. She slammed the door and locked it. Mor didn't hear any satisfying shatter, so she assumed some magic had stopped them. Ugh. Tears rolled down her face and fell into the bowl she was cradling in her lap. Why was she always just a tool to someone? For once, she had thought she was more than a barely useful pawn.

Someone knocked on the door. Mor didn't dignify it with a response. Also, she may have been crying too hard, but she wasn't going to go there. Fuck 'em. She was going to eat all the popcorn.

"Mor open the door, I can explain - we can explain."

"Fuck off!"

"Dammit Mor! You do not understand what is happening!"

"I understand plenty, jackass!" Mor was starting to get angry instead of sad. She much preferred that.

"No, you really fucking don't understand!" Atreyu knocked again. When she didn't respond she heard a muffled, "fuck this," and then the door burst open. All her - the - guys were standing there looking pissed. Well, she was pissed too. They came in and she gave them an icy stare as she ate her popcorn.

Ben finally shook his head. "You really think we would do that to you?"

"What, so when you meet your mate you're gonna say 'Sorry, love of my eternal life, I have to wait until this human dies but then I'm all yours!'" Mor rolled her eyes. "I think we all know that won't fucking work."

"Dammit, Mor! The reason I was in the coffee shop that day was because I sensed you when I drove through town!" Atreyu yelled at her, just as angry as she was.

"I don't even know what that fucking means!!!" She yelled.

"It means YOU are my mate!" He yelled, then stomped over, yanked away her popcorn, and kissed her silly. "You, you stubborn, beautiful, ridiculous woman." His voice softened. "You are my mate."

"Oh." Mor froze. "Oh shit." She looked at the others with wide eyes.

"Yes, you're their mate too."

"Oh shit. Shit. Shit. Shit." She put her head in her hands.

"Haven't you figured it out yet?" Sebastian's voice was soft.

"You're the center of our world." Max's voice caressed her.

"You won't get rid of us." Ben finished.

Only one thing she could do with this right now. She stood up, went to the kitchen, and sat down with a pint of ice cream.

CHAPTER 18

*I*ce cream was supposed to help to process. Mor sat and worked her way through the pint of pistachio while the guys sat across from her. She ignored them. This was insane. They were basically immortal and for some fucked up reason they thought she was their mate. The human. She could not wrap her head around that. So, ice cream.

"Mor - " Ben started.

She waved her spoon at him. Nope. Not ready to talk. Thankfully, they sat quietly until she finished her ice cream. With a sigh, Mor sat her spoon down and looked up at them. "When were you planning on telling me?"

Atreyu shifted uncomfortably. "Well, my original plan was to talk with everyone once they all had a chance to meet you and then we could talk to you...." He trailed off.

Mor eyed Ben. "So your reaction to me?"

"Fear." His answer was quick. "I had just come home from my parents trying to force me to marry Marissa, only to be confronted by my mate in my home."

"At least you're honest," She muttered. "So I get that things kept

181

happening, but why would you not find a few minutes to tell me this?!"

"That's not really fair, Mor." Max chastised her. "This is not a 'few minutes' discussion. We are talking about our mate - our life."

"How do you know that? If I have more than one mate, then how do you know you only have one? It doesn't make sense."

"Maybe because you're human you can't sense it. When you are with your mate and the full match is present, we feel complete." Sebastian answered her, leaning forward on his elbows.

Mor nodded slowly. Maybe that was why she had felt so comfortable with them. She wasn't crazy, she was feeling the bond in a muted human way. "I'm guessing that's why I trusted y'all right away."

Ben nodded. "Most likely."

"So how did you go from wanting me as far from you as I could get to tracking me down?"

"When you left...we all felt broken." His head hung and he ran an agitated hand through his short hair. "It felt like a piece of us was torn away."

"I felt that too. It's why I pulled over. I couldn't see because I was crying so hard."

"Then when we went after you and we found your car...I was terrified. I had let you down because of my fears." Now he looked at her. His face was drawn with pain. Mor didn't say anything. "And then we kept failing you. We've been attacked, you were taken again and tortured. And now..." He made generalized gesture. "Now we can't even protect our own home. We had to call for help."

Now Mor stood up and went around to Ben. She put her arm around him and pulled him into her. "Ben. Do you think less of me for needing help?"

"Well, no, but you aren't..."

"Aren't what?" Frustration seeped into her voice. "Aren't strong? Aren't tough enough? Because I'm still here. After the years of mental and emotional abuse. After being kidnapped. After being tortured at my *family's* request so that I would hire my uterus out to fucking John Davis. So don't fucking say that I'm not strong enough." Mor had gotten angry as she spoke. The cabinets banged open, making them all jump. "What the fuck, guys? Can't y'all keep it under control? I'm allowed to be mad."

"That wasn't us, Mor." Ben shook his head. "We can't even figure out why the fuck things are going wrong in this house!" He sighed heavily and wrapped his arms around her. "I'm sorry, you're right. You are incredibly strong. I think we just haven't focused on that because you're human and we just...want to keep you safe." He sighed.

"So again, I ask. Why did you all hold out on me? If it was this important and I'm your special mate or whatever the fuck you call it, then you *should have made time.*" They all flinched.

"You're right." Max said. "We should have. But how would you have reacted? My guess is you wouldn't have believed us, or argued, or ran away."

"I'd argue with good reason! You can't be mated to me. I'm a human."

"That doesn't really matter, clearly." Sebastian rolled his eyes. "And you just made Max's point for him."

"Well, I - " Mor sputtered. Shit. He was right. "Look, I'm just saying that it doesn't make sense. I'm human. I'm finite. I can't be whatever it is you need." She pulled away and ran out the back to the patio. She heard the guys yelling for her, but she didn't stop. Once she was outside, Mor sank down into the grass. She could feel them watching her, but at least they had the sense to stay back. Ice cream didn't fix it. What a let down. Although she really shouldn't be surprised movies were wrong about that. She sat there for a long time, watching the sun go down.

Cassandra came to find her as the sun sank down behind the trees. She quietly sat down next to her. "It's hard finding your mates."

"It won't work."

"What won't work, dear?"

"You coming out here to convince me to accept them."

Her laugh was not what Mor had expected. It was hard and long. "Oh my dear child. I'm not out here to do that." She chuckled again.

"The bond will drive you together. The harder you fight it, the more painful it is for all of you." She smiled gently at her.

"What do you mean?" Mor couldn't help her curiosity. Even though it was definitely not going to work. She was positive. Mostly.

"The magic that creates the mate bond is not well understood. We believe it flows from the very heart of the Fae realm. What we do know is that if you fight it you end up miserable." She paused thoughtfully. "It's also never been wrong." She patted her hand. "While a human has never been a mate that I'm aware of, I'm sure that the magic has not made a mistake here."

"I don't know."

"No one knows the future, child. All we know is our past and the choices we can make now. The question you need to ask is do you want to be without them?"

They sat in silence, watching the stars come out. It was beautiful. What did she want? Did she want to be with them? Even if it was just for now. Did she want to leave? Maybe she should. If she did, then maybe they could find someone more worthy of them. At the thought of leaving, Mor felt a sharp pain. It was emotional but it also felt like her heart was being physically ripped from her body. The thought of leaving them was bad, but it was the thought of them being with someone else that really pushed her over the edge. She bent over, gasping and clutching at her chest.

"Ah, did you think about leaving them? Or....?" Cassandra lifted an eyebrow. "My guess is you thought about them with someone else. I've felt that, as well. When I first met Michael he was - ah - spending time with another. I thought to stay out of the way because they had been together for many years. But it ate at me and at him. Eventually, she actually brought us together. We're still very good friends."

"So you didn't know Isabella then?" She was so curious how it would work.

"No, we knew we were missing someone but it didn't click until Isabella." She smiled softly. "Now we feel complete." She stood and looked down at her. "Are you ready to go in? Your mates are currently pacing in the kitchen trying to decide how best to convince you while giving you space."

"Just...one more question." Mor blushed. She really didn't want to ask Atreyu's mom this question. "You know what, never mind."

"Oh no, dear, get your questions out now." She stared at her with a serene but firm look on her face.

"It's no big deal. Really." She held up her hands and forced a smile.

"Dear, you are not going back in there until you ask." Her face hardened.

"Ugh! Fine. How do you, um, complete the bond?" She was mortified because she was pretty sure what the answer was.

Cassandra laughed again. "Dear, when you get to be as old as I am you are quite a bit more...frank...about these things." She held a hand down to Mor and pulled her up when she took her hand. "Sex, dear. What other way would there be to complete a mate bond?" She looked back in at the guys, all watching from the porch window. Her face took on a clinical expression as she watched them. "I do believe you will have an excellent time. Atreyu looks just like his father and I know what he is capable of. And his friends have grown up to be quite handsome." She winked at her again and then laughed at Mor's blush. "Sex is very much part of life, dear." She patted Mor's hand. "Best you get used to it. The mate bond will do interesting things to you once it's completed." Cassandra tugged on her hand, leading her inside.

Now her face felt like it was on fire. "Erm." It was one thing to have fun times with the guys and it was another to talk to a mother about it. Especially the mother of one of them. Mor followed her inside but as soon as they were in, Cassandra let go of her and left her to face the guys. "So. I don't know how this is going to work and I still think there is some sort of mistake, but I don't want to be without you." The last part was not what she meant to say. But there it was. It was probably the most truthful, anyway.

"Really?" Sebastian took a hesitant step toward Mor.

"Yes. Really."

The guys rushed her and Mor was wrapped in four sets of arms. The longer they stood there, the more she could feel them all relax.

Something clicked once they all acknowledged what was happening. Well, once they *all* knew what was happening and acknowledged it.

"I'm still upset that y'all didn't tell me this sooner." Her voice was muffled against them.

"You're right." Ben spoke up first.

"We shouldn't keep things from you." She felt Max lean in and kiss her head.

"If you do it again, I will definitely yell and cuss at you."

"You do that anyway." The deep rumble of Atreyu's chuckle moved through her.

"Well, I promise to do it extra."

"Alright, children, let's get back to work now that the drama is finished." The sharp voice of Isabella cracked through the room.

"Geez, mom, you can't give us five minutes?"

"You've had more than that to get this straightened out. Now, there was an attack while you were all moping about."

That jarred them all. They broke apart and went to the War Room. Sebastian and Max both grabbed Mor's hands as they walked in. "So what happened, Isabella? We didn't feel anything." Sebastian squeezed her hand before letting it go and walking over to the table.

Isabella gestured and one of the maps became a - hologram? "That's cool!" Isabell gave Mor a sharp stare.

"Mor's never seen anything like this, mom."

"Yeah…I just learned magic was real like two weeks ago."

Isabella just stared at her before turning back to the magic hologram thing. "The first attack was on the back side of the property." It lit up in red. "This second attack was on the East side. They tried to dig underneath."

"What stopped them?" Max was all business.

"Adair set wards on the ground to search for attack that way." Michael had come in to the room after them.

"Where is he now?"

"Your brother ran to Fae for a quick errand. He gave me the key for the wards."

"How was the attack repelled, Michael?" Ben stared at the map like it would somehow spit out answers.

"The wards did it. Adair was very thorough." His smile was proud.

Mor wandered away from the table, feeling out of place as they debated who was most likely to be doing this and where another attack may happen. Max sat with her while the debate raged. Isabella was convinced they should just retreat to Fae while Ben and Sebastian felt they should press to find out who it was. Atreyu, Cassandra and Michael were undecided.

Thankfully, Trisha came to interrupt them and called them for a late dinner. Michael and Cassandra kept conversation up with Mor, Max, Sebastian, and Atreyu while Ben and Isabella muttered over strategy. Trisha snapped at them several times, but they just ignored her and continued on. Occasionally, Sebastian chimed in with suggestions for defensive options. By the time dessert was finished, they were all frustrated.

Adair still hadn't made it back when they all went to bed. His parents weren't worried, so Mor decided not to worry either. Surely, they would know if it was dangerous. After getting ready for bed, she hesitated going back out to her - their - room. It felt different now, bigger, going to get in the bed that fit all of them. She had thought it would be weird when they did that, but figured it was a need to protect. Now, she knew it was because they all felt itchy? Wrong? When they weren't together. A thought occurred to her as she was standing hesitantly in the bathroom.

Before she could stop herself, because Mor's filter had apparently started disappearing when she met Atreyu, she went into the room and said, "Did I mess up something between y'all?"

Sebastian looked up, startled. He was the only one in the room. "What do you mean, darling?"

Her face blazed. That was the other thing she couldn't stop doing here. Word vomit and flaming face. "Um, Trisha said you weren't but were any of you....you know...together?"

Sebastian stared at her, nonplussed. "No, Mor. Although two of my fathers do frequently entertain each other none of us had that relationship."

"So why are you all so comfortable sleeping in a big bed together?"

"We've known each other for two hundred years. We've spent time camping, at war, fucking, and living together." He said it like that was all the answer she needed.

Something registered. "Fucking?"

"Mmmmm, I love that that is the word you picked up on. Yes, darling, we've had practice sharing while we waited for you."

Her face blasted up again. "Why won't my face stop doing this?!" She muttered it to herself, but by his smirk he heard. Speaking louder she said, "I'm not sure what all those things have to do with you being comfortable in a bed together."

"We trust one another implicitly. The most important reason, though, is that you are here. None of us want to be apart from you. So, it's either rotate and we all suffer or we all sleep in here." He shrugged. "It was really no question at all, darling."

"Oh." She couldn't think of anything else to say.

"Come lay down with me, darling." He patted the bed next to him and lifted the blankets.

Mor crawled across the bed and snuggled up to him. She started dozing but couldn't fall asleep. Eventually, she felt the others join them one by one. When they were all there, sleep swiftly came over her.

That night she had crazy dreams. Dreams of places she had never been. Dreams of Tom and John attacking. Dreams of a woman with flowing blonde hair and three men standing behind her. When she woke, the guys were still asleep. Mor tried to snuggle back down into the mattress when she realized they weren't on the mattress. They were floating in the fucking air!

"What the fuck!" As soon as Mor said it they crashed into the mattress.

Her guys jumped up, ready for battle, surrounding her. "What happened?" Ben was abrupt.

"We were floating. In the air. Above the bed."

"What?" Max turned to give Mor a confused look.

"Floating. In the air." She pointed up, needlessly.

"Okay, someone's magic needs to get their shit together." Atreyu was grumpier than usual. Maybe floating did that to you? Or the crashing?

Michael, Cassandra, and Isabella crashed into the room. "What's happening?" Isabella demanded.

They all looked at Mor where she still sat in the middle of the bed. "We were floating in the air." Not sure where else they would float, but she felt it was really important that everyone realize they were in the air. Mor scooted to the edge of the bed and Max and Sebastian sat next to her, taking her hands in theirs.

Isabella gave her a hard look. "Why do I feel like I am not getting the full picture?"

"Weird things have been happening, Mom."

"Define 'weird'." Isabella's voice was tight with annoyance.

"Things breaking, doors closing and opening, floating apparently." Max shrugged. "We haven't figured out which of us doesn't have it locked down. I assume it's because of the newness of the mating bond."

Cassandra looked thoughtful. "I don't think that's it." She stared at Mor, hard. "There's something about you....I can't quite place it." She shrugged, dismissing whatever it was she was thinking. "I can tell you it isn't any of you boys. The signature is different."

"Therefore, as my lovely mate is trying to say, there are only two options. One, there is some foreign object that was brought into this house that is causing the magic malfunction." Michael looked thoughtfully at Cassandra.

"Or two," Isabella was staring Mor down, "Mor is the source of the magic."

CHAPTER 19

"Nooooo." Mor's voice was incredulous. "I've never done anything remotely magical."

"What was your childhood like?" Mor was pretty sure Isabella wasn't capable of sounding soft. She was always in battle mode.

"Not fun." Elaboration was not needed, or so she thought.

"Be specific."

Heaving a sigh, Mor continued, "Emotionally abusive. Suppressive. I had to meet a certain standard both in how I looked and how I acted." Jaw clenched, she stopped talking. She took a deep breath to calm herself.

"Exactly." Isabella's voice was triumphant. "That level of suppression would affect all parts of you, not just your personality." Her face was all business.

"Do humans have magic?" Max spoke up.

Michael hesitated before answering. "Yes. But we have only encountered a few of them."

"I feel like we're missing something." Sebastian wrapped an arm around Mor's shoulders.

Cassandra gave them a sad look. "You are."

"Love, I don't think you should." Michael's face was closed off.

"No, they have a right to know. They need to know." She slowly walked over and knelt in front of Mor where she sat on the edge of the bed. "Every human mage we have known went mad."

Mor drew back in horror, her grip tightening on Max and Sebastian's hands. "What do you mean?"

Isabella came and stood beside Cassandra. "She means that every human mage we met went insane with the use of magic. The more they used, the deeper the insanity went."

"We don't even know if it's her." Max wrapped his arm around her waist so she was snugged up to both Fae. "It could be any one of us losing control because we just met our mate."

"Max is right." Atreyu came to stand near Mor. She looked up at him, panic starting to rise to the surface. He pushed forward a little, nudging his mothers back with his presence.

"Loves, why don't we give them some space?" Michael waited for Cassandra and Isabella to walk over to him before leading them out of the room.

"Guys..."

"No, Mor." Ben knelt in front of her, taking her hands in his. "We do not know what this is. There is so much happening right now, that it can't be a coincidence. *None of us* will jump to conclusions." He looked each of them in the eyes. "We need to focus on what is happening now. We will deal with anything else later, as a family." He made eye contact with each of them, waiting until he got a nod from each. When he got to Mor, Ben added, "It doesn't matter what it is, we will figure it out." When she nodded, he pulled her in for a hug and whispered, "We've got you."

"Hey. What's happening?" Adair's voice sounded from the door to the kitchen.

Their heads whipped around to stare at him. "Faelan! You've brought Faelan!" Atreyu gasped and ran toward the door. Faelan met him halfway and they collapsed on the floor together. Faelan climbed into his lap and started licking his face. "My sweet pup, I missed you!" Faelan was yipping between licks, for all the world looking like he was talking to Atreyu.

"So anyone want to tell me what's happening?"

Ben grunted. "On top of the magic attacks, we've had some strange magic...incidences...inside the house. Your mothers think Mor is a human mage and is going to go insane."

"Huh. Seems like I missed something big." He looked over at Mor. "Feeling crazy yet?" His grin took the bite out of the statement.

She laughed. "You'll be one of the first to know."

"Excellent! It'll give me time to get away from you." He winked at her.

The guys broke into smiles as Mor took a deep breath and stood. "Come on, let's get your parents back in here. We need to figure out who is attacking us - me."

Sebastian slipped his arms around Mor's waist. "You sure you're ready?"

"Yeah. The sooner we get this done the sooner we can figure everything else out."

"Dad! Moms!" Adair yelled.

"Moms? Really?" Mor raised her eyebrows.

"It's easier than 'Mom, Mom' or 'Mom Isabella, Mom Cassandra.'" He shrugged, making Mor laugh.

Michael walked back in with Cassandra and Isabella. "I assume we're ready to get back to finding these creeps?"

"Yes. We'll deal with anything else after this threat is taken care of." Sebastian's voice was hard.

Atreyu finally extricated himself from Faelan as they all went downstairs to the War Room. "What's the plan?"

"We have to find a way to draw them out." Michael leaned forward on the table.

"Of course." Isabella glanced over at Ben. "Where do you think would be the most advantageous for us to set up an ambush?"

The guys all leaned forward, staring at the map. "What about down there? On the West side of property? There's a small ravine right on the other side of the wards."

They all stared at the spot Ben pointed out. Isabella pointed at it and it rose up into the middle of the table. She stared at for a few minutes, walking around the table to look at it from all angles. "I think this could work."

"We could set up so we are just inside the wards, cloaked." Ben nodded.

"How are we going to set up the trap?" Atreyu leaned further in.

"What about a magic net? We can set it up high." Sebastian said.

"I think all of us out there, too. Maybe spread out down the border to make sure we don't miss these assholes."

"Michael, I don't want any of you out there."

"Cassandra, love, you know we have to."

Mor had sat quietly while they talked. "How are we going to lure them there?" They all fell silent. "Do we have something to attract them?"

Isabella huffed as she looked around the table. "Is no one else going to suggest it?" No one looked at her. "Obviously, Mor needs to be our bait."

"No!"

"Absolutely not!

"We are not letting our mate out there!"

"Mom, how could you say that?"

Ben, Sebastian, Max and Atreyu all spoke at once. Mor shook her head at them. "She's right. How else would we be able to lure them in? Do we have anything else they want? Really, we don't even know *what* they fucking want, beside my uterus which doesn't actually make sense at this point. I'm the best shot."

"I don't like this." Ben said.

"You think I want to be bait?" Mor snapped. "I just want this to be over!"

Atreyu frowned and walked around the table. He took Mor into his arms. "Beautiful, if this is what you want to do, then we'll make it work." He looked at Isabella, eyes narrowed and voice harsh. "But we will find a way to be with her on the other side of the wards. I am not leaving her out there by herself."

"You are bordering on insolence, son." Her face softened, "But because I know how the bond can be…I'll let it pass." Isabella looked back at the ravine floating above the table.

"What about placing them up above? In the trees?" Adair said.

"That could work."

"One of us needs to be with her at all times." Max stepped up next to Mor. "Every time we leave her alone, shit happens."

Isabella glared, opening her mouth to snap something when Cassandra touched her arm. "I remember you struggling with the new bond too, love."

Her face softened. "You're right." She looked around the table at all of us. "Very well. Now, we have to make it look believable. Mor, you need to look like you've run away. Maybe stop and cry when you get to that point? We'll have the guys follow you cloaked so you won't be able to see them."

"When do we want to do this?" Mor straightened up. She was finished with being a victim.

"Well, maybe tom -" Isabella cut off with a curse when a loud *BOOM* sounded and the house shook. "Fuck!"

"What was that?" Eyes wide, Mor stared at the ceiling, flinching when a second *boom* sounded and the house shook.

Isabella went into general mode. "Adair, head out to the West. Ben go East. Sebastian, North. Atreyu - " She stopped. "No?"

"We told you. One of us with Mor at all times. I'm the best at shielding so I'll take her and Trisha into the office."

She huffed. "Fine. Max, go South."

"What about me?" Cassandra's voice was soft.

"Go with Atreyu. Michael will stay with me to help." Cassandra nodded and ran off.

"And you?" Mor asked.

"I will try and figure out where this is coming from. Go now!" She closed her eyes and raised her face to the ceiling.

Atreyu pulled Mor into the office. Trisha and Cassandra were already waiting. After he set the wards, he pulled her into his lap. Hours passed and they just sat, wrapped up in each other as the attack continued on the house. Fear coursed through her. Fear for her guys.

Fear for Isabella and Micheal. Fear for all of them trapped in here. She was shaking as she thought of everything that could go wrong."Mor, they're going to be fine." His voice was a soft whisper. Cassandra and Trisha sat in a corner, quietly talking, not bothering them.

"How do you know I'm worrying?"

He chuckled. "One, you're shaking and I can feel it. Two, you have a cute crinkle between your eyes. Three, you have no idea what those guys are capable of, so it would be normal for you to worry."

"Maybe you should tell me so I don't worry so much."

"Hmm, maybe you're right." He settled Mor against him a little more comfortably and leaned back against the wall. "Well, Max used to be a Medic for the remnants of the Fae Royal Army, Sebastian was like a Lieutenant, and Ben was a Captain."

Mor laughed a little, "Must be why he is so bossy. What about you?"

"I was a Pathfinder. Basically, I was a scout."

"So is this supposed to make me feel better?"

"It should." His expression was cocky. "The royal family was already missing when we joined, but the army was still trying to defend the empty throne. There were a lot of people fighting to get into the palace and therefore claim the throne." He looked sad for just a moment.

"What happened?"

"Eventually, one of our High Mages set a spell around the castle. As long as the ward holds, at least one of the royal family lives. If it ever falls, then the throne will be up for grabs." He shrugged. "After that, the army was disbanded. We weren't needed to protect anymore. So we moved here. It helped that Ben's family had really started pressuring him. And there were things with me."

"What about Max's family?"

"They had already disowned him probably a century before."

Mor hesitated before asking, "What happened with you?"

Atreyu paused before opening his mouth to say something when there was a knock on the door. His mouth snapped shut as he listened for the pattern. When the third knock finished, Atreyu raised his hands and broke the wards. Ben was standing on the other side, looking a little worse for wear. Mor ran to him, throwing her arms around him. "Are you okay? Sebastian, Max?"

"They're fine, love." He sounded exhausted.

"I'm good too!" Adair yelled from another room.

"Let's go sit down." Atreyu suggested from behind Mor.

They all went into the War Room and sat around the table. Ben leaned his head into his hands. "We saw who it was. It was Tom and John." He looked over at Mor. "I'm so sorry we didn't catch them."

"I'm just glad you're okay."

"They attacked me at the same time. They were throwing fire first, which I had a great time turning back on them," he smirked briefly, "But then they hit me with darkness? I'd never seen anything like it."

Isabella paled. "Describe it."

"It was like a wave of dark. I could see it coming, but nothing broke it. When it hit me, I couldn't see, couldn't speak."

"What did you do?" Mor's voice was quiet as she gripped his arm.

"Surrounded myself with fire and waited for my brothers." He shrugged. "I knew they were coming and I just had to hold out. But the dark seemed to pull my strength from me. If they hadn't gotten there when they did…"

"We've seen that before." Cassandra's voice soft.

"When?" Sebastian snapped. "We need to know how to defeat it. The only thing that saved Ben today was that we all showed up and chased them off while they stood there arguing."

"What were they arguing about?" Michael asked from where he stood behind Cassandra with his hands on her shoulders.

"Whether to kill him or take him." Max's voice was hard.

"Did they say anything else? Anything that may give us a hint at what they want?" Isabella snapped out the questions.

"John was yelling that Mor is the key. That they needed her before her birthday." Sebastian said glancing at Mor.

"Fuuuuuck." It just slipped out of her. Tomorrow was her birthday.

"How do we fight this?" Ben looked at Isabella.

"It takes a lot. When we fought this before it took all of us. We had to combine our magic."

"That doesn't sound too bad." A cocky smile started to stretch across Atreyu's face.

"Think again, son." Michael's voice was serious. "You have to blend your magic until it's seamless and then direct it at your target. You have to be one mind, essentially."

"What you are not understanding is that these are human mages who are most likely insane. They won't care if they drain themselves dry because they will not think about it. They will only think about what the magic is driving them to do." Standing, Isabella walked out of the room. "I need a drink for this."

"At least we know it's me they're after. So I'll be excellent bait."

"No, we are *not* following that plan now." Max's eyes narrowed and his voice was fierce.

Mor shook her head. "We have to stop them. If they're...insane... then they won't stop coming until they get what they want. And they know what you are, probably. Which means that they may try to follow us even if we decide to just move to Fae."

"We will not put you in danger." Sebastian was shaking his head, his face full of regret. "We'll find another way."

"Mor, you have to understand. We just found you. Now that we *know* they want you, there is no way we will allow you to place yourself in danger." Ben patted her hand.

"Allow?" Her voice was low as she stood up. Emotion rose in her too fast for her to stop it.

"That's right. Our job is to keep you safe, beautiful." Atreyu rubbed her back, not hearing the warning in her voice.

"*Allow?!*" Mor raised her voice, her anger cracking through the room. "You do not get to dictate to me! I have spent my life being told how to act, what to say, what to wear, who to talk to, what to do!" Her voice rose with her anger. "I have been nothing more than a pawn moved around to please other people!" They were staring at her, eyes wide. "I will not be used as a pawn again! You will not make decisions for me! I have had enough of that to last me a life time!"

"Woah, Mor. Why don't you take a deep breath?" Atreyu said.

"DO NOT tell me what to do." Her voice echoed across the room.

"So, your hair is floating." Max had stayed where he was sitting and was staring at her calmly.

"What?" Mor blinked at him, surprise bringing her out of her anger.

"Your hair. It's floating around your head. And there are sparks coming from your hands."

"Oh shit."

"So maybe you should take a breath with me." He took a slow, deep breath. Mor kept her eyes focused on Max, trying to match his breathing, struggling to get herself under control. She looked down at her hands, panicking when she saw the sparks flying from her hands. "Mor! Breathe with me. Slow. In. Out."

"I'm trying!" Sparks flew from her hands and hit the table. When Mor's eyes widened with fear, Ben simply reached out and gathered the flames in his hands.

"Mor." Max pulled her attention back to him. "In. Out." She started to look down but Max focused her, "No, sweetie. Look at me. Only me." She focused back on him. Taking deep breaths, she matched him. "That's it. Nice and slow." He started walking toward her. When he got to her, Max slipped his hands into hers. "That's it, sweetie. No one is going to tell you what to do."

"You *all* just did that!" Her voice started rising again as anger flared. Mor shook her head, trying to stop it.

"We were wrong."

"You were wrong?" Her head snapped up to look at Max.

"We were wrong."

Mor felt a hand brush up her arm to caress her neck. She turned to see Ben standing next to her, his face serious. "I was wrong."

"Wrong?" Mor was having trouble focusing through the waves of feeling coursing through her. She felt like she was being pulled apart and she needed to make sure that they understood.

Sebastian squeezed one of her hands. "We won't tell you what to do."

A caress on her other arm. "We are yours." Atreyu whispered before kissing Mor under her ear.

Sebastian rested his hand on her back. "Command us." He kissed her on the back of her neck.

"Mine?"

"Yours." Four voices whispered across her skin. Mor sighed, sinking into their arms, tears falling as her anger broke into sadness that she couldn't hold back anymore.

CHAPTER 20

*M*or gasped as everything hit her at once. She couldn't stop crying. For the pain her family put her through and the pain of not having a real family until now. The pain of years of being silent. Of being pushed around and told what to do. Of her family - *her family!* - ordering her tortured and now attacking her new home. Her guys didn't let go even as Mor's knees went out. They held her as she broke apart and mourned with her. Held her as she struggled to put herself back together again. They just held her in their arms until she was able to breathe without crying.

She took a shaky breath. They pulled back a little bit but didn't let go. Mor slowly stopped crying enough to say, "I'm sorry. I don't know what's going on with me. I just can't seem to get a handle on myself." She shook her head. "I was just so angry and now..." Her breath hitched but she managed to keep the tears from starting again. "Maybe your parents are right, Atreyu. What are we going to do?"

"Shh, Mor. You have nothing to apologize for." Max kissed her softly.

"It doesn't matter what happens, we're yours." Atreyu nuzzled her neck. "We will figure this out, together."

"But I don't know who I am. My fingers sparked. My hair fucking floated! My *hair floated*! I just flipped out at you for wanting to keep me safe! What if I try to hurt you?"

Sebastian brushed her hair back from her face. "Darling, it doesn't matter to us."

"We will be with you no matter what. And like Atreyu said, we'll figure it out together. You aren't alone in this." Ben murmured in her ear.

Mor nodded and the guys helped her stand up. She felt unsteady. She needed to be stronger than this. She would not allow her adopted family to make her decisions ever again. They would never affect her future with Atreyu, Max, Ben, and Sebastian. Her future was holding her together so she could rebuild herself and be - Mor. Straightening her spine, she pulled herself together, ready to fight for this new future. There was no way she would let anyone take it from her. Besides, she could have a real breakdown after all this was finished.

"I - we - can do this." The guys smiled at her. "Sooo. My hair floats. And my fingers spark. And I can't seem to control my emotions." Mor paused thoughtfully, "And I'm probably going insane."

"Fuck that." Sebastian scoffed.

"You think we'd let you go insane." Atreyu grinned down at her. "You got another thing coming if you think we would ever let you fall apart."

Mor started to pull back, emotion rising in her again. "You think to tell me what to do?"

"Mor." Max took her attention, both hands on her face. "We will help you until you decide what you need. You decide." He took a deep breath, waiting for her. "You. Not us. What do you need?"

She paused, struggling to regain control of herself and trying to match Max's breathing. Why couldn't she hold it together? Now that she was breathing again she could see how crazy she was being. What *did* she need? Did she need someone defending her? Did she need to hide from this attack? Fuck that.

Before, Mor would have let someone tell her what to do. She would have sat back and followed directions. That is what her adopted family had trained her to do. Jump? How fucking high? Now,

Mor was a different woman. She had been supported. She had been given choices. She had survived being tortured. She had been terrified and come through it.

Now, Mor knew she had a team behind her. One who would support her even if she chose danger. It didn't matter if she was safe as long as she had her choice and her guys backing her up. Mor had learned that safety was not what it was cracked up to be. She had spent years making the safe choice, going with the flow, and not rocking the boat. That boat had fucking capsized and her guys had been the ones to help her back up again.

"I got this." Mor's voice was strong as she looked each one of her guys in the eyes. "I will be the bait." Her eyes met Isabella's as she walked back in the room with a drink in her hand.

"Do you understand what that means?"

"Probably not. I'm going to do it either way, though. My brother and John can't be allowed to continue with whatever it is they're doing. My gut says it would be a really bad idea to ignore them. And I'm learning to pay attention to my instincts." She smiled at her guys.

"Darling. You're hair is floating again." Sebastian pressed himself against her. "It's sexy."

"Of course it's fucking floating. I apparently have magic and I'm going to be bait. Let it fucking float." Mor looked back at him, annoyance flitting across her face before she controlled herself. She reached out to grip his arm and he winked at her.

"This needs to be finished." Isabella shook her head. "I'm sorry that we don't have another way. We will have you run to this spot." She pointed to the map. "Faelan will run with you - I can magic him to track to the ravine so you can follow him. Ben will run with you, cloaked. Atreyu, Max and Sebastian will be waiting in the trees above you." She highlighted the trees but hesitated before speaking again. "We need to know why they are doing this. Try to draw it out of them."

Mor nodded, "When will we do this?"

"Tonight. We'll make it late so it looks like you snuck out to run away." She answered.

"Fine." Ben stood up. "We are going to spend time with our mate. I'm sure you all can find something to do." He pulled Mor to her feet and led them out of the room. After a brief stop in the kitchen, they all went down to the movie room. The next few hours were spent laughing, watching dumb movies, and just being together.

"It's almost over." Mor whispered from where she was curled up in Sebastian's arms.

"It almost is." He kissed her hair. "So, what's your favorite cake? We have to celebrate your birthday tomorrow."

"Ugh. Birthday."

"Darling, we are going to celebrate you and teach you how to have fun on a birthday."

"Fine."

"Cake?" He prompted.

"Um. I've never had cake." The silence in the room was deafening. Mor picked up her head to look at the guys staring at her.

"You've never had cake?" Atreyu's voice was incredulous.

"Well, no. It didn't fit into the 'diet plan' I was on to make sure I was 'marriage ready'." She shrugged and muttered, "Which is maybe why I thought ice cream would fix how I was feeling."

Atreyu snorted before coughing to cover his laugh and said, "Fuck that. We're having - like - eight cakes tomorrow." He glanced at his watch, "I'm going to talk to Trisha about it. We have a few minutes before we have to go." He was gone up the stairs before anyone could say anything.

Max rubbed his hands together. "We are going to have more fun than you on your birthday! I've never introduced anyone to cake!" He grinned. "I'm going to talk to Trisha, too!"

Mor's gaze bounced between Sebastian and Ben. "Do y'all need to talk to her too?"

Ben chuckled, "No, I think they've probably got it covered." He stood and came to kneel in front of Mor in Sebastian's lap. "I can think of better things to do." He leaned in and claimed her mouth, kissing her deep.

Sebastian groaned. "That's a much better idea." Bending his head he started trailing kisses along Mor's neck. Hands slid up her shirt to cup her breasts and another hand slid down into her pants.

Just as the hand dipped into the top of her panties the door to the movie room banged open. "It's ti- oh shit, my bad." Adair laughed. "So sorry to be a cockblock, but it's time. You can always make it up to her on her birthday." He winked and then jogged laughing out of the room.

"Damn." Mor grumbled.

"He's right, though. We'll definitely be making it up to you on your birthday." Standing, Ben pulled Mor up so Sebastian could get up. Both guys reached down to adjust themselves.

"Sorry." Mor glanced down at the hard bulges and licked her lips. When they both groaned she looked up to see them staring at her mouth. "Oops."

Sebastian heaved a sigh. "Come on, darling, let's get this over with so we can get back to playing."

Mor followed them out, slipping her hands into theirs and squeezing. When they got to the top of the stairs they found everyone waiting for them in the War Room. Adair smirked at them while Isabella rolled her eyes. Micheal and Cassandra smiled knowingly. Max and Atreyu just smiled as they came over to kiss her. "We get to play next time, too." Atreyu whispered in her ear before tugging on her ear lobe once with his teeth.

"Were we that bad?" Isabella snapped at Cassandra.

"Oh yes, we were definitely that bad." She smacked Isabella's ass. "We're still that bad, so cut them some slack."

Isabella rolled her eyes again but Mor thought she saw a smile flicker across her face. "Mor, I'm going to cast the cloaking spell over all of us. You will not be able to see us. Make sure you're crying and holding on to Faelan - he'll lead you to the right spot." She made eye contact with every person in the room. "As soon as you are cloaked, get to your places. And whatever you do, do not let them act together. If they do, they are likely to cast the darkness spell."

"Can't you just fight it like you did before?" Adair asked.

"No. The cloaking spell will drain me and the last time we fought this it took every drop of our combined magic. It took weeks to recover from."

"Oh."

"Yes. Oh." She looked around the room. "Trisha, do you want to join us or will you be staying here at the house?"

"I'd just be in the way, Isabella. My magic is no meant for combat."

"Very well. I suggest the office." She looked at Mor. "Are you ready? Once they're cloaked, everyone but Ben will go. Give them a few minutes head start. We don't have a lot of time." When Mor nodded, she gestured for her to stand to the side of the room with Trisha. Isabella closed her eyes and began swaying as she murmured. She clapped her hands and they all disappeared.

"Well. Guess it's time then, lass." Trisha gently pressed Mor's hand. "Trust yer family, lass. Tomorrow we'll be celebrating yer birthday with eight cakes. The boyos insisted." She winked before heading to the office.

Mor took a deep breath and walked into the kitchen to stare out at the night through the patio doors. Faelan whined by her side. "Crying. I have to cry." Her eyes felt dry. It seemed like she had spent days crying. Well, really she had been crying a lot lately. After tonight, she would be stronger. She would learn how to handle her magic and would learn to defend herself physically and magically.

"Cry." Mor focused on what had brought her here. She thought about what had happened with her 'family' and what they had put her through over the years. Tears started falling. She looked down at Faelan. "This is the last time I cry over them," She whispered before she slipped open the sliding glass door, gripped his ruff, and started to run.

She felt a light pressure on her back and knew Ben was with her. *Nope!* Mor couldn't think of that right now. If she thought about that, then she'd stop crying. She felt Faelan tug her to the right and turned with him, running through the trees and trying not to trip in the dark. Ahead she saw a dip in the ground. *There!* That was the ravine. When Faelan slowed and stopped, Mor sank onto the ground and wrapped her arms around him. She buried her face in his fur and focused on her shitty family to keep up the crying.

"Well, well, well. What do we have here?"

Mor's head snapped up. "John? What are you doing here?" Holy fuck that was fast. Did everyone have time to get in place? *Stay confused,* Mor thought, *don't let him know!*

"Why, I'm here for you, dear fiancé." He smirked down at her from the top of the ravine.

"I'm not your fiancé. And you were supposed to be arrested."

"Come now, Moreen. I know you've been living with those damn Fae. I know you felt our attacks."

Fuck, fuck, fuck. He did know what they were. Which meant this probably went deeper than any of them thought. "How do you know that? Who are you? Are you Fae too?"

"I'm human, which is more than I can say for that trash you've been associating with." He sneered, taking a step closer.

"Stop playing with her." A voice snapped out from behind Mor.

Mor turned to look, "Tom? What the fuck do you want?"

Tom snarled. "You watch your mouth, you dirty little slut. All you had to do was marry John before your birthday and we wouldn't have to worry about you anymore!"

Mor felt Ben put his hand on her back. She had to get more out of them. "Why? Why is it so important? He can go get a trophy wife anywhere. Women who will be happy to be a kept woman and spend his money while he fucks whatever he wants."

Tom jumped down into the ravine and slapped her across the face. Mor gasped at the pain and held her face. She felt a flicker of - something - inside of herself. "I told you to watch your mouth."

"Please! Tom! I'm your sister! Just tell me why you're doing this!"

Both men laughed. John shook his head, still chuckling, "Sister." He was still shaking his head as an evil smile spread across his face. "You were never his sister. You were always a tool. They just needed to raise you long enough for the spells binding you to come undone. I paid your 'family' quite well to babysit you until you were old enough for me."

"I don't know what you are talking about! What spells? I just learned about magic two weeks ago!"

Tom sneered down at her. "Have strange things been happening around you lately, Moreen? Things going bump in the night? It's the binding coming undone." He looked up at John. "We need to do this now. It's just a few minutes until midnight and then it will be much harder to take the magic from her." He grinned down at her, "And far more painful. Can't say that would disappoint me much."

Suddenly, Mor felt Ben grab the back of her shirt and yank her back. She saw Tom fall to the ground with a grunt and Faelan jump at John. "Run, Mor! Back to the wards!" Ben yelled. She heard thumps all around her as she turned to run.

"NO!" John flung a hand at her and a bolt flew from it, striking at her feet and making her fall. "YOU WILL NOT ESCAPE ME!" He screamed. John flinched as something struck him and then he was defending himself from invisible blows. Mor tried to stand but collapsed when her ankle wouldn't support her. Crawling, she headed toward the wards.

There was a *BOOM* behind her and she turned to look. John was standing at the bottom of the ravine. Mor couldn't see Ben and Tom. Faelan was whimpering at the base of a tree. Sebastian was prowling behind John but Atreyu was on the ground, bleeding. Max was crawling toward him, one eye on John. "Stop now, Moreen. I have waited far too long for this moment. You will be mine." He started walking toward her. Sebastian tried to attack but John gestured and he was flung backwards.

Mor felt someone behind her. Cassandra grabbed her by the arms and started dragging her toward the wards while Michael and Isabella stepped in front. A shield started glowing in front of them.

John laughed and waved his hand. Michael, Cassandra, and Isabella were blown aside. He stalked over to stand in front of her. "Did you really think you could get away from me? I searched for your family for hundreds of years after they fled from me. I killed them one by one after taking their powers. And you are all that is left." He leaned over and grabbed Mor by the hair, pulling her upright. "Your slut of a mother bound your magic thinking it would keep you safe from me." He smirked, hand tightening in her hair. "Luckily for me, there are always greedy humans to be bought so I wouldn't have to lower myself to raising you. I will drain your power and force you to give me heirs since you are the last of the line." He kissed her, forcing his tongue into her mouth as she struggled against him. "And once I have your power I will take the throne on Fae and on Earth."

Rage like she had never felt before rose in Mor. She felt something fill her, starting with the connection her feet had with the earth. The power rose through her, giving life to her rage. She glowed with it and sparks started falling from her hands.

"What's this? What's happening?" John looked confused, his hand loosening in her hair.

Mor brought her hands up and pushed him. Energy arced from her hands into his body, forcing him back. His face fell into a grimace of pain as he let go of her hair. "No." He shook his head. "No! NO!" He looked frantically around. "I've waited too long for this!" Desperately, he reached a hand out toward her and a black rope shot out of his hands, shooting toward Mor.

She cocked her head to the side and then brushed it aside. When she touched it the rope disintegrated. "How are you doing this?" Fear appeared on John's face.

Tom came flying at Mor from the side, hitting her in the head with a tree branch. Dazed, Mor wasn't able to stop John as he ran toward her, grabbed her arm with one hand and placing the other on her forehead. "Grab her arms! Hold her still!"

Tom wrenched Mor's arms behind her back. "Got you now, bitch."

Pain worse than she had felt with Dr. Smith coursed through her head. It felt like knives were carving into her brain and then pulling the pieces out. Mor screamed, rage and pain fueling her. The light surrounding her grew brighter. She felt heat pouring off of her as air began swirling around them. Tom started cursing as the heat increased.

Letting go he yelled, "Hurry! I can't hold her anymore!"

John screamed, grabbing Mor's head with both hands. "You will be mine!"

"You will not be taking me." Mor's voice was chilly. It sounded more resonant, like a bell. She felt panic begin to war with the rage that was filling her. She forced down the panic - time for panic after the bad guy was gone. The glow surrounding Mor became incandescent and John was flung backwards.

"NO!" He ran back toward Mor.

She held her hand out and shoved it forward, acting on instinct. John flew through the air, hitting a tree with a loud thunk. He looked at her, fear and anger warring on his face before turning and running. Tom rushed after him, looking back once, his face filled with hate.

Mor stared after them, waiting for them to come back. When they didn't, she gasped as the fear and anxiety she had been holding back crashed into her. Running over to where Max was working on Atreyu, she fell to her knees, "Will he be okay? What happened?"

Max didn't look at her from where he was steadily stitching Atreyu up. "He'll be fine." Max grunted. "Just going to be down for a few days. Need to get this stitched before he wakes up."

"Where's Ben? Sebastian?"

Max grunted as he kept working, "Sebastian is over by that tree. He's knocked out but okay."

"I'm here, Mor." Ben came up from behind a hill. "They got away again. I'm sorry." He stopped short when he saw her. "You're glowing. Your ears...your *eyes*..."

"My ears?" Mor reached up to touch them. They were...pointed? She looked down. Her skin was still glowing faintly and sparks gently danced across her skin. "What happened?" She reached up and brushed her hair back as it floated in front of her face. "I don't understand."

Soft footsteps behind her made Mor turn. Michael gasped when he saw her. Cassandra smiled like someone had just given her a piece of candy. Isabella merely nodded, a strangely satisfied look on her face. All three went to one knee in front of her and bowing their heads.

"Happy Birthday, Your Majesty."

AFTERWORD

Thank you so much for taking the time to read this! This has been a wild ride for me and I hope you enjoyed the end results. I will be working on book two, hopefully getting it out as soon as possible.

I also want to thank my Mom for instilling a love of reading and writing in me. Last, thank you to the rest of my parents and my grandparents for supporting me in all my crazy ideas.

You can find me on Facebook at https://www.facebook.com/eva.blackwing.7 and join my reader group Eva's Elementals at https://www.facebook.com/groups/957627227922105/

If you love Instagram find me at https://www.instagram.com/evablackwing/

Made in United States
North Haven, CT
14 October 2021